# THE GIRLS NEXT DOOR

Also by Mel Sherratt

**Mel Sherratt books**

*Somewhere to Hide*
*Behind a Closed Door*
*Fighting for Survival*
*Written in the Scars*
*Taunting the Dead*
*Follow the Leader*
*Only the Brave*
*Watching over You*

**Marcie Steele books**

*Stirred With Love*
*The Little Market Stall of Hope and Happiness*
*The Second Chance Shoe Shop*

# THE GIRLS NEXT DOOR

MEL SHERRATT

bookouture

Published by Bookouture, an imprint of StoryFire Ltd.

23 Sussex Road, Ickenham, UB10 8PN,
United Kingdom

www.bookouture.com



ISBN 978-1-78681-091-5
eBook ISBN 978-1-78681-090-8

# THE FIGHT – APRIL 2015

Katie Trent dragged her feet as she walked down the street towards the park. Her best friend, Jess, was ill and already she felt lost without her, even though lately she seemed to be glued to the hip of her boyfriend, Cayden.

When Jess had rang to say she wasn't able to go out that night, Katie had suggested calling to see her instead of going to meet Nathan. Nathan was her new boyfriend – but not by choice. It was Cayden who had wanted her to get friendly with him. He saw Nathan as their inroad, their ticket to more involvement with the Barker brothers.

Katie didn't really like him that much. Although she knew some of her other friends were envious because he was attractive in a bad-boy way, his moods were volatile and she hadn't wanted to meet him unless it was in a foursome.

But Jess had been adamant that she should go without her, said it was important that she keep up the act. It was all right for Jess, she thought. She didn't have to have Nathan's tongue rammed down her throat. She shuddered involuntarily.

The weather was warm for the end of April, the night sky clear but darkening by the minute as it edged towards 8 p.m. Katie tapped along in her heels, feeling grown-up in her new ankle boots. She was wearing Jess's top and a leather jacket that she'd told her mum was a knock-off from a cheap shop in Stockleigh, rather than costing her a fortune from Topshop. Her parents didn't approve of her wearing too much make-up, so once she'd left her house she'd added some more. She hoped it made her seem more mature, helping to hide her nerves a little.

On the Mitchell Estate, she headed across Reginald Square, turned the corner and crossed Davy Road into the park. There was grass on either side of the gravel path that led up to the children's play area, the lawn sloping up to her right. In the distance was the subway she and her friends hung around inside of when it was raining.

Her heart sank as she spotted Nathan with two other boys at the top of the bank. It was all right when Cayden and Jess were with her, but Nathan was two years older, so his friends were older too. If Jess was with her, she would feel safe. Her feet stopping abruptly, she turned to leave. Jess would go mad but suddenly she didn't care.

'Katie!'

She paused before turning around to see Nathan beckoning to her. She couldn't back down now, so she started walking towards him again.

'Where's your mate?' Nathan asked as she drew level with them. He threw an arm possessively around her shoulders. 'That bimbo Jess?'

'She's not a bimbo!' Katie tried to sound outraged, but her voice didn't carry as much authority as she had hoped.

The two boys with Nathan began to snigger. She had seen them both before several times: Twins Tom and Craig Cartwright. They were all wide-eyed and their mood seemed a little oppressive. Craig was checking his phone and Tom kept looking over towards the path that led into the subway.

'So you're all alone.' Nathan asked a question that obviously needed no answer. 'It'll be nice to get to know you at last, once we've sorted some business out.'

Katie tried not to grimace as he thrust his face nearer to hers, his breath rank. He'd definitely been taking something.

'Do you want a smoke?' he asked, pushing a spliff to her lips.

'No, thanks.' Katie disliked it with a passion after watching her granddad smoke forty a day and die a painful death from lung cancer. Alcohol she was fine with, and the odd happy pill. But these boys had taken more than that, it seemed. Nathan's pupils were like black bullet holes.

'So where is Jess?' he asked again, looking at his watch before glancing down the bank.

'She's poorly.'

Nathan pulled a sad face. 'Don't worry, we'll keep you company. Won't we, lads?'

Katie swallowed. Being on her own with Nathan would be bad enough but with these two loons as well? She had to be home by ten anyway, but she would stay for an hour and then maybe slip off on the pretence of getting some lager or something. She'd kill Jess when she got her hands on her. That bloody Cayden!

'He's on his way,' said Craig, pointing down below. They all followed the direction of his finger.

Katie could see someone walking along the path. He wore baggy jeans, trainers and a black hoodie with a yellow emblem on the back, the hood pulled up so his face was almost hidden.

'Who's that?' she asked, sensing the mood darkening even further.

'Travis Barker – and he's going to get what's coming to him.' Nathan began to jog down the bank towards him.

Tom threw his cigarette to the ground, grinding it out with the toe of his boot before following Nathan, Craig hot on his heels.

Katie watched them sneaking up on the figure. Just as he was about to disappear into the subway, she saw Nathan punch him in the side of the head. The boy, taken by surprise, dropped to his knees before scrambling up and turning to face them. Nathan punched him in the face this time. So did Craig. Tom drew back his foot and aimed a kick at him when he dropped to the floor for a second time.

As if they were a pack of wild dogs, they rained punches and kicks down on the boy as he tried to curl up into a ball. For a moment Katie froze, unsure how to stem the rage that was coming from them. Then she saw Nathan flick out a knife.

'No,' she whispered.

Rigid with fear, she watched Nathan thrust the knife into the boy's stomach. It was as if time stood still as he pulled it out and then stabbed him repeatedly.

'Stop! Please!' Katie screamed and ran down the bank towards them as they continued their attack. Finding courage she didn't know she had, she pushed first Craig and then Tom away as hard as she could, hoping it would snap them out of the red mist that must have descended.

Nathan glared at her but dropped the knife.

She scrambled across to the boy and knelt down beside him. There was blood coming from his mouth and he was making gurgling noises as he fought for breath. His hood fell from his face, and Katie recoiled. It wasn't a boy. It was a girl.

And Katie knew her.

'Deanna? Oh, no, Deanna.' She pulled her into her arms and looked up at the boys. 'This isn't Travis. It's his sister!'

'It's a girl?' Tom grabbed hold of his hair with both hands. 'Shit, what did we do?'

'Call an ambulance!' Katie cried.

'She's dead, isn't she?' Craig turned to Nathan. 'This is your fault! No one mentioned anything about a knife!'

Nathan shook his head vehemently. 'She's breathing, look!'

'But she's bleeding!' Craig pointed at Deanna.

Katie held Deanna as she thrashed about, trying to catch her breath. 'Call for an ambulance,' she screamed. 'If she dies, we're all in trouble!'

The enormity of what had happened began to dawn on Nathan, and he gripped the collar of Katie's jacket. He pushed his face close to hers.

'If you say anything, you're dead, do you hear me? I'll come after you and then I'll come after your family.' He let go and began to run.

'She needs an ambulance!' Katie yelled. But Tom and Craig followed Nathan's lead and ran too.

Left with Deanna in her arms, all Katie could do was cry.

*Please don't let her die.*

Deanna gasped, blood pouring from her mouth.

'Try not to speak,' Katie whispered, as she retrieved her phone from her jacket pocket. 'The ambulance will be here soon. They'll sort you out and get you better again.'

*Please don't let her die.*

'Ambulance please,' Katie sobbed. 'My friend has been stabbed.' As she told the operator where they were, she gasped as Deanna's eyes glazed over. She felt her body go limp in her arms. 'No, Deanna, please! Deanna!' She hugged her close, tears dripping into her hair.

It felt like hours but it was a matter of minutes before she heard the siren of the emergency services.

'I'm so sorry,' she repeated, looking down at Deanna. 'I have to go too. I can't stay here or else I'll be in trouble.'

As two paramedics came into view at the top of the hill, she waved to alert them. They rushed down the bank towards her.

Katie gently laid Deanna's head down on the grass. 'I'm so sorry,' she repeated. Then she too stood up and ran.

# FRIDAY

9 October 2015

# ONE

Detective Sergeant Eden Berrisford glanced at the young woman walking down the path next to her and sighed.

'You're twenty-six and it's your wedding,' she said, as they reached the pavement. 'If you can't stand up to your future mother-in-law before the big day, then you're going to have a lot of problems in the long run.'

'I don't think I'm ever going to be able to stand up to her. She can't say a word wrong in Seth's eyes. She's always interfering. She even comes around our house when we're at work and starts tidying up.'

'I wish someone would do that for me.'

Detective Constable Amy Nichols threw her a look as Eden smirked.

They walked down the road to where Eden's car was parked. It was 3.30 p.m. and with the predicted storm gathering, it was dark enough for the reflectors on the doors to be working. Not yet turned from autumn to winter, the nights were getting shorter, but the clocks weren't due to go back for another two weeks.

'Jeez, it's blowing a gale out here,' Eden complained. 'It seems to be getting worse by the minute. I'm glad I'm not on duty this evening.'

'There's definitely a storm brewing in there, Sarge.' Amy raised her eyebrows. 'I'd like to punch him myself if I could, the arrogant git.'

Eden and Amy had been taking a statement from a woman and her partner who were being terrorised by her ex-husband. Eden had had several run-ins with the man over the years she had been in the force, so knew when it came down to it that the woman wouldn't press charges. She was too scared, and even now that they could put the evidence in front of the CPS without the victims' consent, there wasn't enough of it to satisfy a conviction. Instead, all Eden could do was build up a file in the hope that she could persuade the woman to go down that route one day.

A call came through on the radio.

'D429 to control room,' said Eden, after listening. 'We're in the area right now so we'll knock on and have a word. Show us responding.'

'Received with thanks, D429.'

Even though she rarely got involved with day-to-day complaints now, Eden would never turn her back on the residents of Stockleigh. She wasn't a jobsworth who thought things were beneath her now that she was a sergeant. Not like some at the station she could mention.

She glanced at Amy, seeing a kind pair of eyes underneath a straight fringe, a mass of blonde hair she wore in a long bob framing her oval face. They'd been working closely together for a month now and even though Amy's small frame was a contrast to Eden's height, she'd shown a punchy side to her that gave Eden the impression that most things didn't faze her and that she could stick up for herself. So it was nice to see she had a caring side about her too: Amy seemed torn between having what she wanted and upsetting anyone with regards to her own wedding.

'Why don't you tell your future mother-in-law that you'll compromise a little if she does?' Eden said as they marched up another path. 'You'll wear frills and cover up your arms if she wears a black bag and matching eyeliner.'

'I'd be dead if I said that to her,' Amy said, laughing.

Eden glanced at the front door as a face appeared in the glass panel at its side.

They heard a bolt being drawn back, and a small elderly man popped his head around the doorframe.

'Mr Percival?' Eden placed her warrant card up to the gap, vaguely recognising the man's face.

'You're too bloody late as usual,' he snapped. The door was slammed in their faces.

Eden raised her eyebrows at Amy before they heard the chain being removed and the door opening again. They stepped into the bungalow as the man shuffled back inside with the aid of a walking stick. As soon as they were in the living room, Eden spotted a framed wedding photograph on the wall and remembered where she knew the man from. She'd have recognised the woman in it anywhere. She had visited Mr Percival at a previous property many years ago, when she was on probation. Mrs Percival had died in her sleep and she had been the first officer on scene. It had been her first dead body, and if she remembered rightly he had made her a cup of tea when she had burst into tears at the sight of the woman lying peacefully in her bed.

He didn't recognise her though, as he began to rant, arms waving, a stern look on his weathered face.

'This is the third time this month they've nicked it,' he told them, turning back to them slowly. 'They use it for a bit of fun and then they leave it wherever the battery runs out. I'm stranded every time it goes missing. I don't know what else to do. I don't have anywhere to keep it, and the council won't make me a ramp so I can get it in here – not that I have the room, but at least I could get up every morning and it would still be here. I missed the two thirty race at the bookies. Little bastards.'

'Do you know who has taken it, Mr Percival?' said Eden.

'Lived here all my life I have,' he continued. 'Never known anything like it. And no, I didn't see them. I've just got back from the shops and I left it outside. I only went to have a pee because I was desperate. Doctor gave me some stronger water tablets and the buggers are working overtime. I came back and it was gone.'

Eden stared out of the window. The Hopwood Estate stood on the other side of the bank of grass that dipped down to a brook that ran the length of the road. Rows and rows of houses and six-to-a-block flats clustered together in squares. It was like a rabbit warren if you didn't know your way around and housed many of the families that gave Eden and her colleagues the most trouble. Smack bang in the middle of it was the Horse & Hound pub, where most of the estate's residents could be found morning, noon or night. It was always the first port of call for the police when a warrant was issued for someone's arrest. She wondered which little scrote had taken to thieving this time. It was all a game to them.

Once Amy had taken down the details, there was nothing else they could do. 'I'll get someone onto this once we get back to the station, and we'll have a drive around to see if we can see any—' She stopped as a mobility scooter raced past the window, driven by a teenager who was screaming at the top of his voice as if he was in the Wild West on bare horseback. 'Won't be a moment, Mr Percival.'

Eden ran out of the bungalow with Amy on her tail. Having the advantage of an unmarked car and plain clothes, they weren't spotted immediately by the thief, but as soon as he saw them giving chase, he sped up as much as he could.

'You won't catch me, lardarses!' the boy shouted, throwing them a finger as he pushed the lever on full power.

'If you don't bring that back right this minute,' Eden yelled, 'I'll shove it right up *your*—'

Amy came rushing past Eden and gained on the scooter. She had nearly reached it, her hand outstretched as it veered off the road and up over the pavement.

The teenager wobbled and lost control as it hit the grass verge. It toppled over, tipping the driver off with it. As the scooter went one way, Amy legged him over and Eden got out her cuffs.

'Liam Matson, I'm arresting you for the theft of a mobility scooter.' Eden's breath was heavy. 'You do not have to say anything. But it may harm your defence if you do not mention when questioned something that you later rely on in court. Anything you do say may be given in evidence. Do you understand?'

'You're hurting me!' he cried. 'Police brutality!'

'I intend to hurt you, you selfish little shit.' Eden pulled him to his feet as Amy came back up the grass verge, pushing the scooter. They reached the road again and Eden put him in the back of her car before radioing through for a uniform to come and pick him up. She might have done the collar, but she sure as hell wasn't doing the paperwork if she could get away with it.

'What do I do with this, Sarge?' Amy nodded in the direction of the scooter.

'You'll look quite fetching on it.' Eden grinned. 'You can have the pleasure of driving it back to Mr Percival.'

Amy's eyes widened. 'Why me? Can't uniform do it when they get here?'

'Call it your initiation test.'

'For what?' Amy frowned.

'YouTube. The last time I did that it was all over social media by the time I got back to the nick, and I'm not having that again.'

'I thought you were partial to scooters,' Amy teased. 'You know, with you owning a Lambretta?'

'I'll have you know it has to have a flyscreen with sixteen mirrors, chrome work and air horns for me to be interested in it.' Eden grinned. 'Now get on and drive. I promise not to take any photos to share.'

# TWO

Cayden Blackwell pulled up the hood of his jacket as the wind battled with it. It had stopped raining heavily, but it was still spitting the fine stuff. He was going to be soaked through if he didn't get to Jess's soon. He checked his watch: 5.30 p.m. He'd better hurry.

Trust him to say he would call for Jess and bring her back to his house. The only reason he was over that way was because he'd needed to see his friend, and his mum would be suspicious if Travis Barker called at their house. For starters, she'd want to know why he was there, darkening her door, and then what he wanted with Cayden. Then she'd probably tell him to keep out of Travis's way – or worse, tell Travis to sling his hook.

Even though Travis Barker was a known troublemaker, Cayden was hoping he'd be his ticket to earning some good cash – not just the odd twenty quid here and there that he was accustomed to. He wanted in with some of the bigger jobs he knew Travis was involved with now.

With business out of the way, he couldn't wait to see Jess, especially knowing that his house was empty and they could get it on in peace for once. Last night had been parents' evening, and as his brother had been doing well in his first year at high school, their mum and dad were taking him out for a pizza. They'd offered to take Cayden too but he'd declined, saying he needed to study for his exams. Well, that would be right if he was studying anatomy.

All he wanted to do was get his hands on Jess. Tonight there would be no little Lloyd to run in and interrupt them. No Mum to knock on the door with a cup of tea for them both, on the pretext of caring when all she wanted was to make sure they didn't do anything 'untoward' under her roof. No Dad to give them a leery grin and crack wise remarks every time he saw them. It was beyond embarrassing at times.

Cayden and Jess had started dating a couple of months before her best friend, Katie Trent, had been sent to a secure unit and three of his friends had been placed on remand in a youth offending institution for the murder of Deanna Barker. He'd fancied Jess long before then, but she had been the most popular girl in school and he hadn't been the most popular boy. She wasn't a sleep-around. Some had said she was a tough nut to crack, but it hadn't bothered him. They'd messed around a few times now and while his olds were out, they'd have time to do it again. He felt an unfurling in his groin. Maybe she could do something about that, he smirked, like she had the last time his house had been empty.

Cayden lived on The Cavendales, a walled estate with over fifty large detached houses. It backed onto fields on the outskirts of Stockleigh. Peppermint Avenue was a small cul-de-sac with only seven houses. His parents ran their own IT business and had moved in when the houses had first been erected in 2003. Last year they had built him and Lloyd a loft room above the double garage. Yet even that hadn't meant he and Jess could get any peace as his brother often came storming in, purposely. Tonight they would have a good two hours to mess around before anyone was home.

The pavements were like a ghost town; the only thing out was passing cars. Bright headlights shone in the fading light and rainwater splashed up as tyres hit the puddles that had formed in the past hour.

Cayden pulled in his collar as he crossed Railton Drive and headed into the cut-through that would take him onto the main road and back to Jess's house. He wondered whether to call in at Shop&Save for a couple of cans and some chocolate. Residents on The Cavendales had fought against having any kind of shop, for fear of bringing in gangs of youths to hang around and cause trouble. They hadn't even been able to get a pub, not like on the Mitchell Estate where some of his mates lived. So most of the time, he and Jess hung around away from home.

Earplugs in, he listened to music on his phone, watching where his feet were treading to avoid the puddles that had collected on the tarmac. He checked through his messages to see if there was anything from Travis about their conversation earlier but there was nothing new.

Music blaring, he wasn't able to hear footfall behind him. He felt a crack to the back of his legs and he dropped to the floor, cursing as the knees of his jeans began to soak in the rainwater. He stood up quickly, pulling his earplugs out and hanging them around his neck.

'What the hell is your problem?' Cayden's brow furrowed. He'd expected it to be someone he knew fooling around, playing a joke that had gone a little too far. But facing him was what looked like a man, dressed in dark clothes and boots and wearing a balaclava. He had a piece of three-by-two wood raised in the air.

'I don't want any trouble, mate.' Cayden held up a hand in surrender.

The man came towards him again and smashed the wood across the side of his face. Pain shot through Cayden, the blow knocking him off balance once more. He fell backwards onto the path, his phone sliding across the surface of the wet tarmac.

As the man came at him for the third time, Cayden tried to get up, but the wood was brought down on his shoulder before he could put a knee to the ground. There was nothing for it but to curl up into a ball.

He pushed himself as close as he could to the chain-link railings that surrounded the community centre to his right. Dazed, he couldn't do anything to stop the blows raining down on him. He lost count at six when a kick to the stomach had him turning onto his side in agony. A stamp on his hand resulted in a sickly crack.

'No. Please,' he managed to say, blood filling his mouth where his lip had split.

But the man didn't stop. One final hit in the face and Cayden's nose exploded, blood gushing out of both nostrils before he lost consciousness.

# THREE

Laura Mountford sighed to herself as she picked up the jacket that was hanging over the bannister at the bottom of the stairs. She hung it up on the coat peg a few feet away, where it should have been.

'Jess, how many times do I have to tell you to put your things away when you come home!' She sighed as she walked through to the kitchen. 'It only takes a few seconds longer.'

'I'm going out soon,' Jess replied. 'I'll be putting it back on.'

'I've already moved it. You know I can't stand how untidy it looks.'

'Chill out, Mum. It's only a jacket.'

Laura shook her head in frustration. At sixteen, Jess had such a defiant attitude. She'd inherited her father's quick temper, anger clear to see in her steely blue eyes without the added body language of folded arms and the pout. If only Neil were here to chastise her now, she sighed, resigning herself to handling the situation as best she could.

'Would you like me to make you a cheese sandwich for your supper?' Sarah, her elder daughter, asked as she buttered herself a slice of toast.

'Please, if you can be quick.' Laura nodded gratefully. 'I'm already running late, clearing up after this one.' She turned to Jess again. 'The bathroom was a tip too. Why you can't pick up after yourself is anyone's guess.'

Jess stood up so quickly that her chair scraped across the tiled floor with an excruciating screech. 'Mum! I've only just got in from school. I've been nagged at all day there too.'

'What for?' Laura stared at her pointedly. 'You're not in trouble again, are you? I told you after the last time—'

'I meant in general! Why do you always think I'm in trouble?'

'Because you usually are,' Sarah joined in. 'Mum's only going by past experience.'

'Don't you start, Goodie Two-Shoes, or else I'm going out right now.'

'Less of the cheek, young lady.' Laura gnawed at her bottom lip. She sounded like her late mother. Young lady was as patronising as she could get.

'It's funny how you'll listen to teenagers on CrisisChat, but when it comes down to your own daughters, you haven't got time for us.'

Laura recoiled at the harshness in Jess's voice. 'Of course I have time for you!'

'You're never here.'

'That's not fair,' she snapped.

'It's not true either,' noted Sarah.

'My job pays the bills,' Laura added. 'It pays for you to have treats.'

'Not many,' Jess muttered before storming out of the room with a bang of the door. Laura jumped, startled at the noise. Little minx.

Sarah rolled her eyes. 'She'll calm down eventually. I don't know what's wrong with her.'

'It's probably because Deanna Barker's trial is coming up next week. It's all everyone is talking about. It's going to be a tough few weeks, I guess.'

'I know. I went into a shop during my lunch break and heard the shopkeeper talking about it. Two women on the bus home were chatting about it. It's going to be the centre of everyone's world for a while.'

'Don't remind me,' said Laura.

It had been a dreadful blow when Deanna had been murdered. Even now Laura realised how lucky Jess was not to be in a secure unit with her friend Katie, waiting for her trial to begin on Monday. If Jess hadn't been ill, who knows what might have happened.

She looked out of the kitchen window. Already it was dark, the stormy weather blowing the trees about, making leaving the house even less appealing.

'I can't believe she's going out in this weather at all,' Laura added. 'What are you doing this evening?'

'Brad is finishing at seven so he's coming round straight from work.'

Brad was Sarah's boyfriend, and at twenty-one was two years older than her. They'd been together for just over a year, and Laura really liked him. He worked hard as a trainee manager at an insurance brokers. Friday was his late night and the office didn't close until 7 p.m. as they called up customers for prospective sales. Most times he'd call round with a takeaway and a bottle of wine for the two of them. Laura knew that Sarah always looked forward to it, and it was good that they got to share a little time alone. They were saving up for their own home – something she knew would take a long time with the way house prices had risen in the area lately. Still, she wasn't in any hurry to see her firstborn leave the nest yet.

Upstairs, she could hear Jess stomping around. She turned to leave the room, but decided to stay with Sarah a while longer. It was peaceful here, just the two of them.

In truth, Laura couldn't have had two more different daughters if she'd tried. The only similarity between them was their blonde hair and tall, lithe figures. Where Sarah was shy and good to talk to, clever and methodical, Jess was wild, outgoing and a worry every time she went out of the door.

Although, to be fair, though Laura and her sister, Eden, looked similar, they too had very different personalities. They both had jobs that involved caring, both listening to people's troubles and dealing with life's dramas. But Eden had a tough streak about her too. She needed it for her job in the police force, and anyone could see that she loved nothing more than wrestling someone to the ground whenever necessary. Laura would run a mile if anything kicked off in front of her. Just like Sarah would. Whereas Jess would probably stay and fight.

For the past few months, Jess had hooked up with a boy from school, Cayden Blackwell. The Blackwells lived a few streets away, on an estate that the Mountfords used to live on. Over the course of the summer, Laura had got to know Cayden but even now was unsure about him. He seemed too cocky for her liking, but that could be because he was only sixteen.

Knowing that her daughter was changing from a sulky schoolgirl into a young and confident woman, she'd tried having the mother–daughter conversation several times, but Jess had always stormed off. Jess had said that she found the whole thing embarrassing, and talking to her mum was the last thing she wanted to do. Mainly if Laura wanted to say anything to Jess, she had to use Sarah as chief negotiator and peacemaker.

'Sorry to leave her with you like this.' Laura touched her daughter's arm.

Sarah shrugged. 'She'll be fine when you're gone and there's just the two of us. I don't know why she had a mood on her just then. She was okay when she came in from school. I know she misses you being around.'

'You think so?' Laura sighed. 'She has a funny way of showing it.'

'It's the digs about the helpline that give it away for me, and she's always talking about Andrea, Cayden's mum. You know what teenagers are like. They think everyone else's mum is cool.' Sarah wiped her hands of toast crumbs and got up to put the plate in the dishwasher.

'If we saw more of each other, the house would be a battle ground,' Laura remarked. 'We're too alike to get on.'

'Maybe,' Sarah agreed. 'But I was used to you working at CrisisChat every night, and I know I'm no trouble. It's a shame you can't change your shifts now so that you're at home for some evenings at least. I'd like to have you around too. Sometimes I feel like my sister's mother and father rolled into one.'

'I'm sorry.' Laura stood up and gave her a hug. 'I know how hard it is for you, but I have to work. I can't change my hours – you know how many times I've tried. And you know how long it took me to get this job. I was out of work for months when I was made redundant, and it wasn't nice. At least this way we get to have some treats.'

Sarah hugged her back. 'And we both love you for it.'

Laura gave her a faint smile. She tried her best, and yet sometimes she knew it wasn't enough. Just lately, Jess had been giving her lip, hanging around with the wrong people and coming and going a lot more than Laura felt comfortable with. Laura knew it was typical teenage behaviour, pushing the boundaries, trying to see how far she could go. At times Laura met her halfway, but at others Jess would grind her down and she'd give in too easily. She did ground her if she didn't do as she was told. Trouble was, that didn't work when Laura wasn't around in the evenings to see that Jess stayed in.

She picked up the sandwich that Sarah had wrapped in silver foil and put it in her bag. Two chocolate biscuits from the barrel and she was ready to face her shift.

Hesitating in the hallway, she dashed upstairs and knocked on Jess's bedroom door.

'What?' came her daughter's dulcet tones.

She pushed the door open. The room, decorated in pale pastel colours, was moderately tidy after the previous night, when Laura had moaned at Jess until she had shifted the mess from the floor.

There was another pile of clothes at the bottom of the bed, and she could see several pairs of discarded shoes. Knowing Jess, she would change her clothes at least twice more before she decided on what she was wearing that evening. The rest would be either slung to the floor or shoved in her wardrobe out of sight.

'Are you okay now?' she asked, not wanting to step inside the room and crowd her.

'I'm fine.'

'All I ask is that you keep the place tidy. I have to go to work. I can't be there for you all the time and you have to help your sister.'

Silence followed. Laura changed tactics.

'It's still horrible outside. Wear your beanie hat to stop your hair from frizzing.'

That brought a smile to Jess's lips. Jess lived in her beanie hat whenever she could and Laura was always telling her to remove it. She'd bought her two new ones last Christmas – a purple, black and white stripy one and a grey one – but she still wore the one that had belonged to her father, even though it was a little on the big side for her.

'If you'll be at Cayden's house, you can stay out until eleven as long as he walks you home.'

'Okay.'

'And there's a fiver tucked behind the bread bin if you want to get you and Cayden something to eat.'

'Thanks, Mum! We can grab chips later.'

Laura smiled. She despaired of herself at times for being a pushover, but she needed Jess to know that she cared. It was hard being a single parent now that she was a widow, but she did her best to provide for her girls, and if she had to give in every now and then it didn't make her a bad parent. It probably made her more use in her job to parents in a similar situation.

Children had to grow up some day and be trusted.

# FOUR

Jess had indeed changed her top three times before settling on the outfit she was wearing now. She loved fashion and even though she didn't like to be a sheep, she always wore the latest styles. That's why she and Cayden had started to work for Travis Barker. Earning a little money here and there enabled her to have clothes she wouldn't be able to afford if she had to ask her mum all the time. Even if her mum had money to spare, she would insist on Jess getting cheaper versions of the same designs. She just didn't seem to understand how hard it was to keep up with peer pressure to look good.

Sarah was in the living room watching the evening news when she went in to say goodbye.

'What time will Brad be here?' Jess asked as she wrapped her scarf around her neck.

'He'll be about an hour,' said Sarah.

'So you'll be all loved up. Glad I'm going out.'

'Pot. Kettle. I take it you're going to see Cayden?'

'Yes, he's going to be later than planned now so I'm meeting him over by Shop&Save and then going back to his house.' Jess flicked her hair back from her face.

'Why don't you go straight there? It's still raining.'

'I'm not sure.' Jess shrugged.

'Well, just be careful when you do get together.' Sarah looked at her knowingly.

'You sound like Mum! I'm not about to get pregnant and be tied down with a kid for the rest of my life.'

'You went to the clinic then?'

Jess nodded, blushing a little.

'Good, at least you have protection now. And if it is Cayden that you love, then see he treats you well. You know you can say no whenever you like. He shouldn't force you to do anything.'

'He doesn't.' Jess shook her head. 'And he won't, because if he does, he'll get a swift kick in the balls and never come near me again.'

Sarah laughed. 'I wish I had your attitude, little sis.' She stood up and gave her an impromptu hug. 'You're so sassy, even if you are a spoilt brat and try my patience all the time.'

Jess hugged her sister back. They were closer than either of them chose to admit.

'Be home before Mum is due in, won't you?' Sarah added as Jess left the room.

'Yep.' Jess nipped in the kitchen and took a chocolate bar from the shelf in the fridge. 'Mum gave me some money. I might get some chips later,' she shouted through.

'You've just had something to eat!'

'I'm a growing girl!'

Jess took her jacket from the peg where her mum had put it and rushed out of the house. She pulled her beanie hat out of the pocket, pushed it on and put her hood up against the rain. It took her a few minutes to walk to the main road and by this time her jacket was soaked. She would kill Cayden when she saw him. It had taken her ages to do her hair and it was going to be a frizz bomb with the wind lashing the rain under her hood, soaking her hat too. Why couldn't she have just gone to his house? It was much closer, and now she'd have to walk further to get there as well.

On the high street, the lights of the supermarket just ahead, she passed Caffè Nero, wondering if she could get Cayden to buy her something nice to take with them. She loved their chocolate muffins.

Blocking her way further up on the pavement was a group of boys she knew from school.

'Wahey, Jess,' shouted one above the level of the wind as she approached them. 'Whassup?'

'Nothing.' She pushed past him, much to the amusement of the others.

'Playing hard to get, I see?' he shouted back at her. 'You'll be mine one day, Jess Mountford, just you wait and see.' He put his hand on his crotch and licked his top lip provocatively.

'In your dreams.' Jess turned to him and, walking backwards, flicked him the finger before continuing on her way. She could hear them laughing and it made her sad. If she had been with Katie, they would be laughing now too. She hoped Katie would be found not guilty at the end of the trial so she could come home again. Even though someone had died, Jess couldn't believe what had happened, how wrong everything had gone that night.

The past six months had been the longest of her life since Katie had been locked up. More to the point, she couldn't believe *she* hadn't been locked up with her. If she hadn't been laid down with a bad cold, she would have been out that night with her. So too would Cayden. She shuddered involuntarily, thinking again how lucky she was.

She and Katie had been best friends since they were twelve, when Katie and her family had moved into The Cavendales. Katie lived in Orchard Way, which, back then, was the next cul-de-sac to their house. They'd been inseparable, and when Katie had been charged under the law of joint enterprise because there wasn't sufficient evidence to say whether or not she had been involved in the murder of Deanna Barker, she'd been placed in a secure unit and taken away straight after the charge. To Jess, it was like losing a sister. Katie was her rock, her soulmate, and it had taken ages to adjust to her not being around. She hoped she was acquitted at the trial. She knew that Katie was innocent.

She pressed on down the street, past the entrance to the supermarket, where another group of kids were hanging around, trying to escape the rain, no doubt, rather than go home.

Jess had lived in Stockleigh all her life, and even though she was lucky enough to live on the edge of a nice area, she and her friends always hung around on the Mitchell Estate. Some properties were owned, some rented out by private landlords, but the majority were owned by Mitchell Housing Association. The high school they all attended was halfway between there and where she lived. She couldn't wait to leave next year.

She was saving the money she earned on the sly so she could move somewhere bigger like London, Birmingham or Manchester – somewhere with a bit more life. Jess loved going shopping in Manchester. She couldn't wait until she was old enough to stay out overnight and try out all the pubs and clubs. Apart from the youth club, which she would never be seen dead in, there wasn't much else to do around their area, which is why she and Cayden mostly met their friends on the Mitchell Estate and made some noise. It was a great way to let off steam.

At the corner of the building she turned and walked across the car park, holding on to her hood as the wind nearly took her off her feet. Thank God she and Cayden would be indoors again soon.

She took out her phone as she walked to call Cayden, to tell him she was there. She was already ten minutes late and he was nowhere around. There was no reply and, frowning, she sent a message urging him to hurry up.

The rain began to come down heavier and she cursed, running under the shelter that housed the shopping trolleys. Huddled in there, she heard someone shout. She turned to see a man jogging towards her.

'Excuse me,' he said, trying to catch his breath as he drew level. 'You haven't seen a little white dog, have you?'

Jess shook her head. 'No, sorry.'

'He's only tiny. I'm afraid he might be run over if I don't find him. He's a terrier. Are you sure you didn't see him?'

'Sorry.'

'My little girl will be heartbroken if I've lost him. Jackson!' he shouted and walked past her. 'Jackson!'

She watched for a few moments as he continued to shout the dog's name, looking in-between the parked cars, bending down on his knees to see if he could spot him. She and Sarah had never been able to have a dog, no matter how much they had protested. She hoped he found it soon.

She checked the time on the screen of her phone. Where was Cayden?

The man was back.

'No sign of him?' she asked, realising how stupid she sounded as soon as she had said it.

The man shook his head, raised his hands to his side and then down again. 'I'll keep looking for a while. He can't be far.'

'What was his name?' she asked, coming out of the shelter.

'Jackson. I saw him last down here.' He pointed and walked on ahead.

Jess followed behind him, trying to focus through the rain. 'Are you sure your dog would have gone this way?' she asked, glancing around.

'He's only a small thing, he could be anywhere.'

'Have you got any chocolate or anything? Maybe—'

As they passed a small white van, he lurched at her, punching her full in the face.

Jess staggered back with the force, hot pain pulsing through her, but she managed to stay on her feet. She put a hand to her mouth, feeling liquid running between her fingers and a pain that almost took her breath away.

'My nose – it's bleeding!' she cried. Disoriented and confused, before she knew it he had grabbed her around the neck and pulled her backwards. She screamed, hoping it would carry above the noise of the wind, and tried to pull his arm away. But he covered her mouth.

He dragged her to the van. As she fought to get his hand from her mouth so she could shout again, he opened the door and shoved her inside. She lunged at him as he tried to close the door. He pushed her back inside, but she came at him again. This time he punched her to the side of her head and she fell to the floor of the van in a daze.

Before she could do anything else, he had wrapped a woollen scarf tightly around her mouth and done the same with duct tape around her wrists and ankles.

She heard a door slam and the engine start. There was only a tiny window and she couldn't see who he was. Shock setting in, she burst into tears. She didn't know where she was going, and she didn't know who had taken her.

The van began to move. It left the car park seconds later.

# FIVE

The city of Stockleigh, based in the West Midlands, had a population of just short of 200,000 residents. Schooling was slightly above the national average, the level of unemployment below. Many of its residents owned their own homes, family and friends living within a few miles of each other. It had a middle-class feel about it, but the majority of its residents would argue they were the new race of middle-working class.

With more of a town than a city feel about it, it still managed to be home to a university with a good reputation, two colleges of further education and a business-training centre. Only ten years ago, the city council had erected a new, larger shopping centre, where most high street stores opened branches, incorporating a large eating area and eight-screen cinema. There were a few pockets of deprivation, such as the Mitchell Estate in the south and the Hopwood Estate not too far from the centre of the city, but for the most part it was a good place to live.

At thirty-nine, Eden had worked at Stockleigh Police Station since leaving university almost eighteen years ago. Joining as a police constable, she'd completed years on the beat before taking exams and training on the job to be a detective constable, before earning a place in the domestic violence unit, which, although harrowing at times, she had found tremendously rewarding.

As part of a new government initiative, Safe Streets, she had been put forward for a newly restructured post as detective sergeant running the Community Intelligence Team. It was a secondment for twelve months so she'd be able to return to her previous position if the initiative wasn't successful or, as was often the way with such things, lost its funding despite its success.

Eden had been thrilled to be asked. It seemed her skills in working with people to worm out information had been noted. Over the past few years, she'd managed to help solve a few crimes that the higher ranking and longer serving detectives hadn't been able to get to the root of. Many times, officers asked her to get involved in coercing people into doing things they were scared to do for fear of the repercussions, like giving evidence to lock away someone who would undoubtedly commit the same crime again if left on the streets.

When she'd been told about the position, she had jumped at the chance. With a sixteen-year-old daughter, Casey, and an estranged husband, Danny, long gone, the extra pay from a promotion was a welcome relief. It meant learning how to manage staff, but she didn't mind that because she got to do what she loved, which was getting down and dirty to wheedle out any necessary information.

Their new team had only been working together for four weeks, so they were still finding their feet. Along with Amy there was another detective constable, Jordan Ashcroft. They were all supported by Detective Inspector Sean Whittaker, who had been given the role to manage them alongside the murder investigation team.

Their nickname had quickly become 'the sticking plaster team' but it was an affable joke that she didn't mind. And if it helped to solve a crime, then, well, the DI was always up for a curry across the road at the Red Onion or a pint down the way at the White Lion.

She hadn't even had to leave the building, just locate to the opposite corner of the room. She'd stayed close to CID and her colleagues in the domestic violence unit, which would ensure she was still in the thick of things. Information passing and gathering was crucial in their line of work. Their offices were on a large open-plan floor, which they shared with too many filing cabinets and overflowing waste paper bins.

'What are you lucky pair up to tonight?' Eden asked Jordan and Amy, who were sitting at their desks opposite.

'I'm going out for a pint or two,' said Jordan, clicking a few buttons on his keyboard before looking up. 'If I don't pick up a bird, I'll grab a curry and cry into my tikka masala.'

'As if you'd ever be short of a woman,' Eden teased, even though she knew he wouldn't be looking for anyone special. Jordan was twenty-nine and had been working in their station for two years after starting his career in Manchester. She knew him well enough to know that, although he had a cheeky-boy personality, he wasn't the type to go looking for one-night conquests. In any case, he still seemed to be broken-hearted from the recent break-up of his three-year relationship with his first love and wasn't looking for a woman to take her place.

He was far too suave to be a copper really. A male model would have been more apt, with the six-pack he kept well hidden, his chiselled features, brown eyes, skin and hair. To the men, he was one of the lads, and to the women, he was eye candy. Both had their advantages and disadvantages, but Eden was more thankful for his placid nature. His ability to keep calm during many an incident that she knew she might have struggled with was fresh and it also put people at ease.

Jordan was keen and fun to be around too, and Amy adored him in a sisterly way, teasing him constantly about his dreamy eyes getting him results, which was true. Eden glanced over to see her throwing Jordan a huge smile.

'How about you, Amy?' Eden leaned across to pinch a Jaffa Cake from the box her colleague was devouring. 'Have you got anything planned, other than murdering your future mother-in-law?'

'Ha ha.' Amy gave her a sarcastic smile. 'I'm coming in to catch up on some paperwork.' She pointed to a tray. 'Got tons of it.'

'Well, no matter what, we'd better get prepared for the fireworks when Deanna Barker's trial begins on Monday. We have to be prepared for things to escalate until it's over.' Eden leaned forward on her elbows and rested her chin in the crook of her hands, brown eyes serious now. 'And we have to be prepared for things to escalate after the trial too – whichever way things go.'

# SIX

Cayden tried to open his eyes. One stayed shut; the other felt watery. One hand hurt so badly he couldn't move it. He pressed the tentative and shaky fingertips of the other to his face, wincing at their touch.

He lay there for a few seconds while he tried to breathe, before he eventually pulled himself to sitting, resting his back on the fence. His head wouldn't stop spinning, his vision blurry.

The last thing he could remember was curling up into a ball as the man came at him. He wondered if it was a random attack or if it had been planned. He certainly hadn't provoked the man, so there was no need for him to just act out like that.

Was this part of the plan that he hadn't been told about?

After a minute, he turned and pushed himself to his feet. Swaying for a few seconds, he reached into his pocket for his phone, and that's when it all came rushing back. He remembered the hit that had knocked his legs from under him, the force of the wood when it came crashing down and his inability to find time to put up any resistance. Had his attacker spoken? No, he couldn't remember anything else.

He walked along the path, holding on to the fencing to stay upright. He'd have to go back home, call his parents from there. The cut-through was darker in the middle where he was but there was a street light ahead. He began to take slow steps, stumbling to one knee on more than one occasion. His breath was coming in rasps, his nose unable to take in air.

Was his nose broken? He put a hand to it and groaned as fresh pain erupted inside his head.

Even if he couldn't get home, he could get to the supermarket. Someone would ring his parents. As he inched forward, he spotted something glistening on the path. It was his phone. He stooped, careful not to topple. He turned it over. The screen was intact. He should be able to make a call with one hand.

He pressed Mum, but after a few rings it went to voicemail. Crying out as pain shot through his head again, he held on to the railing and threw up.

Step by step he walked slowly along the path, each metre taking him nearer to safety. Through his quickly swelling eye he could see it was getting lighter, but he had to stop.

He tried to think what had happened back there. Who would attack him so viciously? He couldn't recall much about his attacker now, but he was hoping he didn't know him. If it *was* someone he knew, he would sure as hell be after getting him back. Unless this had something to do with Travis double-crossing him. He'd thought he seemed a little jumpier than usual when he'd met him.

He set off again a minute later, clutching his stomach. If he could just make it to the supermarket, someone would help him.

He made it to the end of the path and into the street. The entrance to the shop was just above him. He needed to activate the automatic doors.

A few more steps and he fell to his knees before lying down on his back. The last thing he remembered before he blacked out again was people rushing over to him.

# SEVEN

Claire Mornington was on her way to meet up with her friend Stacey before heading off to hang around the shops, down on the Mitchell Estate. She flicked long dark hair from out of her face as it battled with the wind.

It was so blustery, she wondered if anyone would be out, or if the night would be wasted as everyone was indoors. They couldn't even crash at their friend Jess's and put up with her namby-pamby sister because she was going over to her boyfriend, Cayden's, house.

Even though Claire was hanging around with the same gang, she still missed Deanna Barker. Even now, six months later, it was hard to imagine that she was dead. Claire would often imagine that Deanna would come walking down the road, linking arms with Katie, and say that she'd played a silly joke on them all. It just didn't seem real that she had been murdered by Nathan Lucas. Everyone knew that he carried a knife – he'd pulled it out lots of times. But no one had been certain he would use it. Claire had thought he was all mouth until that day.

She still wondered what had provoked them to act like they did. Sure, they were all into having a laugh at other people's expense, dishing out the odd slap and punch every now and then as a dare. But the brutality of it, along with it being people she had thought of as friends, had hit home hard. It had also rocked their community.

She heard a car slow down and someone shout her name. She took a step towards the rear door as the window slowly went down.

'What do you want?' she asked.

The door opened, and hands reached out and seized her. Before she had time to react, she was pulled into the back seat. The door slammed behind her and the car screeched off.

'What the hell are you doing?' She tried to sit upright, scrambling for the door handle.

The person by her side wore a balaclava. She was pushed down on the back seat, straddled and her arms forced up above her head.

'Get off me!' she screamed, fear bursting out of her as she tried to free herself. A strip of duct tape was pressed roughly to her lips. She screamed but it came out muffled.

She glanced around quickly. What were they going to do with her? Where would they take her? Who were they?

Panic ripping through her, she began to buck, still screaming behind the tape. Tears poured down her face as she struggled with her fear.

'Shut the fuck up.'

She drew in a breath as he searched through her pockets, emptying them. His hands roamed over her breasts, his face stopping an inch from hers as their eyes connected. She bucked even more before he moved.

Minutes later, the car took a sharp left and the handbrake was pulled up sharply. The car whizzed round to a halt. The door beside her opened, and she was pulled from the seat. She landed heavily on the floor.

She scrambled to her feet, trying to get up, but she was pushed in the back. Crying openly now, she looked up at them. They wore dark shoes, jeans and black jackets. She wanted to rip the tape from her mouth and scream, but she didn't dare. Instead she sat, frozen, until they came towards her.

She curled up in a ball, but one reached for her legs and pulled them out straight, while the other held on to her arms again.

Not a word was spoken between them as she groaned, her head flailing from side to side.

The one who had pulled her into the car straddled her legs and began to open her jeans.

*No, please.*

She kicked out as her arms were held above her head. But she was no match for them. Her jeans were pulled off. Her shoes were removed too. With the wind howling around her, she began to shiver. Ohmigod – the lower half of her body was partially naked.

'This is a warning to keep your mouth shut. You tell anyone what's been going on and you're dead. Do you understand?'

It was the same voice as before. This time she recognised it.

'Do you understand?'

She nodded fervently.

The two people moved away. With a sob, Claire scrambled across the grass away from them.

They got back into the car; she heard doors slamming and the engine restarting. The car skidded away.

Gasping for breath in the cold night air, she pulled at the tape and then sat for a moment. Everything looked so different in the dark.

Where was she? Buildings loomed up around her as she concentrated on focusing, and she realised it might be a block of garages. There were no lights nearby, only in the distance, she guessed a couple of minutes' walk away.

Where were her jeans and shoes? She tried to make out any shapes. They would be in a pile near to each other, or strewn across the area, but she couldn't see them. She searched around with her hands for a while, before getting up, treading into large puddles of water that had accumulated.

They had taken everything from her pockets. She had no phone, no money, no way of getting home other than to walk barefoot and half naked. She had no idea where she was.

Not caring what she was treading in, she pushed herself up and stumbled out of the lane, hoping to figure out where she was when she got to a main road. Then she began to run.

# EIGHT

The office block where Laura worked was in the city centre. A few minutes before 6 p.m., she parked her car and dashed into the building. She had been at CrisisChat for five years now, after qualifying as a counsellor just after Neil was killed, in 2007. The helpline had found their own funding at first, then been given a government grant for the next nine years. There were two years left from this round of funding before the money ran out and the not-for-profit charity would have to start bidding for more.

Laura had volunteered at Samaritans for several years before coming to CrisisChat, but the fact that she had to do a night shift once a month became too much when she had both girls. Neil didn't like it either – said it wasn't safe. And after one suicide attempt too many from the callers, she called it a day.

After that had come regular hours working in the offices of Warren's Electrical Supplies, doing the filing, accounting, invoicing. The work was okay and her colleagues fine to a point, but she missed the feeling that she was helping people, so she trained to be a counsellor in her spare time. Which was just as well, as she was made redundant not long after she qualified.

When the job had come up at CrisisChat, she'd applied thinking she wouldn't have enough experience. She'd been pleasantly surprised to find that they were willing to train her on the job, recognising that many of her skills were transferrable to their clientele.

She knew the job had been meant for her as soon as she'd first stepped into the building. And not many people wanted to do the graveyard shift either. It was only because she needed the money. It was thirty hours a week, unsociable hours due to its nature, but even when the shifts had their low moments, Laura would always bounce back when she got home, closed the door on that world and switched off as she thanked her lucky stars it wasn't a part of hers.

CrisisChat was located on the third floor of a block of offices just off Stockleigh high street. Laura walked up the final flight of stairs with a puff and pushed the door to her office open. It was a tiny attic room, hardly big enough for the staff who manned it.

At the nearest desk sat her colleague Nicola. She was a small woman in her mid-forties, with short spiky hair pushed down by her headphones. She waved as Laura came in, whilst continuing her conversation with the person on the other end of the line.

Both women had probably heard most things on the phones at the helpline. Laura tried not to take it personally when someone shouted down the phone at her, cussed and roared at her to get rid of their anger. Teenagers would laugh as well as cry. Occasionally, she'd learned too much and had suffered for days when she'd heard horrific stories. She could never tell if the words were true or a pack of lies told to garner attention. But she would never judge. Nicola wouldn't either, which is why they were both good at their jobs.

There were three of them on the helpline. Marian, the third member of the team, worked early afternoons. There were only ever one or two of them at a time on shift. It was all the charity could fund. Which was why they were a close team.

Laura made the universal sign for a cuppa, and when Nicola nodded vehemently she went over to the far end of the room where there were tea and coffee facilities. She flicked on the kettle before removing her coat and going back to Nicola to collect her mug.

Nicola put a finger over the mute button. 'It's Leah Burton again,' she explained. 'She seems okay, fed up of Mum and Dad, but just wants to talk. She's been on for the past fifteen minutes.'

Nicola removed her finger and began to speak to Leah. Laura shook her head as she listened to the broken conversation. Leah was a regular caller and always talked over them. But they were just there to listen for the most part.

Ten minutes later, coffee had been made and Leah was still talking. Laura put on her headphones, ready for the next call, but the lines stayed quiet. She sent a quick message to Sarah asking her to remove a joint of meat from the freezer, which she had forgotten to do before leaving the house.

Finally, Nicola took off her headphones. With a huge sigh, she laid her head on the desk.

'Thank goodness for that,' she said. 'I was beginning to think I'd never see my bed this evening.'

'You could have given the call to me,' said Laura. 'I would have chatted to Leah, save you staying late.'

'Oh, I'm fine. What have I got to go home to except Sherlock?' Sherlock was Nicola's cat. 'How are you, by the way? Is Jess still causing you grief?'

Laura nodded. 'She's still being her usual teenage self. She thinks she can come and go as she pleases, and she treats the house like a hotel.' She clasped a hand to her mouth. 'I'm doing it again. I sound like my mother.' She groaned and put her head on the desk too.

'Been there, done that,' said Nicola. 'Three times, and one still to go.' She quivered. 'I'm dreading it already.'

The women smiled at each other before sitting up again.

'It's never-ending – both here and at home. Has anyone mentioned the trial yet?' Laura asked as she drew her hair into a ponytail and tied it back with the band around her wrist.

Nicola shook her head. 'I'm surprised though. It's going to hit everyone next week, isn't it?'

Laura was already dreading it. She and Katie's mum, Maxine, had been friends since the Trents had moved into The Cavendales and long after she and the girls had moved out. Jess and Katie had grown closer still at high school.

It had been hard for Jess when Katie had been charged. Even their house seemed empty for a while, with no laughter as the girls shared an in-joke, no loud music and bangs as they practised dancing, no sounds of feet thundering up and down the stairs.

Laura had missed Katie as much as Jess. It had been like losing a breath of fresh air. Jess had been lost without her friend, so much so that at one point Laura had thought she might be suffering from depression. But gradually over time Jess had accepted that Katie would be gone for a while and kept hoping that justice would be done and she would come home at the end of the trial.

'I can't even begin to imagine how Maxine will be feeling,' she said.

'I hope they do right by Katie,' said Nicola. 'She doesn't deserve to get a sentence for something she didn't do.'

Laura shivered as she heard the wind howling through the single-glazed window by her side and pulled her long cardigan into her chest. She made a mental note to find time to ring Maxine in the morning. She needed as much support as she could get. It must be such an ordeal to think that your child was facing a charge of murder for something she hadn't done.

# NINE

Jess whimpered. The van was moving at speed. Panic had set in long before she had worked out that she wouldn't be heard if she screamed. As she bumped around in the back, her eyes filled with tears as she remembered helping the man to look for a dog. And then she recalled him hitting her and then dragging her into a small white van. She hadn't even had a chance to see the registration number.

The tears fell then as her thoughts went into overdrive. Had he been trawling around looking for someone – anyone? Was he a paedophile, after a young girl? Maybe he'd seen her waiting for Cayden and had seized his opportunity.

She tried to close her mind off to the dark thoughts. She wanted to bang her feet on the floor, alert him that she was awake, but something made her stay quiet. Maybe it was best to store up all her anger for when she needed it. For when the back door opened again.

Someone would have noticed him dragging her into the van. Someone would find her before he harmed her, wouldn't they? She tried to remember what he looked like, in case the police needed her to do a photofit. He had looked normal. There was nothing odd about him. He was average height, average weight. He wore a black bomber jacket and jeans, rolled up at the bottom. His head was covered by a woollen hat, but there was no hair showing around its edges. She couldn't recall anything about his face except his eyes. And they had seemed friendly enough, at the time. He had seemed worried about finding his dog.

There hadn't been a dog, she knew now.

Where would he take her?

Slowly, her eyes grew accustomed to the dark. A few minutes later, the van slowed down and her heart began to beat a drum inside her chest. She tried to listen in case she could hear any familiar sounds as it drew to a complete halt. There were beeps, and she could see yellow flashes. They must have stopped at a crossing. But it was only seconds before the car was on the move again.

The driver sped up and took a sharp left, and her head hit the side of the van as she struggled to steady herself. She groaned at the sudden pain. By the time the van stopped she'd be so travel sick he could do anything to her and she wouldn't be able to put up a fight.

Then her eyes widened. Cayden! He would be waiting for her. He would call her to see where she was. She manoeuvred her hands to reach her jacket pocket, but she could feel from the outside that it was empty. He must have taken her phone.

She wondered if he'd got it with him now or if he'd left it in the car park. He could have thrown it out of the van. If he had, the police would find it and be alerted. They would watch the CCTV footage from the big camera she saw every day, see her being manhandled into the van. They would see the number plate, find the owner and then what? They would follow the CCTV footage and see where he took her. But there wasn't coverage everywhere in the city.

A sob escaped her. She couldn't reach Cayden. She couldn't call her mum. She couldn't call her auntie Eden, who would know what to do. She couldn't get in touch with anyone. She was at his mercy.

She tried to reassure herself. The police would find her. Eden would find her. She wouldn't let her down.

But she could be dead by then.

What if he wanted to rape her and then murder her afterwards? What happened if he was taking her to the docks ready to ship out of the country and sell as a sex slave? What happened if he was a warped bastard who wanted to carry out weird experiments on her? What if. . .

Keep calm, she repeated inwardly over and over, hoping it would work to stop her hyperventilating. Instead, each time they passed a street light and a ray of light came through the tiny window, her eyes searched around the sides and the floor of the van, hoping to see something she could use to defend herself when the door was opened again, take the man by surprise.

Seconds later she burst into tears again, shaking uncontrollably, but not through being cold. There was nothing in the back of the van except her. Nothing she could use as a weapon.

All she could do now was wait until it stopped – and pray he wouldn't kill her.

# TEN

Maxine Trent got out of her car and locked it quickly before struggling to put up her umbrella as she walked across the car park. Thinking better of it when it blew inside out within seconds, she took it down again.

By the entrance, she craned her head as she drew level with an ambulance, its lights flashing, but she couldn't see anything.

Drenched as she entered Shop&Save, she shook her head, pulling strands of red hair away from her face where it had been lashed about.

Her stomach lurched as she saw how many people were in the store. She felt eyes on her immediately, and she quickly lowered her gaze. Once Katie's trial started on Monday, she and her family would be all over the media again – in the newspapers, on radio and television. They wouldn't be able to go anywhere for the next few weeks and had all been dreading the thought for ages now.

Ever since Katie had been charged, their family had been targeted. Maxine thought back on some of the nasty things that had happened to them. If she hadn't been a part of it all, if she had been reading about it in the local newspaper, she wouldn't have believed it could have been reality.

Every night for several weeks, there had been something pushed through their letterbox. Handwritten notes saying they would die if they didn't move away, which the police could do nothing about because they couldn't find out who the culprit was. Dog crap had been shoved through on a regular basis. A firework in the middle of May caused a hole in the hall carpet – but luckily nothing else.

At one time there had even been a toe tag delivered, pushed through in a small brown envelope with Katie's name written on it. When her ten-year-old son, Matty, had come into the kitchen with it, Maxine had soon realised that it was a luggage label carefully made to look the part. And it had done its job – she had been scared to death at the sight of it.

Things had calmed down a bit over the summer, but she knew it was bound to start again. Everywhere she went, Maxine could almost feel the anger simmering, ready to burst forward. Once the trial was over, what happened if Katie was found guilty? They'd have to move. They wouldn't be safe in their homes.

And the trial was going to be so intrusive. Lots of people had condemned her daughter even though she knew that Katie was innocent. A mother can feel it in her bones. No one would tell her otherwise. Sure, they had all been present when it happened, but it had been Nathan Lucas who had committed the act that led to Deanna Barker's death. All three boys were aged eighteen, barely adults in her eyes. Only Katie had been sixteen and then only just.

Her husband, Phil, hadn't been coping well these past few weeks. They were supposed to be going to see Katie on Sunday morning, but it was looking likely that she would have to go by herself again. Phil hadn't been to Ashcroft House to see Katie for the past month, and it had been easier to go alone rather than cause too much of a fuss.

Even so, with everything that had gone wrong since that night, and their family being victimised constantly, at least they were all still alive. Maxine would never forget the moment when she had stood outside the church at a memorial for Deanna and Lulu, Deanna's mum, had launched herself at them. It wasn't their fault what had happened, but she had felt Lulu Barker's grief as she blamed all four teenagers for her daughter's death. Lulu had a go at one of the other mothers too: anyone related to the families involved had become a target.

Maxine picked up bread and a small bottle of milk and added them to a basket, wondering what else she needed to tide them over until she went shopping on Sunday afternoon. She doubted any of them would want to eat much that weekend. Her stomach churned at the thought of the weeks ahead. She wished she could get the trial over and done with, even if the verdict didn't go in their favour.

'What the fuck are you doing in here?'

Maxine turned to see who had addressed her, her shoulders dropping as much as her temperature when she saw who it was. If she remembered rightly, this was Travis, Lulu Barker's youngest son. He was tall, her head only reaching his shoulder, which gave him an intimidation win straight off. He had a tiny scar on his chin, the kind caused by accident rather than malicious intent, yet he had the remnants of bruising around his cheek and temple on one side. But it was his eyes that bore into hers, trying to send hatred to her very soul, that scared her the most.

Maxine tried to move further into the store, but he blocked her way.

'I asked you a question.' He prodded her sharply in the shoulder.

'Please leave me alone.' She walked around him and made her way quickly through the aisles to the self-service tills. The bread and milk would have to suffice for now.

But Travis followed her. He stood next to her, an aura of menace coming from him.

'I'm coming after your little lad if that bitch gets away with it,' he said. 'Because she needs to be locked up for good. A life for a life, that's what I reckon.'

Maxine pushed her shopping into a bag as quickly as she could.

Travis moved closer. She could feel his breath on the side of her face as he pointed a finger near to her eye. 'Are you listening to me?' he seethed.

No one in the shop came to her aid. She had been condemned the same as her daughter. Guilty until proven innocent. She paid for the shopping as quickly as she could and marched out, hoping he wouldn't follow her. If he did, she would go back inside and ring Phil. But even then it would be too late. She knew he'd be after revenge for what had happened to Deanna. She'd seen him several times over the past six months, and he'd always shouted something nasty to her but kept his distance. Now he had her cornered like a scared animal.

Regardless of the relentless wind and rain, her steps were quick as she glanced behind her, but he wasn't there. Her eyes brimmed with tears, and she could feel her hands shaking as she carried the bag to her car. How dare he threaten to hurt Matty!

Taking one last look around the car park, she got into her car and slammed down the locks. She sat while she caught her breath, hands pressed to the steering wheel to stop them shaking. She couldn't even attempt to put her key in the lock.

Looking in the rear-view mirror, half expecting someone to creep up from the back seat, all she could see was fear reflected in her eyes. And this was before the trial started. She'd just had another taste of how intrusive, how unbearable things were going to become again.

Maxine didn't know which verdict she was dreading the most. There was no way she wanted Katie to be sentenced for murder. She wanted her daughter to come home. But what would happen if she was freed? What would the Barkers do then if justice wasn't dished out to their satisfaction?

Would they always have to live their lives looking over their shoulders?

Katie – April 2015

Dear Mum,

I thought I would be coming home today. I wanted to say sorry to Deanna's family for what happened. And I have to tell you too. I haven't had time to go through it all properly with you, and I need you to understand so that you can help me.

I wished I'd never gone out that night. I should have been with Jess, but you know she was poorly, and she had Cayden to look after her. Now I have blood on my hands.

I ran away because Nathan Lucas threatened to hurt me, and you and Dad and Matty. I couldn't chance that. When I reached the end of our street, I didn't know what to do. I didn't know what you would say. I knew you would be angry that I hadn't stayed behind to face the music, like you always taught me to do.

I came straight home, but I couldn't go in. How could I tell you what had happened, what I had been witness to? No, what I had been *involved* in. What if you didn't believe I hadn't done anything? Nathan could say it was me. He'd probably lie to save his own skin. But then I remembered there would be cameras. CCTV would show what really happened.

I never thought that would go against me.

Trouble had been brewing between some of the boys for ages, Mum, because of the Barker brothers. It was only a matter of time before something like this happened. But someone dying hadn't been part of the plan. Cayden told me to play the game, but I didn't want to pretend that Nathan was my boyfriend. I didn't like him that much. I tried to explain to Jess and Cayden how much he frightened me, but neither of them listened.

Every time I squeeze my eyes shut I can still see Deanna's face, blood pouring from her mouth before her eyes glazed over and her chest stopped moving. I keep seeing Nathan pushing the knife in, pulling the knife out. I didn't know he was going to do that, I swear. I didn't know they were going to jump Travis, not that it makes a difference really. Deanna was wearing her brother's hoodie. But I had no idea they were going to attack anyone that night.

The judge said we are all evil. I'm not evil, am I? They were waiting for Travis, Mum. They had it all planned, but I didn't know. I stayed on the top of the grass verge because I was thinking I might just go home. The mood wasn't good and I didn't want to be with them all night. Not without Jess.

But then I saw them laying into Deanna. You taught me that three on one isn't fair. I couldn't stand and do nothing. So I ran down to them. I pushed them all off – you believe me, don't you? I wasn't goading them like the judge said. I didn't panic when it all went wrong. I didn't know it was going to happen. I swear.

Nathan backed off, but he kept on waving the knife around. No one dared go near him. And then I saw it was Deanna, Mum. She was hurt real bad – her face looked a right mess. They were all like animals. I rang for an ambulance and as soon as I saw the paramedics running towards Deanna, I ran too.

She was dead before they got there. I held her in my arms, Mum. She didn't die alone.

I'm in a dream, aren't I? I'm going to wake up any moment and be safe at home in my bed. Deanna Barker will be alive and Nathan Lucas will have played a trick on me. Because I can't believe what's happened. It isn't real, is it?

This is a mistake. I am not guilty of murder. I have to come home. I can't bear to think of having no life beyond living here. I have to be cleared at the trial. They can't find me guilty. There isn't enough evidence.

You have to get me out of here, Mum.

I miss you so much.

Love you loads,

Katie x

# ELEVEN

At her desk, Eden was familiarising herself with her paperwork for court on Monday morning. Before the death of sixteen-year-old Deanna Barker, there had been five children in the Barker family. Now there were four brothers between the ages of seventeen and twenty-two. The eldest two were serving time in prison, both for armed robbery. The younger two, Damien and Travis, were living off the family reputation while gaining ones of their own.

Eden had been the first on scene at Deanna's murder. Over the next few days, working as part of the murder investigation team, she had been appalled at what she had learned, how Deanna had been kicked and punched with a pack mentality that was usually seen only on screen.

She still wasn't sure of the extent of the involvement of sixteen-year-old Katie Trent, but CCTV footage clearly showed the young girl standing back and doing nothing for a while as the boys laid into Deanna. Even though she had pushed them away shortly afterwards, and stayed with Deanna until the paramedics had arrived, it hadn't gone in her favour. A case of mistaken identity hadn't washed with the judge.

The fact that Katie had run away had gone against her too. The judge, sending her to a secure unit until the date of the trial, questioned whether she knew exactly what was going to happen, had stood by and watched it and then panicked when it had all come to fruition.

'You two haven't had many run-ins with the Barker brothers yet, have you?' she asked, looking at Amy and then Jordan.

'No,' they replied in unison.

'I had to interview Katie Trent, and her story of events was different from the judge's interpretation,' Eden explained. 'Katie said she'd been scared of Nathan Lucas and the boys and had frozen when they had started to attack Deanna, who at the time she had thought was her brother, Travis.

'When she saw the knife go into Deanna's stomach, Katie reacted and pushed them all off. But by then it was too late. I asked why she ran, and Katie said through fear of what Nathan would do if she spoke out about it, threatening her and her family. It had all been captured on CCTV anyway, although Tom Cartwright had given us Nathan's name, stating that he was the ringleader.'

'Do you really think they'll cause any trouble?' Amy's hand had moved towards the box of Jaffa Cakes again. 'I know I wouldn't want to mess with their mum, if I were either Travis or Damien.'

Eden sniggered. Lulu Barker did have a worse reputation than her boys at times.

'I know so,' she replied. 'The word on the street is there will be trouble if the verdict doesn't go in their favour.'

'But joint enterprise is hardly cut and dried, Sarge, is it?' Jordan joined in, sitting back in his chair to stretch out his legs under the desk.

Eden shook her head. 'In some cases I agree with it, but others? Never judge a book by its cover.'

'Surely just being in the wrong place at the wrong time when a crime is committed isn't sufficient for a murder charge?' queried Amy.

'It's an old law that doesn't fit in modern society,' said Jordan.

'Being in the wrong place at the wrong time is only part of it. And not necessarily a chargeable offence.' Eden looked at Amy. 'The law of joint enterprise is when there isn't sufficient evidence to say what or who dished out the fatal blow. Anything those kids said could have goaded Nathan Lucas into attacking Deanna Barker with a knife.'

'But *he* was the one who was holding the knife, Sarge,' said Amy, wiping her hands of cake remnants. 'I just don't understand how they can all be guilty of murder.'

'It's a tough law,' agreed Eden, 'but it stands, and it will have to be abided by. I just hope the jury sees sense, and that there is enough evidence, or lack of it, to get Katie Trent off. We don't want the judge to make an example of her. It would devastate Katie and her family.'

'Like you said, though, Sarge,' said Amy, 'if she's guilty then it's up to the jury to find that out.'

Eden sighed. 'I'm not looking forward to giving evidence, put it that way.'

Amy stretched her arms above her head and yawned loudly.

'Go on then, bugger off home, you two,' said Eden, sounding more like their mother than she had intended.

As they pulled their coats from the back of their chairs, Eden glanced at a pile of paperwork on her desk. She ran a hand through her short blonde hair. There were only a few staff left in their office now, Friday night calling to them. She sighed loud and long, knowing that she should at least tackle some of it before leaving.

'Are you coming too, Sarge?' Jordan asked, as if to rub salt in her wounds.

'Not yet.' Eden pointed to her in tray as she read from her computer screen. 'I need to catch up on a few things first. Oh, damn!'

'What's up, Sarge?'

'Maxine Trent has been threatened by Travis Barker in Shop&Save. He's saying he'll harm her son if things don't go his way next week.' She looked up at them, knowing that she needed to delegate this despite wanting to be reactive herself.

'Sorry, but one of you needs to go and visit. Any takers or are you drawing straws?'

'I'll go,' said Jordan. 'I can catch up on my drinking time.'

'Anyone ever tell you that you're a diamond?' Amy grinned widely.

'All the time, honey.' Jordan's tone was ironic.

Eden nodded. 'Thanks, Jordan.'

Once they'd gone, Eden sighed again, into the quiet of their corner. While she enjoyed looking after staff, she also appreciated time alone. She sent a quick text message to her sister to see if Sunday lunch was still on before staring at the paperwork in her in tray again. With a grimace, she went to make a coffee before sitting down to tackle it.

# TWELVE

Ruby Peters sat in the bus shelter waiting for her friend Stacey to turn up. After receiving a message to say she was on her way, Ruby had legged it out of the house. She'd been trying to get out for ages, but her mother wanted her to watch Dean while she sorted out her Avon orders.

She checked her watch, wondering whether to have the cigarette she'd pinched before she'd come out or to wait until Stacey arrived so they could share it. They shared most things: clothes, taste in music, even the odd boyfriend or two, although never at the same time.

She glanced down the street, but she couldn't see her friend. Stuff it. She got the cigarette out of her pocket and lit up. Then she stood up, sucking in and blowing out the smoke as she looked up and down the street to see if she could see anyone.

It was only just after 6.30 p.m. yet everywhere seemed deserted. Even though it was Friday evening – no school in the morning – there was no one around because of the drizzling rain being swept along by the howling gale. As her olds would say, it wasn't fit enough for a dog to be out.

A noise behind her made her jump. It sounded as if someone had thrown a pebble at the glass. She turned to look but could see nothing but dark shadows in the hedges. The bus shelter backed on to a playing field that led across to the shops that they would be going to once Stacey showed her face.

She sat down on the tiny bench again. All that could be seen in the darkness was the lit tip of the cigarette glowing redder and redder as she inhaled. She'd started smoking when she was fourteen. When she could afford to buy a packet she would, but the majority she either pinched from her mum or her nan – or she begged off other people. Although nowadays not as many people smoked. It wasn't seen as being cool any more, and Ruby was desperate to give up. She wasn't trying those e-cigarettes though. Not until there was more evidence on the damage they might cause. Everything alien to a body would do more harm than good, even the lesser of two evils, in her opinion.

Another noise.

'Stacey, is that you?' She stood up, dropping the cigarette butt into the bin before blowing out the remaining smoke. 'Stacey? Stop pissing about.' She stepped out onto the pavement again.

Two figures came from the bushes, dressed in dark clothes and wearing balaclavas. Ruby screamed as they each grabbed one of her arms and pulled her behind the hedge.

They pushed her to the ground, one with his hand over her mouth as she tried to scream. She kicked out as the other straddled her torso, his knees holding down her upper arms, while the first held her hands together above her head.

She tried to see the eyes behind the balaclava, but she couldn't. She was sure they were men as she bucked underneath the one straddling her, the horror of assault going through her mind. She was metres away from the road and they could do anything.

With fear mounting, she heard tape being pulled from a roll and ripped off. A piece was pressed hastily across her mouth.

Then, without a word, the person on top of her drew out a large pair of scissors from his pocket. He pushed her cheek into the wet grass. Ruby tried to resist but, with a few swift cuts, he hacked at her hair, chopping it off on one side to just above the ear. Ruby sobbed, struggling for breath beneath the tape as he moved across to the other side and did the same.

By the time her attacker got off her, the majority of her hair lay on the grass either side of her.

She heard laughter. It was definitely male, but she couldn't tell who it was. Then they were off, running across the field. Ruby lay there for a few moments, paralysed with fear. Urine soaked through her jeans.

And then she was ripping the tape from her mouth, big gulping sobs escaping her the whole time, tears pouring down her face. When she looked down there was a note pressed in the band of her jeans.

*KEEP YOUR MOUTH SHUT.*

She pushed herself up to standing and staggered back towards the road. Why would anyone want to do that to her? Neither of the people who had attacked her had spoken, so she was unsure who they were, but she could hazard a guess.

She put a hand to the side of her face; felt chunks of what used to be long hair. Her beautiful hair. She sobbed. She must look like a scarecrow.

As soon as she was on the main road again, she ran.

# THIRTEEN

Jess froze as the van slowed. She heard what sounded like a garage door going up, then the van moved forward again and the engine was killed. Her heart racing, she gulped down air in an attempt to stop the panic from building up. She couldn't breathe properly with the scarf around her mouth.

The van door opened and slammed shut. The garage door was pulled down. Everything sounded so loud.

When the rear door to the van opened, bright light stung her eyes. She squinted until she could see the face of her abductor. He had removed his hat and his hair was short, fair. His skin was pale, dark rings around his eyes. He seemed mid-forties at a guess.

He reached a hand inside. Jess screamed but it came out as a groan because of the scarf. He pulled her out of the van by her arms, keeping a firm grip on her. She placed her taped feet on the floor carefully and submitted. For now. She tried not to panic because she couldn't defend herself.

'You'd better behave,' the man said, 'or I have something to knock you out with. Do you understand?'

Jess nodded.

He slammed the van door and kept hold of her arm. 'I'm not removing the scarf from your mouth until I know you won't scream the place down.'

A tear rolled down her cheek. He was going to keep her here, wherever here was. She glanced around. She was right: she was in a garage. He could do anything to her and no one would know.

He pushed her forward as her eyes flicked around her surroundings. Shelving on one wall, containing lots of detritus. There was a door in front of them. As he tugged her towards it, she tried to see if there was anything useful to pick up if she could get away from him. Paint tins, paint brushes in turpentine, screws.

He opened the door and pushed her forward. When she missed the step because her eyes were trained on a hammer she'd spotted, he cursed as he pulled her upright again and switched on a light.

They were in a kitchen. It was a cheap but modern Formica job, units to three sides and a table on the far wall. Double doors led through to a living room and another door to their left was closed. A window over the sink had a roller blind pulled down. The worktops were covered in newspapers, leaflets, letters. There were dishes piled up in the sink, and the table was laden with food containers, a packet of cereal, a bottle of milk and the carcass of a cooked chicken left out to rot. The smell assaulted her. It was the odour of grunge, as if the room hadn't seen air for weeks. Behind the scarf, she gagged.

'This way.' He took her arm again.

Jess had no choice, but still her eyes combed every surface, trying to remember things to grab if she had the chance. She spotted a knife sticking out of the sink, a saucepan that could do some harm if she could whack it across his face. There was a kettle she could pull off its base and throw at him.

He opened the door on the left and dragged her into a hallway. This too was dark, a strip of wallpaper peeling off in a corner at the skirting board. At the bottom of the stairs he turned to go up, but she froze. She could see her reflection in the long hall mirror. A pale, petrified young girl, her face covered in blood. She couldn't let him take her up the stairs. She tried to pull her arm away but his grip tightened.

'I need you out of sight,' he said, pushing her again. 'No one will see you up here. Besides, I have a special room for you.'

Jess pulled away from him, kicking out with all her might.

'Calm down!' he cried.

She resisted again, and he pushed her forward. She fell on the stairs, hitting her head on the banister. Groaning didn't make any difference as he dragged her up the last few steps and into a room at the back of the house.

He pushed her down onto a bed. The room was in darkness. She couldn't see a thing. Was this a holding room? Somewhere to keep her before moving her to somewhere else? But then he flicked on a lamp.

'The house next door is empty,' he told her. 'So there's no point banging on the walls, and there's nothing behind except a field. So no silly tricks.'

Jess never said a word as she watched him get up and leave. She heard a lock being fastened before she began to whimper. She glanced around the room. The walls were a pale shade of pink, the carpet grey, the wardrobe in front of her a pale grey too. The duvet cover and curtains were swirls of pinks and purples, whites and greys, a modern take on a sixties design. By the side of the bed, a book, *The Girl on the Train*, sat on a bedside cabinet next to an alarm clock, a postcard in the middle of it to mark the page it had been read up to. She spotted a bucket in the corner of the room and gasped again.

She curled up on the bed and burst into tears. She couldn't even get under the covers, as she couldn't pull them over her. The light in the room was dim, and there was no bulb in the main fitting above her head.

It was nearing 6.30 p.m. Four and a half hours until her mum got home from work. She would miss her then. She would start looking for her. Or maybe Cayden would have got fed up of waiting, unable to get an answer from her on his phone. He would call for her, alert Sarah, who would get in touch with Mum. She would contact Eden and then everyone would start to look for her.

She lay shivering, again looking around the room for something to use if he ever untied her hands. There was a dressing table too, with a large mirror, but there was nothing else.

She stared at herself, seeing the mess he had made of her with his fist. Oh God, what was he going to do to her?

Tears poured down her face as she drew her knees into her chest. No one knew where she was.

# FOURTEEN

He went back downstairs after locking the door. He paced the living room, running a hand over his head. The bitch had to learn a lesson. It was her fault everything had gone wrong. Everything he had lived for had been lost on that night and nothing he did could ever bring her back. She was locked away in his memory.

It had taken brute strength to stay sober enough to keep his wits about him. Now he had the girl, he could catch up on what he'd missed. He poured a glass of whiskey. Only a little bit, mind. He needed to stay on alert.

He took her phone from his pocket and scrolled through it. There were messages from Stacey, Ruby, Claire mostly and Cayden – was that the boy he'd beaten up?

As he read through each feed to try to capture her tone, he found out she was popular, that she had a sister called Sarah, and there were lots of texts from her mum and someone called Eden.

He took a look through the photos. There were so many of the girl doing that trout-pout thing. Why did young women do that? It was the most unsightly thing he could think of.

Then he came across the boy. Photo after photo of the two of them together. Yes, that was Cayden, although he might not have too perfect a nose now. He smirked. Having said that, it was nothing to be proud of. He was old enough to be his father, and he had taken him by surprise. Doing him over that hard hadn't been the plan, but he had been bigger than he'd expected and had youth on his side. He looked at his bruised hands, ran a finger over his knuckles.

After reading a few more messages, he now had the right tone to send a text when necessary. He went through to the kitchen, opened the fridge and took out a can of lager. Opening it, he drank a good half of it in one go, cocking his ear up to the ceiling to see if she was making any noise. It was quiet.

He banged his fist down onto the worktop, knocking a cup and a plate as he did so. The noise made a jolt in the silence. He banged his fist again and kicked out at the kitchen unit.

*My beautiful girl. Why did you leave me?*

Squeezing his eyes shut tight, he clung onto the worktop and groaned loudly through gritted teeth. He needed to keep his anger inside, locked away until Monday. Because if he didn't, Lord knows what he would be capable of.

# FIFTEEN

Jordan drove through the gated entrance of The Cavendales, an estate that he had big ambitions to live on in the future. The estate smacked of being someone, doing well in life and generally having money. He loved the individual designs of some of the larger properties at the back, with their top-of-the-range vehicles parked outside, or hidden away inside double or triple garages.

The Trents' residence was one of the smaller houses on The Cavendales, built before the larger executive houses had been erected, and was at the head of a pleasant cul-de-sac. The branches of the nearest tree were taking a good battering in the storm that was gathering momentum. Jordan held on to his car door as he got out, for fear of it coming away from its hinges if a gust of wind caught it.

Maxine Trent opened the door before he had a chance to knock. She ushered him inside.

'It's horrible out there,' she said, closing the night out for a while. 'Can I get you a coffee?'

'Yes, thanks. Black, no sugar, please.'

Jordan didn't want a drink, only ever finished a few mouthfuls, but he found it a great way to build up a rapport. Many a good conversation had been had over a cuppa of some sort.

Maxine showed him through into the living room. It was a large open-plan space with a dining area at the rear and seating around a television and fire at the front. While he waited for her to come back, he scanned the images of a young girl and boy that were everywhere: over the fireplace, on the back wall, sitting on a small table. It was sad to think of them separated for so long.

It wasn't the first time he'd visited. Over the past six months, since their daughter, Katie, had been sent to a secure unit, Jordan had been called out several times for reports of harassment and anti-social behaviour. He'd got to know Maxine and her husband well, and had played football in the garden with their son, Matty.

Maxine came in and placed a tray with three mugs on the coffee table.

'What happened?' Jordan asked, taking a seat on the settee when asked to do so.

'Oh, it's nothing now.' Maxine waved a hand dismissively in the air. 'I just felt a bit threatened by Travis Barker, but now I think I overreacted. Everything is bound to be raw for their family with the trial coming up next week.'

'Even so,' said Jordan, 'it doesn't give anyone the right to threaten you. What did he say?'

Maxine sat down in an armchair and relayed the incident to him. She was a lovely woman, warm and family orientated, and Jordan couldn't help pitying her. It had been sad to watch her deterioration over the past few months. She had lost more weight, he noticed. Her jeans and jumper were practically hanging off her small frame, and her hair had lost its shine. She looked as if she was ready to shrink into herself, make herself as small as possible.

But Jordan knew she had a fighting streak too. She had shown so much courage so far, and his gut feeling was that she would survive the outcome of the trial, as well as get through what had happened this evening.

'Would you like me to have a word with Travis?' he asked after she had finished talking. He was met with the shake of a head.

'I don't want to make matters worse.' Maxine clenched and unclenched her hands into fists as she spoke.

'He shouldn't be allowed to intimidate you, no matter what.' Jordan paused. 'It's up to you though.'

A noise at the door and he turned to see Phil Trent standing in the doorway. Phil looked as if he had just come out of the shower – his hair was wet and he wore casual clothes.

Jordan had got to know him too, found him a straight and fair man. He loved the dynamic between him and his wife. They were a team, and they seemed to be in a happy relationship, despite the trouble they'd been thrust into.

'Hi, Jordan,' Phil greeted him as if he were an old friend.

'Mr Trent.' Jordan nodded his acknowledgement.

'I've just been telling Jordan that I overreacted,' Maxine explained as Phil came into the room.

'No, you didn't.' Phil shook his head.

'He wasn't going to harm anyone, least of all Matty,' she replied.

'Travis Barker is an arrogant idiot, but no one threatens my wife.'

Jordan's heart went out to Phil. He couldn't begin to imagine how he must feel being unable to protect his family.

'I agree but —' Maxine paused for a moment. 'Let's just leave it for now.'

Phil sighed. 'If you wish.'

'You know I'm right.'

Phil perched himself on the arm of the chair Maxine was sitting on. He pulled her near, giving her shoulder a squeeze.

'I know,' he told her, giving Jordan a look of frustration.

Jordan put his notebook away and stood up. 'I hope everything goes well for you next week,' he said, looking down at them both. 'Neither of you deserve what you've been through.'

'Thanks. Do you have children?' Maxine asked him.

Jordan shook his head. 'Sadly not yet. I was hoping to by now, but I have the broken heart that comes before settling down.'

Maxine gave him a faint smile.

Once in his car again, Jordan rang the control room, signed off and headed home. Part of him wanted to curl up on the sofa and be safe and warm in his own world. Part of him wanted to go out and party, because life's too short.

He hoped that the life's-too-short version won by the time he had come out of the shower and washed the day away.

# SIXTEEN

Eden hadn't managed to start any paperwork. Several staff members had come over to ask her to look into or check out things, the DI had emailed asking for some stats about the last SWAPs meeting she'd been at and the cleaner had started on the hoovering in their office already. The drone was driving her mad, even though she loved Margaret, who had been working there as long as she could recall.

Eden had wanted to shift most of the paperwork from her desk to someone else's all week, but even if she did do it all tonight, which wasn't a possibility, there would be another pile to take its place by the following weekend. The job was paperwork, paperwork, paperwork, and now she had staff management, strategies and red tape to contend with as well.

'You still here?'

Eden looked up to see Sean standing next to her. Sean had been a police constable for as long as she had but had joined CID three years before her and had been promoted to inspector early last year.

A bear of a man in his late-forties with short and neat hair, he towered over her even though she was above average height at five foot nine. He wore sharply cut navy trousers and a white shirt, the knot in his multi-coloured tie fastened as tight as it had been that morning. Sleeves rolled up to the elbow were the only thing that showed a bit of dishevelment. Even at this late hour she could smell a faint whiff of his aftershave as he pulled up a chair to sit next to her. Much better than eau de sweat.

'I'm all yours if you need me, boss.' Eden smiled.

'Oh, it's nothing important.' He sat down and removed the glasses he hated but had to wear for close-up work. 'I was just wondering how you were getting on? It's been a month since you started in the role. Your mumsy skills seem to be coming on just fine.'

If anyone else had said that, Eden would have felt insulted but, coming from Sean, it was acceptable. To say she loved her job would make her sound weird. Who would want to deal with insolent people, moaners of the first degree, violent crimes and the day-to-day drudgery that she and her officers had to put up with?

But Eden *did* love it all. She enjoyed being in the thick of things, especially when she had helped either prevent a situation from escalating or made someone feel better by doing something small that had a huge impact for that individual.

It wasn't so much job satisfaction but job contentment. Of course some days were worse than others, as with any other job. And the times she had been assaulted had evened out now. You'd expect anti-social behaviour and low-level domestic violence on a regular basis from the two social housing estates in Stockleigh, but even residents in the larger houses, such as those on The Cavendales, caused just as much trouble behind closed doors. Often, despite their wealth, they seemed more devious in their attempts to get away with things.

'I can't help it if I want to nurture my staff rather than drag them up to do things the old and often naughty way,' she acknowledged.

Sean slid over the box of Jaffa Cakes, looking disappointed that there were only two left.

'I won't tell if you don't,' Eden urged. 'I'll get some more in this weekend. Talking of weekends, you got anything good planned?'

'I'm due out with Lucy this evening. Another fiftieth bash that reminds me of my advancing years.'

'Don't remind me. I've my big four-o next year. Is Lucy organising you a party?'

'She'd better not be or else there might be a murder.'

'Ah, you know you love her, boss.'

'Speaking of which – how are you getting on with this new fella? Joe, isn't it?'

'It is, and. . .' she looked at him from the corner of her eye, 'it's none of your business.'

'I'm only trying to show I care. . .'

Eden shook her head. 'You've never been good at the "how are you doing" thing, have you?' She rolled her eyes in jest. 'The job is fine. I'm fine. Everything's fine. You don't need to worry.'

Sean slapped his thigh before standing up. 'In that case, I'm off. And don't forget to get your photo taken for the new ID card.'

'I won't,' she said over her shoulder.

Actually, Eden had been putting off changing the current photo for a while now. On that one she was nine years younger, keen and eager with a huge grin to prove it. Her blonde hair had been long, with a full fringe that had framed dark brown eyes, still twinkling. Her face was slightly thinner. She'd always tried to keep herself in shape.

It had often been a bone of contention between Eden and Casey as fashions had come and gone that Eden remained firmly in the 1960s, with tight-legged trousers, pinafore dresses and short skirts that she wore with opaque tights and knee-length boots. At work it was cropped fitted jackets with thin lapels and large-collared blouses. She remembered Casey being mortified when the sixties had come back into fashion for her own age group last year, although not so much when she realised she could fit into her mother's clothes and borrow them all.

Now Eden's hair was short, giving her the look of a younger Twiggy, and the nickname to go with it, and even though she had gained no more than a few kilos since then, it was enough to make a difference to how she felt, if not how she looked. She couldn't do anything about the body that had started to sag through age, despite her attempts at keeping it fit and healthy, nor the lines that were appearing around her eyes. And she'd need glasses soon too, although she wouldn't admit that to anyone.

So much had happened during the past nine years that she preferred to forget about much of that too.

She checked the clock on the wall again. She'd been on shift for near on twelve hours. The office was emptying around her. Stuff the paperwork. It was time she headed home. Joe was coming over at eight.

Now that she was looking forward to.

# SEVENTEEN

Stacey Goodwin walked along the pathway by the side of Theodore House. She was meeting her friend, Claire, at half past six but was already ten minutes late. She braced herself as the wind almost blew her off her feet again, and wondered if they should go over to Cayden's house and hang out with him and Jess. She knew Cayden wouldn't like it, and maybe Jess would want time alone with him, but it was freezing out here, and she didn't fancy walking around the streets.

As she walked, she scrolled through her messages until she found her conversation with Ahmed. They'd exchanged numbers last week and had been sending texts ever since. There had been the odd photo between them, some Snapchats and lots of texts.

Ahmed made her laugh. She'd known him for ages from school but only recently begun to fancy him. He had a dry sense of humour, and she'd often crease up with laughter as he was daring enough to take on a teacher, giving out lip. Yesterday, she'd got into trouble with him as they had sat together and sniggered through double maths. Honestly, she'd only had to look at him and she'd got the giggles. Eventually, they'd been sent out of the class and had ended up with detention.

She grinned widely, already wishing her life away as she wanted it to be Monday. She and Ahmed were going on their first date. He was taking her to Cineworld. She'd been planning what to wear and had been hoping to discuss it with her friends that night.

She was only a few feet along the path when she was seized from behind. She cried out, but it was carried away on the wind. Then a hand was over her mouth. Another hand snaked around her waist.

Pulled into the bushes, she landed on her knees with a smack. A handful of her hair was grabbed, forcing her face upwards. Someone else appeared and a strip of duct tape was pressed across her lips.

Fear coursed through her, and she tried to kick out. She wondered if anyone would be looking out from the flats. They were all a bunch of nosy gits on the ground floor, all the old-and-wrinklies. Maybe one of them had seen her being dragged out of sight and had alerted the police. But they wouldn't get here in time. They were going to rape her, and no one could hear her as she couldn't scream.

Tears stung her eyes as they flitted from one figure to the other, trying to take in as much detail as she could. One man stood at her side, the other in front of her. They were both tall and of average build, wearing dark clothes and balaclavas, black gloves.

Without saying a word, one pressed his hands on her shoulders, holding her down. His feet were either side of her legs so she was unable to move.

The other man squatted beside her. She looked down, eyes widening as she saw he had a large tin of paint.

What the hell. . .? Surely he wasn't going to. . .

He prised off the lid with a small knife, and she began to whimper. She tried to claw at the man behind her, who kept a firm grip on her shoulders.

The man in front held up the can. She groaned loudly, squeezing her eyes shut as he tipped the contents over her head. The liquid dripped down over her hair, her clothes, down onto her knees, puddling in-between her legs on the grass. The fumes began to sting her eyes.

She heard laughter; it sounded male. And then a phone clicking as it took photos.

And then suddenly she was pushed forward as the man behind her let go. She fell face first in the grass.

She stayed still for a moment, hoping they wouldn't begin to kick her while she was down. Her body tensed against the onslaught she imagined would be next. But there was nothing but the noise of the wind and rain.

She wiped at her fringe, taking most of the paint with it away from her face. Her breath came in shallow gasps as she sat up. Looking around from side to side to see where the men were, it took her a few seconds to realise they had gone.

Stacey pulled the tape from her mouth and gasped as she took in air. Quickly she wiped at her face with the sleeves of her coat. The liquid mingled with tears and snot, running down her face. She wiped at her neck, her hands covered in the stuff now.

They had pushed something into her pocket. She reached inside, and her paint-covered fingers clasped something. It was a piece of lined paper folded in half, the kind found in any notebook. Thick black felt-tip writing in uneven capitals.

*KEEP YOUR MOUTH SHUT.*

Her hands shook as she read the words. Keep her mouth shut about what? As far as she knew, she hadn't done anything wrong lately. Was this to do with the trial next week, or something else?

But suddenly she didn't care. She stood up, staggering forward, and then she began to run, sobbing with every step. There was no one on the path, no one in the car park as she ran through the stormy weather.

She didn't even care that Claire would be waiting for her. All she wanted was to be back home again before anything else happened to her.

# EIGHTEEN

Eden was listening to the radio while driving home, her fingers tapping to the beat of the song. Yes, she hadn't done everything she had intended to do today, but it had been a good one all the same. Nothing drastic had happened. The residents of Stockleigh had behaved themselves, for the most part.

In her line of work, everything could change with one phone call and they were very fortunate if they ever got time to catch up. So even if she had a pile of paperwork on her desk, she could live with that.

The weather was so miserable that there weren't too many people about. But a flash of white caught her eye as someone dashed along the pavement to her right. She frowned and, indicating quickly, pulled over to the kerb and parked up.

The girl was a few metres behind her. Her jacket was ruined, her long hair covered in white paint, which had dripped onto her jeans, and there was a huge stain on both thighs. Her boots had paint splashes on them too. As she drew nearer, Eden recognised her.

'Stacey?' she said. 'Stacey, what's happened?'

The girl stopped, taking a breath between sobs. 'They covered me in paint,' she cried, shaking uncontrollably as Eden held on to her arm.

'Who did?'

'I don't know,' Stacey gasped. 'There were two of them and they were in dark clothes and balaclavas and they poured the paint over me, and it will never come off, and it's stinging my eyes. What am I—'

'Slow down, Stacey.' Eden tried to calm her down. 'It's okay. You're safe now.'

'But look at me! I'm such a mess.'

'I know but it can all be sorted. Where do you live?'

'29, Hardman Road.'

Eden blew out her breath. It would only take a matter of minutes to get the girl home. She couldn't leave her on the street like this.

She took an elbow that was paint-free and ushered Stacey towards her car. 'Come on, I'll give you a lift.'

Eden opened the boot of her car and searched around until she found what she was looking for. Next to a box of latex gloves and a roll of crime scene tape was a pile of black bin liners. She swiftly covered the passenger seat and the foot well of the car with them. Before Stacey got in, she handed her a handful of paper towels from a box. 'Wipe your face but be careful not to splash the paint into your eyes.'

She started the engine and got back into the traffic. 'Do you know who did this to you, Stacey?' she asked.

'No,' Stacey replied.

'Do you know *why* someone would do this to you then?'

'No. They just jumped me.'

'Where were you?'

'On the pathway through from Theodore House. I was going to meet Claire, my friend.'

'And then what happened?'

'Someone grabbed me and dragged me behind the hedge.'

'And you didn't see who it was?' Eden had one eye on the road and one eye on the girl.

'I told you, I don't know!' Stacey burst into tears.

'Okay, let's get you home.'

Eden said nothing else until she pulled up outside Stacey's house. 'I'll take you in and call for an officer to take a statement,' she said then.

'No!' Stacey almost shrank in the seat. 'I'll be okay. Please, just leave me here.'

'I'll do nothing of the sort.' Eden removed her seat belt. 'Come on, it won't take me a minute.'

Eden raced round to the passenger seat to help her out.

'My eyes are stinging,' said Stacey, as she helped her up the path.

'Let's get you inside. Do you have a key?' Not waiting for a response, Eden rapped on the front door anyway.

A woman opened the door and came rushing at them. 'Stacey! What on earth happened?'

'Mum!' Stacey burst into tears.

'I found her running along the high street,' Eden explained. 'It seems someone has played a practical joke on her, but she won't say who.'

'Come through to the kitchen,' Sandra beckoned Stacey, 'and be mindful of the rug. Keep to the laminate flooring. I can remove the paint from that.'

Eden followed them into the house as Stacey began to cry harder.

'Who did this to you?' Sandra asked.

'I don't know. I didn't see.'

'You didn't notice anything about them?' Eden pressed. 'Were they tall, small? Were they male or female?'

'I don't know, and I'd rather not think about it now. I want to go and have a shower.'

'I'd rather you chat to me about this first, see if we can get some details,' said Eden.

'No, you'll just make things worse!' Stacey turned and raced to the bottom of the stairs.

'Stacey, wait!' Sandra shouted after her. 'You're covered in paint!'

But Stacey had disappeared, slamming a door upstairs as she hid away.

Sandra raised her hands in the air and then down again. 'Teenagers. I never know what's going on with her nowadays.' She tutted. 'I hope that paint comes out of the carpet.'

Eden nodded in response. 'I'll leave you to it. Perhaps I can get someone to come and see you in the morning? That's if Stacey, or yourself, wants us to.'

Sandra nodded back. 'Maybe she'll be calm enough to answer some questions then. Thanks for bringing her home.'

Eden left the house and went back to her car. She sighed as she restarted the engine. Well, the day had ended far better for some than for others.

# NINETEEN

Cayden had arrived at the hospital in an ambulance and been placed in the corridor along with three other emergency admissions because A&E was full to capacity. The woman beside him continually sobbed, clutching her stomach. She'd been attached to a drip, but she kept throwing up every few minutes. An elderly man coughed and spluttered on the other side.

After forty minutes, he'd been wheeled into a bay. It was relatively quiet in there, and he relaxed after being seen by the assessment nurse, while he waited for the doctor to come. Already his right eye had swollen so much that he couldn't see out of it, and his ribs hurt like hell. He put up his hand. Two fingers had been strapped together with bandaging.

His phone was in his jacket, which had been placed on the chair at the side of the trolley bed. He wanted to see what damage had been done to his face. He sat up but before he could get it, a man pulled aside the curtain.

'Hi Cayden, I'm Dr Alexander – Jack to my friends – and I like the look of you.' His smile was as friendly as his eyes. 'I can see I can't shake your hand because it's bandaged up, and I won't ask what I can do for you, because I can already see that too. You've a nasty cut above your eye that's going to need stitches.' He reached for some latex gloves and examined Cayden's nose for a few seconds.

'Ow, watch out there!' Cayden moved away from his touch.

'I don't think it's broken, but your eyes are blackening rapidly. I'll get that X-rayed, along with your chest and your hand. You say he kicked you in the stomach?'

Cayden nodded, and then winced as it caused a sharp pain to drive into the back of his eyes.

'Nasty piece of work. Did you know him?'

'I don't think so.'

'You don't remember anything about him?'

'I was hit on the back of my legs and went down on the path,' said Cayden as Jack examined his eyes. 'I turned round and saw someone behind me and then. . . nothing.'

'Recalling some of it is good.'

'Will anything else come back to me?'

'It's difficult to say. Even if you have no injuries to stop you, your brain might not want you to. You'll be in shock too.' Jack moved towards the end of the bed and drew open the curtain. 'I'll be back to you once X-rays are done.'

Cayden threw his legs over the side of the bed and pushed himself upright. Groggily, he sat for a few seconds before standing up. He reached inside the pocket of his jacket for his phone. He had to call Jess. Although he doubted she would still be waiting for him, he wanted to speak to her, needed to let her know what had happened.

When there was no reply, it took him a while but he texted her with his uninjured hand.

*Been beaten up. Am in A&E. Okay but can you come? C x*

A message came back almost immediately.

*Oh no. I waited, I called you. I'm on my way. J x*

Cayden jabbed a finger to connect to Jess's phone, wondering why she had sent a text message rather than ring him straight back. The call rang out and then went to voicemail. He frowned, wincing again. Turning the camera round on his phone, he gasped. His face was a riot of swelling, blood and bruising. His nose definitely looked as if it was broken.

The curtain was drawn back. It was a nurse this time. She sighed as she saw him standing up.

'Come on, up on this bed,' she chastised, patting the mattress.

'Can you give me something for the pain?' he asked, sitting on it again.

'Let me see what the doctor says. He might want you to have the X-rays first.'

'But I can't stand it.'

'I can get you something for now. Do you feel sick at all?'

'A little. How long will I have to stay here for?'

The nurse pushed him gently back to lying. 'We'll need to monitor you for a while. You've had quite a beating there, and I think—'

'Cayden!' Andrea Blackwell came charging into the cubicle. 'Oh, look what he did to you! Did you see who it was?'

'Mum.' Cayden sat up as she held him. He burst into tears, all the stress of the last couple of hours, being on his own, the pain and the fear, finally released. Although his head was pounding, he felt comforted by his mother's arms.

Yet he couldn't tell her the real reason he was feeling so stressed. He needed to catch up with Jess and find out why her phone was ringing out. He hoped it was because she had taken the huff with him, thinking he had stood her up.

When he'd seen Travis earlier, there had been no indication that this would happen. As far as he was aware, hurting him hadn't been part of the overall plan. Nor was anything supposed to be happening to Jess, so he hoped she was okay.

But what was disturbing him most was if it wasn't part of the plan that he knew about, was it one of the Barker brothers who had attacked him – or someone else?

And if it wasn't one of the Barker brothers, then who could it have been?

# TWENTY

Laura had just sat down with another coffee when her phone beeped in a message.

> *Hi Mum. Staying at Stacey's tonight. See you tomorrow, be back around ten. Love you. Jx*

She sighed loudly and rang Jess, but the call was diverted to voicemail. She began to tap out a reply to the message.

'What's up?' asked Nicola, her eyes glued to the screen as she updated her notes.

'Jess says she's staying over at Stacey's house. I specifically told her to be in by eleven because I thought she was staying in with Cayden. I bet they've had a tiff and she's stormed off. I've tried to call her back but it's gone to voicemail.'

'She takes advantage of you,' said Nicola, eyes still on the screen.

'She does not!' Laura's tone was sharp.

Nicola popped her head over the top of the monitor. 'I'm winding you up! She's sixteen, she's bound to change her mind too often and go against your wishes. It's her prerogative.'

'She's just playing on my good nature, thinking I won't mind if she stays out.'

'Well, it isn't a school night.'

'I just worry about her.' Laura looked up at Nicola. 'She's not like Sarah, all meek and mild. She's got an attitude that will get her into trouble.' Laura tried to reach Jess again, but once more it went to voicemail. She replied to the message her sister had sent asking if Sunday lunch was still on. Of course it was, she replied. She loved spending time with Eden and her niece, Casey. Then she put her phone on her desk. She'd try Jess again later.

'Well, that's me done for the night,' said Nicola, glancing at the clock to see it said 7.55 p.m. 'I can definitely hear a glass of red calling my name.'

'Yes, off you go and leave me here to while away the hours alone,' Laura complained.

'You'll be fine. There'll be a call in soon, you mark my words.'

'You'd expect with the stormy weather that they'd all be indoors. It is rather quiet tonight.'

Nicola clasped her hand across her mouth. 'You said the quiet word! You know all hell will let loose the minute I leave, don't you?'

'I don't care. I'd rather be busy than bored.'

But once she was on her own, Laura soon regretted her words. Worrying about Jess always made her miss Neil. Sixteen years of marriage had been over in a shot after a drunk driver had mown him down on a Christmas night out in 2007. Neil had never known anything about it as he had been thrown up into the air, his head connecting with the kerb on his descent. After being kept in a medically induced coma for a week, further tests had shown no signs of life, and she'd had to make the heartbreaking decision to switch off his life support.

At thirty-three years old, her life support had gone too. Their marriage had been solid, and she still missed him now. She and Neil had worked hard since they'd met, starting out in a small two-bedroom terraced house, then moving to a large semi-detached where the girls had their own rooms, and eventually to the property on The Cavendales. They had moved there as soon as the houses were built. Putting a deposit down for a four-bedroom home had been a thrill for both of them – living in it even more so. Luckily, insurance had paid the mortgage when

Neil was killed, but the bills had still come in thick and fast. It had been impossible to keep the house going, and she'd made another agonising choice to downsize.

Even though she had been determined to give her daughters what she and Neil had wanted for them – a beautiful home with a large garden to play in, rooms of their own, in a safe neighbourhood, and something they could all be proud of – it just hadn't been possible on one wage. The girls had been amazing about moving. Their current home was across the high street, only a stone's throw away from The Cavendales and part of a small cluster of semi-detached houses. It had been only a few minutes extra for them both to walk to school, and around the corner from Eden and Casey. And they'd all settled in there really quickly. It had been a blessing in disguise in more ways than one.

The phone rang, interrupting her thoughts. She quickly switched to work mode.

'Good evening, CrisisChat.'

# TWENTY-ONE

Home for Eden and Casey was a detached house on a quiet street in the east of the city. It was an area of Stockleigh that people aspired to move to, in a friendly neighbourhood, with a retail park nearby and within easy reach of the city centre and train station. Eden and Danny had bought the property back in 1995 when they had married, but there were several years left on the mortgage before she could call it her own.

It was all Eden had ever wanted: a sweeping corner plot at the head of a cul-de-sac with a large driveway leading to a double garage, a kitchen overlooking the garden and room for Casey to bring home friends. It backed on to school playing fields and was pleasantly quiet at most times.

Since they had moved in, the house had been completely modernised throughout, and they'd added a large conservatory onto the kitchen, which had made the whole downstairs feel much lighter and airier. The decor was contemporary, sleek chromes and beech, pale walls and lighting. Yet often it didn't feel like home since Danny had gone.

Still, since Laura had moved from The Cavendales, there were no more than a few minutes between them. Eden and her sister had always been close, and although losing both of their parents to cancer in 2010 had been a blow, it had brought them even closer together.

When Neil was killed, Eden had been there for Laura as much as she could. When Danny had walked out, Laura had understood her loss and the feeling of emptiness that she still felt. Often they didn't see eye to eye, especially where Casey and Jess were concerned, but Eden knew that her sister always had her back and vice versa.

After a quick shower, Eden sat on the settee with a glass of wine. The television was on, but she wasn't watching it. Joe was on his way over and Casey was going out, so she was looking forward to some time to chill. Yet she couldn't stop thinking about Stacey Goodwin. Who on earth would pour a tin of paint over someone's head? And why? The girl was only sixteen and surely hadn't made that many enemies yet. And from what she saw, Stacey wasn't too much of a troublemaker – yet someone was out to get her. She made a mental note to visit her again in the morning and see if she had remembered anything else.

Minutes later, Casey popped her head around the door. Eden almost gasped as she spotted her daughter looking like she was in her mid-twenties already. She was made up a little too much for her liking, but she had to admit she'd done the same when she was Casey's age, to give off the look of a mature woman rather than a gangly teenager. Casey's long blonde hair was straightened to a sheen that made it look like it had been dipped in oil. She wore skinny jeans and a white shirt, square-heel ankle boots and was throwing a coat over her shoulders as she spoke.

'Mum, can I have a fiver to spend tonight please?'

'You're a bit dressed up for a youth club,' Eden replied. 'Maybe you might want to tone down the black eyeliner around your eyes a little too.'

Casey did a dramatic eye roll. 'This is fashion,' she sighed.

'I gave you five pounds last night. What have you done with that?'

'We went out.'

'We being you and. . .'

Casey shrugged. 'Just friends.'

'And are you going out with just friends this evening?' Eden raised her eyebrows. She knew that Casey was seeing someone new, a boy from school, but she hadn't told her much about him yet. Said they'd had a few dates but it was nothing special. Although she tried not to interfere too much, it worried Eden because of the people she mixed with on a daily basis. It would be hard enough for Casey to be a copper's daughter anyway.

'Yes,' Casey replied.

It was Eden's turn to sigh. She wasn't made of money, but that wasn't Casey's fault. 'What time does it close? It's eight o'clock now.' She beckoned her into the room as she reached inside her bag for her purse.

'Well, it's nearly finished. But I'd like to grab a coffee with the gang.'

'Where?'

'At Caffè Nero, on the high street.'

Casey wouldn't look her in the eye. Eden opened her purse and checked her notes. Luckily she had a five pound note or else she wouldn't see the change from a ten. She handed it to Casey.

'Thanks.' Casey stood in front of her, reluctant to go.

'What is it?' Eden knew full well it wouldn't be a mother–daughter loving chat, full of advice.

'Can I stay out late tonight? Everyone is meeting at the café and it is Friday night.'

'That's not an excuse to stay out past ten o'clock, though, is it? It's miserable outside.' Eden paused. 'But you can stay out until ten thirty.'

'That only gives me two and a half hours!' Casey protested.

'Well, you should have gone out earlier.' Eden looked at her meaningfully. 'In my day, youth clubs started at six and were over by eight. So I'm not sure who you're going to Caffè Nero with and why you're so secretive, but I still want you home by ten thirty.'

'That's so unfair!' Casey folded her arms.

Eden thought Casey was about to stamp her feet, but she wouldn't give in. 'It is what it is.' She leaned back into the settee again.

'Only because you want to make it awkward for me. I'm surprised you care enough to want me home early anyway, when Joe is coming over. I'd think you'd rather spend your precious time with him.'

'You're wasting *your* precious time arguing with me.' Eden looked up at her pointedly. 'I'm not going to change my mind. And if you're not home on time, I'll come and fetch you.'

'You've had a drink!'

'I can walk that far.'

Casey stood glaring at her. Moments later, there was a knock on the door.

'Hiya.' Joe pushed it open and smiled. 'I let myself in,' he said without need of an explanation.

'Hey.' Eden smiled back. With short, dark hair, blue eyes and a boyish look about him, Joe Atkinson was a sight for sore eyes at the end of a long day. Always neat and tidy, he had a style of dress that most men in their mid-forties wouldn't be able to carry off. He wore a pale blue shirt, and she knew he had a cracking pair of legs underneath his straight-cut jeans, the result of several spinning classes a week. Eden loved to run a hand up his leg, feeling the contours of his muscles, and up. . .

Casey groaned. 'You've given him a key!'

'You know very well that he's had one for a while.' Eden glared back at her. 'And don't question what I do.'

'It's okay for you to do what you want, whereas I have to do as I'm told? That hardly seems fair to me.'

'It's called being a parent and a child. Guess which one you are!'

'I'm sixteen. I'm not a child!'

'Well, stop acting like one then.'

Joe sat down. 'I'll just sit here until the two of you are done,' he said, picking up the TV remote.

'Oh we're finished.' Eden waited for Casey to drop her eyes.

Finally, she did and, after another groan, she stormed out of the front room with a bang of the door.

'And you want to move in with us?' Eden's laugh was sarcastic but to the point.

Last week, after six months of being together, Joe had asked if they could make things more permanent. He wanted to rent out his house and move in with her and Casey.

But Eden wasn't ready for that. More to the point, she wasn't sure she wanted him to. As well as her feelings for Danny, Joe had a sixteen-year-old daughter too – Emma – and there were often fireworks when the two girls got together. It wasn't a case of them getting on, as their parents had hoped, more that each wanted to outdo the other, leading to temper tantrums and tears. It was all so childish, but then again they were juveniles, trying to be adults.

Eden and Joe had met at a parents' evening, their daughters sharing some of the classes at Stockleigh High School. He had sat next to her while he waited to see Mrs Forbes, the maths teacher, and had started to guess what all the teachers were like when they went home. He'd had her in stitches within minutes after suggesting that Mrs Forbes, who was near to retirement, would be hosting Ann Summers' parties for the rest of the teachers.

After she had seen Mrs Forbes, trying desperately not to imagine her doing what Joe had suggested, they had swapped phone numbers. Although a bit shy about going on a date with someone other than Danny, she had enjoyed herself immensely. After several dates, she'd stopped comparing Joe to her ex. They were nothing alike at all.

Maybe that's what had attracted her to him in the first place. And maybe, now that the initial passion had worn off, that was what was holding her back from settling down again. She missed the excitement of being with Danny, despite the ups and downs.

Joe came and sat next to her, slung his arm around her shoulder and kissed her hair.

'Hi, again.' He smiled.

Eden snuggled into his chest, felt herself relaxing.

Despite her home being a battlefield at times, Joe was her light in an almost dark day. Not like Danny, who, even though he still had her heart, had done the unthinkable to her.

# TWENTY-TWO

For the past three hours, Jess had listened to every noise that the house made, as well as concentrating on any sounds from him. She couldn't stop shaking, her nose was hurting where he had punched her and her throat felt sore, dehydration setting in.

What did he want with her? Why had he brought her here? What was he going to do to her?

She tried to shut out the thought that he was going to assault her. Why else would he lock her in a room and leave her there? He was going to keep her as his playmate, use her and abuse her. Maybe he would kill her when he'd had enough. She recalled a film she'd seen with Halle Berry in it, called *Operator* or something. Maybe he would pick up another young girl when he thought she had fulfilled her use. And then she wouldn't be worth bothering about, so he would dispose of her. How long would that take?

All of a sudden everything she had watched that freaked her out came flooding into her mind. *Scream* – don't answer the phone. *The Ring* – don't watch the tape. *The Hole* – don't look into it. All the old films she loved to watch. *Nightmare on Elm Street*, *Poltergeist*, *Psycho*, *The Shining*. She enjoyed anything that would make her jump, the scarier the better.

When her mum was at work she watched *Luther* – he's under the bed, he's in the loft, he's behind you in the car – and *The Fall*. Yet she would always have nightmares after seeing something creepy.

Now it seemed her nightmare had come true – and real life was far scarier.

She heard a door open downstairs. She held her breath as she listened more. Was he coming upstairs to her? She listened carefully. She heard the sound of a kettle boiling, a few tiny bangs as he moved around the kitchen below her. What was he doing? She could smell toast.

She wondered if anyone had missed her yet. Surely Cayden had alerted everyone that she hadn't turned up? The police would already be on to him. Eden would find her.

Footsteps. On the stairs.

She took short breaths. In frustration, she pulled at the tape wound tightly around her wrists again, desperate for them to move enough to be freed so that she could jump at the bastard who held her captive when he came in the room. Take him by surprise, scratch at his face – that always hurt. She remembered how sore her cheek had been when Bethany Swift did it to her. And it scarred for a while too – noticeably.

She froze when she heard a bolt on the door being slid across, a key turning. Why was there a lock? The door opened slowly until it was wide and she could see him. She scrambled to the back of the bed, as close to the wall as she could get, trying not to show him how scared she was. Her eyes would give her away, so she wouldn't look at him. But she needed to.

He stepped inside the room. 'I've brought you something to eat.' He held out a small tray.

Jess could see a mug with steam coming from it and two slices of buttered toast on a plate by its side. How the hell was she going to eat or drink anything with a scarf around her mouth? Her heart began to beat wildly at the thought that he would have to remove it.

'Yes, I know,' he said, as if he was reading her mind. 'I'll take it off, but no one will hear you scream from here. And if you do scream, I'll put it back again. Understood?'

Jess nodded fervently.

'I won't untie your hands though.' He put the tray down on the carpet and stepped towards her.

Every atom in her body screamed at her to move back from him, but she let him undo the scarf, gasped for air for a while and then clamped her mouth shut.

'Eat and drink,' he told her. 'I won't be coming back in here until the morning.'

She tried to speak, but her voice was too hoarse.

'I need the toilet,' she finally managed.

He pointed to the bucket. 'You'll figure it out.'

'No, wait!' she cried as he turned towards the door.

But he didn't look back. Once the door was shut, the lock turned again and the bolt slid across. She held her breath as she waited for him to go down the stairs and then she let it out. Tears poured down her face and her breathing began to escalate again. Why was there a lock on the door? Oh God. She had to get out of that room.

Yet, for some reason, even though the scarf had been removed from her mouth, Jess's first instinct hadn't been to scream as loud and as long as she could. For one, she didn't want to antagonise the man any more than necessary, and if he was telling the truth then no one would hear her anyway. For another, the storm raging outside would carry her cries with it. It would waste her energy, and she needed to conserve that for when the time came for her to make a move.

Nausea washed over her. She didn't want to eat anything, but she needed to keep her strength up. This could be a trick. It might be the last time that she ate in a while.

She ripped the toast into smaller pieces so that she could pick one up in her fingers and reach it to her mouth. It seemed tasteless, and she chewed for a long time before it would go down. The tea was disgusting, weak and too milky for her liking, but she sipped at it anyway. Cupping her hands around the mug, she brought the liquid to her mouth, imagining it was vodka and coke rather than a weak excuse for a cuppa. Jess loved vodka. She and Katie used to drink it whenever they could and would always be buying bottles from the off-licence at the end of the road. It was easy to use her sister's ID. Sarah was nineteen and Jess looked like her on the photo.

It was then that her frustration made her clamp her teeth around the duct tape and pull. The tape was strong, having been wound around several times to make it more secure. She bit it again, wondering if it would weaken any if she wet it with her saliva. She sat back on the bed, back against the wall, and continued to bite.

In a few minutes she had got nowhere, and she sunk her arms down to one side. It was useless. She couldn't get free – and what would she do if she could?

She could rush him as he came through the door the next time.

With that thought, and knowing it would occupy her mind through the long night, she began to nibble at the tape again.

# TWENTY-THREE

Still a little shaken up after the recent confrontation at the supermarket and the visit from the police, Maxine closed the curtains, shutting out the night. It was nearing 10 p.m. and she wanted to watch a film that she had seen advertised, if only to take her mind off things.

She'd been half expecting journalists to be camped outside the door when she got home. They had been quite intrusive after Katie had been arrested, and they hadn't left the family alone for a few weeks afterwards. Maybe they wouldn't start until Monday, once the trial was underway.

She glanced at herself in the mirror above the fireplace before she sat down again. She seemed to have aged so much during the past six months, absorbing all the grief, the pain, the anger, the fear for her daughter and for her family. At least she had the weekend off.

Maxine had worked at Brightware Superstore since her teens. Her first Saturday job had been four hours a day on the tills covering Christmas, then more hours while she was at college until eventually she had stayed on full-time.

She'd taken time off when Katie was born and then had gone back to working thirty hours a week in the staff canteen. Being away from the general public was fun and, as well as the usual office politics, she got to hear all the gossip. It had suited her just fine until she had been the one being gossiped about. Some colleagues had stood by her, some hadn't.

In situations such as these, you certainly got to know who your friends were. She remembered having things chalked up on her locker: murdering scum, killer daughter. The culprit had never been caught, causing her distress because she still didn't know who had wanted to hurt her. It wasn't her fault that Katie had got involved with the wrong crowd. She'd warned her often enough – hoped Matty wouldn't follow in the same footsteps. Hoped this would be enough of a warning to keep him on the straight and narrow.

Maxine would never forget the look of terror on Katie's face as she was led into the dock alongside the three boys. Katie's face had been red and puffy from crying, and it had taken all her strength not to jump over the chairs and go and give her daughter a hug. She looked dreadful, obviously not having had any sleep. And who could blame her? She didn't know what she would be waking up to – a living nightmare for sure.

Over the months since Katie had been placed into the care of Ashcroft House, Maxine had Googled every case on joint enterprise they could find. There were so many teenagers locked up for crimes they had only been witness to, or been dragged into rather than look stupid in front of their peers. Of course most had been guilty but wrong place, wrong time was definitely a truth here.

Some of the stories were horrific, yet some had gangs of teens being put away for the act of one of them. And in this case, Maxine firmly believed, knowing Katie the way she did, that there was no malice intended. She had only been dating Nathan Lucas for a couple of weeks. So, as much as she realised lots of people under the common law of joint enterprise deserved to be charged, there were some innocent people too. And she'd had to shield her daughter from the facts.

There were so many teenagers' mums talking online. In the beginning, she had emailed a few mothers for advice. It had broken her heart as she had read their stories. She hadn't told Phil. He would be mortified that she had gone outside the family. Even Laura wasn't enough. She didn't understand. These mothers did – they were doing exactly the same as she was.

But as well as the support offered, she'd had to listen to their thoughts about their individual cases, their trials, the lesser charges that had been thrown out and longer sentences administered because some had pleaded not guilty.

Going to see a solicitor had been traumatic, but she'd had to look out for her daughter. She needed to do what was best for Katie, even if she had to go through a lot of heartache to stop herself from drowning in despair. She wouldn't give up hope that Katie would be allowed to come home. Hope was all she had now.

Phil came into the room and handed her a glass of wine before sitting next to her on the settee.

'I thought you might need this,' he said, his look solemn.

Maxine's smile was faint as she took it from him. They didn't drink much in the house. They'd share a glass or two during the week, perhaps have the odd bottle if the weather was warm and they were sitting out in the garden, or if it was a celebration, a special occasion or a birthday treat. Spirits were drunk mostly around Christmas. Both of them had grown up with parents who liked their drink a little too much.

They'd built a stable marriage around looking out for each other and had been so happy when Katie had come along and made them into a family. When Matty had followed six years later, a mistake at first but one they had come to relish, their family and their happiness had been complete.

But, like any other family unit, one tiny thing had torn them apart and smashed all their hopes and dreams to smithereens. One night, six months ago, their daughter had been locked up for a crime she hadn't committed.

Phil looked tired too, with bags under his eyes and unusually pale skin. Matty was turning out to be his double, with his dark hair and deep brown eyes, which sparkled a little less than usual. It was sad to see him under as much stress as she was.

Maxine leaned against him for a moment.

'We'll bring her home,' he whispered into her hair. 'They have no right to keep her locked up.'

Katie's solicitor had told them to expect the worst and that they would go on to fight afterwards. Maxine wished she shared her husband's optimism, but being a pessimist at heart meant that she kept her feet firmly on the ground and wouldn't allow herself to feel hopeful in case Katie didn't come home. The likelihood of the judge making an example of all four teenagers in the group seemed a foregone conclusion. This was a case where a young girl had been murdered. A judge might think it had something to do with peer pressure, rivalry, jealousy maybe.

'How are you feeling?' he said.

'Numb, I guess. I'm not sure I want Monday to come, but I can't wait for it to be over too.'

Phil reached for her hand, gave it a quick squeeze. 'I feel numb too, and apprehensive, wondering what's going to happen, and what will happen to us if she doesn't come out. What her sentence will be. What repercussions we'll have if she's acquitted. Either way, we'll be there for her.' He paused. 'She will come home, won't she, Max?'

Tears glistened in his eyes as he pleaded with her to say the words he needed to hear. But she couldn't say them. She just couldn't.

'I – I hope so,' she settled for.

They sat in silence for a few minutes, each with their own thoughts.

'I wonder how she'll be this weekend.' A tear dropped down her face. 'I wish you would come with me to see her.'

Phil stroked her hand. 'She needs her mum, not some dad who can't cope with seeing his little girl locked up. Besides, I can look after Matty.'

'Why did we let her go out that night?' Maxine said suddenly. 'If we had grounded her, then she would have been safe at home—'

'Grounded her for what? We've been over this before. She's a good kid. We brought her up to be respectful. She just got into a scrape with the wrong crowd.'

'Do you really believe that? She's not innocent of everything.'

'I know, but you heard what the police said. They know the good kids and the bad kids around the area, and Katie wasn't known to them – well, apart from Eden because we know her through Laura. Nathan Lucas was known to them all. And Katie was told to keep her mouth shut by Nathan. What would you have done, especially after your recent encounter with Travis Barker?'

That last thought silenced Maxine. What would she have done in Katie's place? When she knew someone was dying and she was being told not to say anything or else she would get it next? Travis had frightened her so much in a couple of minutes, and he had only crowded her space really.

'We have to stay strong,' Phil added.

Maxine nodded.

The next few weeks were going to be hell for them all. There would be intrusions from every media. There would be newspaper journalists and press officers to fend off. There would be more visits from the police. But at least they would get to see Katie.

Phil sniffed and pulled his hand away from hers as he went back into normal mode. He gave a weak smile. 'The last time I wore a suit was at your sister's wedding. How much fun was that!'

Maxine laughed, recalling the fight that had broken out just after the wedding. 'I remember the look on my mum's face as her hat got knocked off and ended up being squashed under the wheels of a Post Office van!'

'And that was without your brother being around to cause an atmosphere.'

It was Maxine's turn to have tears in her eyes. 'Family,' she spoke quietly. 'You can't pick 'em but you sure as hell will defend them to the hilt.'

Katie – April 2015

Dear Mum,

You have to get me out of here. I can stick with it for a couple of nights until you can get me home again, but I'm not guilty of anything. Being escorted to a car and being made to sit in the back knowing that I was going to be taken away from you and Dad and Matty was the scariest thing that has ever happened to me. I wanted to scream, but I didn't have one left in me.

I've been charged with murder and sent to a secure unit until the trial starts on 12 October. How did this happen? I was so sure I would be going home today after being locked up in a prison cell for the past two days.

When I went in front of the judge, I thought they'd realise their mistake and send me home. Not the boys, because they are guilty of attacking Deanna. And Nathan is guilty of murder. He's the one who stabbed Deanna. But *I* tried to stop him, and I tried to help Deanna, but I couldn't save her. I was nowhere near her when Nathan stabbed her. And he didn't stab Deanna – he thought it was Travis.

How are her family? I bet they are so sad. I won't be able to go to the funeral now so will you say sorry to Mrs Barker for me? I wanted to say sorry in person, even though I didn't do anything wrong. She was a nice girl, Deanna. I didn't mix with her much, but she would hang around the shops and the park with us every now and again. She was much cooler than me and Jess, but don't tell Jess I told you.

What's going to happen to me now? How long will I have to be in the secure unit before someone will realise this is all a mistake? I'm so scared. I don't know anyone. You know I don't make friends easily.

I keep crying all the time, remembering the look on your face, and Dad's too, when the judge remanded us all. I shouted to you to help me, but I knew you couldn't. But this isn't right.

What will it be like in prison, Mum? I don't know what to expect.

God, I'm in deep shit, and it isn't even my fault.

Love Katie x

# TWENTY-FOUR

By 11 p.m., Jess had bitten through about an inch of the tape. It wasn't enough to pull her hands apart, for it to split, but it was enough to give her the incentive to keep going.

She wondered what would be happening at her house right now. Would the police have been called or would her mum have to wait for twenty-four hours before she could be reported missing? That's what she'd seen on the television, on news appeals that she'd watched. Maybe teenagers run away every morning on a regular basis and turn up back at home when they're hungry or need a bed again. She hoped Eden would be able to persuade them that this was serious. What would happen to her if they left it too long?

She thought of Cayden too. She hoped he'd rung Sarah or called at her house to see where she was, alert them to the fact she was missing. If he didn't then no one would look for her until now.

No, Sarah would have told her mum that she hadn't come home when she was back from her shift at CrisisChat. Mum would most probably curse and think she had stayed out late deliberately, but she would wait up for her. About midnight she would start to worry. She would call Eden soon. Eden would know what to do.

The police wouldn't know where to look for her though.

She glanced around the room again, trying not to panic. Why was it decorated like this? Was it in readiness for something? Would other men come into the room?

Was she being held for the weekend so that she could be trafficked out of the country? She knew it was possible – she'd just done a project on it at school. They'd been told to research something on the Internet. It had fascinated her at the time. It scared the shit out of her now. Tears burned her eyes again. She wasn't strong enough to get through this.

Questions, questions, questions.

Why had he chosen her?

Where was she?

Would he harm her?

She hoped he wouldn't make her do anything to him – or worse, rape her. She began to cry at the thought.

*Stop it, Jess*, she chastised herself. *You need to stay strong.*

She bit at the tape again to take her mind away from the dark thoughts. *Think of happy things* – holidays and nights out with friends. Hanging around at the park with the girls. Making sure she didn't spend too much of her hard-earned cash on things that would rouse suspicion. She loved going out with Cayden. It was exciting. Now, every time she was with him was more fun than the last, and she wasn't talking about sex. She found their job far more exhilarating. They were like a real-life Bonnie and Clyde.

If she thought about that, about getting out of here to continue to make more money, she would get through this. He shouldn't scare her that much.

She started on the tape again.

# TWENTY-FIVE

As Laura drove home through the rain that was still coming down heavily, she wondered if Jess had gone against her wishes and stayed over at Stacey's house. It didn't worry her that she was staying there. Laura liked Stacey and she got on well with her mum, so safety wasn't an issue. And Jess was sixteen so she could look after herself to a point. But she wouldn't let her youngest get the upper hand. Laura let her get away with some things, let her push her to the limit, but there had to be boundaries. And if Jess had stayed out, without ringing her, just sending a text and then not answering her phone, well, she was going to ground her for the weekend when she got home tomorrow.

The wind nearly blew her into the house as she grappled to put her key in the front door. Once inside, it was quiet. The light was on in the living room, but she found it empty.

'Sarah?' She walked into the kitchen, but there was no one in there either. Upstairs, Sarah's bedroom door was ajar and Laura was surprised to see her asleep under the covers. Usually she waited up for her, especially on a Friday, but tonight she was flaked out.

She sighed when she looked in Jess's bedroom to find it empty of her daughter. She sent another message, telling her to come home as soon as she was up in the morning.

A text message came back before the kettle had boiled.

*Will do. Night mum. Love you. Jx*

Laura couldn't help but smirk. She could just imagine Jess in her jim-jams, tucked up in bed with Stacey watching a scary movie. Jess stayed over at Stacey's house so often that she kept a spare pair of pyjamas there, just in case. She bet they'd have crisps and pop and all sorts of other things that were delicious but no good for them.

In the living room she switched the television on low and sank into the settee with a satisfied sigh. It was good to be home, despite the trials of the night. It hadn't stayed quiet for too long. She'd had two teenagers on, talking about Katie Trent's trial and what would happen to their friends.

It was hard to listen to someone talk about something when she knew the people involved. She couldn't stop doing her job just in case someone she knew rang up, but two in one night was a bit much. These kids were hurting, scared that it could have happened to them. Everyone wanted to see Katie back. She could only hope that their prayers would be answered, although it definitely went against the grain to release her after such a hideous crime had been committed.

She remembered bumping into Lulu Barker two weeks after the murder. She'd tried to send her condolences, but Lulu had turned on her, saying her husband had left her because of what had happened. Lulu hadn't cared that people had turned to stare.

Laura had been mortified but at the same time tried to understand what it must be like to lose a child at such a young age and in such tragic circumstances.

Grief was a strange thing, manifesting itself in many ways. She might have done the same thing if it had been Jess. Lulu's anger had to come out somehow, and that day it had been her turn to get the brunt of it.

Still, at least Jess was alive, and safe and sound, even if she wasn't tucked up in her own bed.

# TWENTY-SIX

He woke with a start. He'd fallen asleep on the settee, the bottle of whiskey on his chest. He glanced around the room – the emptiness was still depressing, but he couldn't be bothered to do anything about it.

It was 4 a.m. The television was on. Was it that he'd heard? He ran a hand over his head before reaching for the remote control. He muted the sound and listened.

Nothing.

He wondered if the girl was asleep. Would she be able to sleep? Did he even care if she slept or not as long as she stayed quiet?

He flipped off the coat he'd covered himself in and went to the top of the stairs. He listened – nothing.

Was she sleeping?

'Are you okay in there?' He knocked on the door.

No reply.

'I said are you okay in there?' He knocked again.

Still no reply.

He paced outside on the landing. She must be asleep.

But then he remembered what had happened to his daughter.

It was her fault.

He needed to stay sober, keep his wits about him. If he hadn't drunk so much, he wouldn't have woken up in a panic.

He went back downstairs to pick up the whiskey bottle. It was nearly empty. At least he had no more of the strong stuff.

He had a few bottles of lager in the fridge. That would tide him over until Monday.

Someone needed to be punished for the death of his daughter. He had to bide his time until he could put the next part of his plan into action.

He picked up a photo frame again, sat looking at the image in front of him, getting angrier by the minute. A beautiful young and vibrant girl smiled back at him.

How he missed his daughter. She had meant everything to him. She was his life and now he was left with nothing. Except pain and hurt and anger and rage burning inside him.

He'd always wanted a girl and had felt blessed when she'd finally come along. She had always been a daddy's girl, a breath of fresh air. He ran a finger over the glass. She had his eyes and her mother's full lips, curled into a smile that lit up her face.

A tear escaped as he tried to remember the last time he had seen her face. He missed her so much. He couldn't breathe without her. Couldn't exist without her. And no one understood how he felt.

But she would soon.

# TWENTY-SEVEN

Behind the door, Jess sat frozen, her hand clasped over her mouth in case she made a sound. Moments later, she breathed a sigh of relief when she heard footsteps going down the stairs.

She thought she'd bitten through enough of the tape to make an impression. She pushed her wrists out as far as they would go, wider and wider, but the tape wouldn't give. She'd been nibbling for hours, taking breaks in-between to stop her lips from drying out too much.

She took another breather, her shoulders drooping. She had to get through the tape. There wasn't much time left until morning. Her thoughts turned to Katie. Her friend had been locked up like this for six months. She hadn't realised how hard it would be for her. Jess had often wondered why Katie had been so low when she had visited. She remembered telling her to get a grip and just get on with things, but now she felt completely embarrassed about it. Even being here for a few hours had been torture, and Katie had been put there by the law.

She had to pee. Although she hadn't had much to drink, it had been ten hours at least since she had last been. She'd been trying not to think about it for ages. Looking at the bucket, she couldn't imagine being able to do anything with her hands tied. But she had crossed her legs long enough.

What happened if she made a noise and he came running in while she was half naked? She bit her lip to stop herself from crying out. Just the thought of what he might do to her was enough to set her off again. But she needed to stay calm.

She took a few deep breaths and sat up, pressing her feet quietly to the floor. She pulled her hands apart again, but still the tape wouldn't loosen.

She stood up and took a step towards the bucket. The floorboard creaked underneath the carpet and she stood statue still. But she couldn't hear anything. She took another few steps until she was level with the bucket. Then she moved her hands to her button. That was easy enough to do, along with unzipping her jeans.

With great effort, she managed to inch the jeans and knickers down each side. It took her a while, the thought of him coming in now enough to stop her flow of urine completely.

She stooped over the bucket, crying silent tears as she prayed he hadn't heard her moving around. Suddenly urine began to come out, and she almost cried with relief. She finished and, with nothing to wipe herself on, began the task of shimmying her clothes back into place.

Getting back to the bed, she collapsed on top of it with the sheer effort. It had been harder than she'd expected to do that with her hands tied. It had also been one of the most humiliating things she had ever done, and she wondered what else he had in store for her. She stared at the bucket, an idea forming.

She crawled under the covers as best as she could and tried to get some sleep. Her mouth was sore and her lips were dry. Even if she got a couple of hours, she needed to rest.

And then she was getting out of here.

# SATURDAY

10 October 2015

# TWENTY-EIGHT

Eden took a sip of her coffee as she sat at the kitchen table. She smiled, still feeling the afterglow of sex from the night before. That was one good thing about a fledgling relationship. Joe hadn't stayed the night though. She'd pushed him out of bed shortly after 3 a.m. She always blamed Casey not being too sure about the relationship, but it was as much her as well.

So now it was 8.15 a.m. and she was alone. Knowing Casey, she would get up later that morning, grab tea and toast and slope back to bed again, read a magazine, chat to her friends on the phone and stay in her jim-jams for as long as possible. She couldn't blame her really.

Eden envied her in a way too. She'd enjoyed nothing better than doing that at the weekend when she was younger with no responsibilities. And at least Casey had come home on time last night. She was a good girl really. She didn't have to worry about her like Laura had to worry about Jess. It was why she had always kept a lookout for her niece whenever it was possible.

She lifted the fridge magnet in the shape of a red high heel and clipped the note she'd written underneath it, hoping that at least some of the jobs listed on it would be done by the time she got home. Joe was coming round again that evening, and she wanted the place to look tidy at least. She wanted to cook him something nice – though Lord knew what and it would have to be a cheap affair. It would involve a trip to the supermarket that afternoon for inspiration as well as supplies.

If she didn't need the money, she wouldn't be going in for extra hours. But having been a single parent for over two years now, every additional penny earned went towards something she could share with Casey or buy for her. She wanted to provide for her daughter as much as any parent and to make up for her father walking out on them both.

She ran her fingers through her hair, wondering whether to wear her tam or not. The weather outside the kitchen window was looking as awful as it had been the night before, Storm Monica still doing its worst. So, although she loved any excuse to wear it, she very much doubted it would even stay on.

So far, October had been a washout. Eden wondered if they might have a good cold snap this winter, with snow and ice to kill the flu germs. Last year had been pretty dire for her, catching two bouts of the nasty stuff and having to drag herself into work. It hadn't been a good idea, especially when Eden had then given it to her colleagues too.

She glanced at her watch to see she'd have to get a move on if she wanted to be in the office for nine. She slipped back upstairs to get her boots. It was definitely the weather for Doc Martens with her skinny black trousers, something she could get away with only at the weekends when she was doing overtime.

As she passed Casey's bedroom, she noticed through the open door that her daughter was sitting up in bed. She tapped on it to get her attention. The room was a double and Casey had managed to cram it with as much stuff as possible. An overflowing bookcase, drawers with clothes sticking out of them, clothes hanging on the wardrobe handles and over a small chair, a shelf full of teddy bears dating back over the years. You could just about make out a colour scheme of duck egg blue and cream underneath all the bright flashes of colour.

To Eden it looked like a tip. To Casey it would be organised chaos. But then again, she and her sister had been the same at her age, and they'd had to share a room until Laura had left home when she married Neil.

'Casey, I'm off now,' she said. 'All being well, I'll be home by lunchtime. I've left you a list of jobs to do downstairs.'

Casey tutted. 'I'm not a skivvy.'

'I agree, but you do want those shoes you saw last week don't you?'

Casey sighed. 'Okay, okay.'

'Joe is coming round this evening. I'm not sure if Emma will be with him or not – I doubt it after the fuss you two caused the last time you met.'

'Thank God for that,' muttered Casey.

'Give me a break,' said Eden. 'I do my best.'

Casey seemed to relent. 'Sorry.'

'Do you realise how lucky you are to have the house to yourself all Saturday morning? Your gran used to hoover around me and your aunt Laura when we wouldn't get up. Always before nine a.m. and always in our room first!'

'I can just imagine her in a pinny and you two shoving your head under the covers at the noise.' Casey giggled.

'She hated me and Laura playing The Jam all the time. She'd say, "Turn that bloody nonsense down. You wouldn't hear that sort of thing in my day."'

'That's what you say to me now!'

Eden smiled. They were so alike, with long limbs, fair skin and brown eyes. Casey's hair was long to her short, but it was as if she was looking down at the girl her mother had harassed with the hoover many years ago. Casey was almost overtaking her in height, especially when she wore the most ridiculous of heels. It was lovely to see her growing up, and yet, in a way, Eden would rather she kept her youth. Often the world was cruel and dark.

'I'm on my phone if you need me.' She leaned over and kissed Casey's forehead. Surprisingly, Casey didn't move away. 'Behave yourself if you have friends over. I don't mind as long as the jobs are done and no one upsets the neighbours.'

'Bye, Mum!' Casey shooed her out of the room.

Going down the stairs, Eden wondered if she was doing the right thing for her girl. She wanted Casey to have a good start in life, and she was sorry in her heart that her lowlife scum father had walked out on her when she was barely fourteen, turning his back on them both completely. Just like her and Laura, it had made the two of them into a tight unit, and Eden knew she was lucky to have her. As children go, Casey wasn't half as bad as some of the kids she had to work with. Not bad at all.

# TWENTY-NINE

Jess woke. Her eyes flitted around the room, unfamiliar with the surroundings. When she realised where she was, tears welled up. How could she have drifted off to sleep when she was in so much danger?

Now she was awake, she began to tear at the tape again. Her mouth was sore, her lips were dry but she kept at it, convinced she would get through it before he came back to her.

She pulled on her hands, feeling the tape give a little more. There was only half a centimetre left now but the more she pulled it, the more the sticky side glued together. She took a quick thirty-second break, drank the last mouthful of the disgusting tea she'd been sipping all night and bit into it again.

She focused on things that made her happy as she attacked the tape. How she would give Cayden the biggest kiss when she saw him. How pleased her mum would be to see her home – and Sarah too – and how much she would hug them both. She thought about Eden and how she would have the whole force out looking for her. They would all be working hard to find out where she was. She had a whole army behind her.

She ripped apart a little bit more of the tape and again pulled her wrists wide. She didn't have much energy, but she carried on pulling, groaning inwardly. And then all her hard work paid off as the tape gave way. She tore at it, pulling it away completely from her hands.

She sat for a moment, waiting, listening. She was sure he would have heard her, even though she knew she had made no noise.

She rubbed her hands together, clenching her fingers and rolling her wrists a few times to ease their stiffness. Then she shimmied to the end of the bed and listened again. Nothing.

She tiptoed across the room. A floorboard creaked and she froze. But still nothing. She wasn't sure why she was expecting him to come clattering through the door to tie her up again, but she wanted to be ready when he did.

Quietly, she opened the top drawer of three and rummaged around. There was a pile of T-shirts, ironed and folded up neatly on one side, and knickers and socks on the other. They were all girls' clothes. Whose were they?

She grimaced as she searched around. It wasn't nice going through someone's personal belongings. Even though everything was clean, it felt wrong, like she was invading someone's personal space. She searched through them all, looking for something, anything. She checked the middle drawer and then knelt down to rummage in the bottom one.

It took a lot of effort to be quiet, as she wanted to scream out in frustration. But she didn't want to alert him to the fact that she was awake. It had taken her hours to rip through that tape with her mouth, and if she didn't get out of the room, it would all be for nothing.

She bent her head down and looked underneath the unit, but there was nothing there either. She turned her head towards the bed. In the far corner there was a shoebox. She reached for it and pulled it out. Sitting on the bed again, she removed the lid.

It was full of mementos. A tiny white teddy bear holding a good-luck sign. A ticket to see Little Mix in concert. A bracelet with charms on it. She picked out a notebook, Keep Calm and Eat Chocolate on its front, and flicked through the pages. There were a few notes about calories and how many it took to walk to the shops and to school. How many calories in an apple, a slice of bread.

Where was the girl, she wondered? This was clearly her room. And then her mind went into overdrive. Her hand clasped over her mouth as she tried not to vomit. He'd kept her here, hadn't he? And he must have killed her. And if he had, he wouldn't think twice about doing it again.

She tried not to hyperventilate, pushing back her tears. She had to keep her wits about her. Her mum said she had an old head on young shoulders. Now was the time to prove it.

She slid the box back under the bed and opened the wardrobe door, wincing as it creaked. She waited, not moving, but there was still no sound from downstairs. There were clothes, things she would wear herself – skinny jeans, long-sleeved T-shirts, leggings and jumpers.

In a bag at the bottom was a load of old make-up. Her hand fell onto a small can of hairspray and she almost laughed out loud. Then there was a brush. She grasped it by the handle and wondered how much it would hurt if she hit out with it.

It was just past nine in the morning. Someone would be looking for her by now. She needed to keep that thought in her mind, stay hopeful that someone would find her.

If she wanted to go home, she had to keep her fear at bay.

# THIRTY

Laura put the iron back onto the board with a sigh. This wasn't really the way she wanted to spend her Saturday mornings, but even though Jess did lots of jobs around the house, she still didn't trust her to iron her school uniform after she'd singed several items.

Five white shirts later and she reached for one of her own blouses. She'd booked Monday off work and was going to court with Maxine and Phil, and she wanted to look smart. The last time she had worn a suit was at her uncle's funeral two years ago. Amazingly she could still fit in it when she tried it on. So adding a more fashionable, coloured blouse it looked decent enough.

There were only two items of Sarah's so she ran the iron over them and switched it off to cool. She checked her phone to see if Jess had replied, but there was nothing. If she didn't contact her soon, she would ring Stacey's mum. Jess would be annoyed, but it would serve her right for being in a mood for something or other. They had parted on good enough terms after their last conversation.

Maybe she realised that she would be in trouble when she got home for not asking her in person. Maybe she was playing it cool. Knowing Jess she would stroll into the house soon, without a care in the world, and she'd moan at her, and then things would go back to how they were before.

Sighing impatiently, she sent her a curt message this time, asking her to ring her straightaway.

'Morning, Mum,' Sarah said, joining her in the kitchen. She covered her mouth with her hand as she stifled a yawn.

'Morning, love. You heard the kettle, I presume? Tea?'

'Thanks. I've got time for a quick one before I leave.' Sarah pulled out a chair to sit down at the table.

'Going shopping?'

'Yes, there's a blue-cross sale on.'

Laura reached for two mugs before turning back to Sarah. 'Did Jess tell you that she'd arranged to stay over at Stacey's last night?'

Sarah shook her head. 'She said she was going to Cayden's house. She told you that, didn't she?'

Laura nodded. 'Then she sent me a message last night to say she was staying with Stacey. I haven't been able to get hold of her since.'

'Her phone is off?' Sarah frowned. 'That's not like Jess.'

'No, her phone is on. I tried to call her back as soon as she sent the message, but it rang out. I've just sent her another message.'

'I wonder if she fell out with Cayden and went to Stacey's instead? The course of true love and all that.'

Laura smiled, remembering back to some of the angst from her teenage years. 'Yes, hardly ever runs smooth.' She glanced at the clock. 'I'll give her ten minutes and then I'll try her again.'

# THIRTY-ONE

Once in the office, Eden threw her keys onto the desk. Coffee first and then head down. She could do so much if she wasn't disturbed. First she logged on to her computer to check the jobs that had come in from the night before. Technically she was here to catch up on paperwork, but she always liked to know what was going on.

As she looked over the actions that she and her team had been allocated, she noticed there had been three more attacks, one reported after another. Two teenage girls and a boy. The report mentioned the names of kids she knew. Eden frowned. Was something about to kick off?

'Morning, Sarge,' said Amy, coming into the room. 'It's still nasty outside, but I come bearing gifts.'

'Give!' Eden clapped her hands like a child before holding them out.

Amy slapped a parcel down into them. Unwrapping the silver foil, Eden groaned in anticipation. Inside was a bacon sandwich. She bit into it, relishing it as if she had never tasted one before.

Amy sat down at her desk and tucked into her sandwich too. 'Anything come in overnight, Sarge?' she asked, once she had eaten her first mouthful.

Eden wiped ketchup from her lips with a paper napkin. 'Uniform were called out early evening. Three people were attacked. All familiar names. And I gave Stacey Goodwin a lift last night. She'd been dragged into the bushes off the side of the path by Theodore House and had a tin of paint thrown over her head.'

'What?' Amy stopped as she was about to take another bite. 'That sounds weird.'

'It does. Obviously she was in a right state so I took her home.'

'With paint all over her? What about The Mooch?'

'You know I carry a roll of black bin liners in the boot of the mini. I practically covered Stacey from head to foot before she sat in the passenger seat. But I couldn't let her walk home like that.'

'Did she say who it was?'

'I couldn't get much out of her, which is why I'd like you to go and see her this morning.'

Amy nodded.

'There was also an attack on Ruby Peters. Bizarrely, someone held her down and cut her long hair to short on either side of her head.' Eden saw Amy frown as she continued. 'Claire Mornington was dragged into a car, driven four miles from home and dumped in a lane. Not only that but they removed her jeans and shoes and took her phone and money so she had to walk home half naked.'

Amy looked outraged. 'That's barbaric!'

Eden nodded. 'As well, someone beat ten barrels of shit out of Cayden Blackwell, our Jess's boyfriend.'

'Ouch.'

'Two of the girls had notes left on them too. *Keep your mouth shut.*'

'Fun and games as usual. Do you think it might have anything to do with the trial?'

'It's possible, although I had hoped it might be quiet at least until it had started.'

'Me too,' Amy agreed.

'Which means that we might have to go out and see some of the SWAPs.'

Stockleigh Working to Achieve Potential had been set up shortly after Deanna Barker's murder in April. It didn't just consist of mothers from the Mitchell Estate, where the murder had taken place, but from all over the city. It was run by Josie Mellor, a housing officer for Mitchell Housing Association. Eden had gone along when Josie had invited her to their first meeting.

Some of the mums in SWAP were doing a great job around the city getting the teens involved in community projects they could be proud of. It took a lot of time to set these things up, and she and Josie got involved as much as they could. Since then, a memorial garden had been created in Deanna's name. A small plot of disused land had been donated by the city council, and the local children and teenagers had raised funds to buy a bench that had a plaque with her name on it. A tree had also been planted in her memory.

Eden flicked through the notes on the screen again. 'This might need nipping in the bud before Monday. How was your morning looking?'

'Oh, you know, the usual paperwork, paperwork, paperwork.' Amy stretched her arms above her head.

'Great. We'll both go out on visits.'

Eden got to work but Cayden Blackwell was playing on her mind. She read the report of his attack and his injuries as noted by the PC on duty last night. Cayden was a bright lad but could be heading for trouble. Eden knew he'd been hanging around with Nathan Lucas before Deanna Barker's murder. She also knew that he'd probably had a lucky escape by being taken out of the equation because he was at Jess's house with her on the night that it happened.

She sat back in her chair and thought of Jess. She was the same age as Casey, but she seemed far more mature. Streetwise beyond her sixteen years, Jess always seemed to be causing worry for Laura. Many times, her sister had asked her to talk things over with Jess about something she had said, attitude given, staying out late. She'd always done that, and it had worked on occasion, but Jess was very headstrong. Sometimes there was just no reasoning with her.

Being a parent was tough. Eden knew only too well how hard it was to juggle being loving and being firm, bringing a child up rather than dragging them up. She could clearly remember her mum reading the riot act to her and her sister on several occasions when they had pushed the boundaries too far.

Eden wondered if it would be worth going to see Lulu Barker, Deanna's mum, too. If these attacks were something to do with the trial next week, then she might be able to calm things down before they escalated too far.

# THIRTY-TWO

After spotting an article headed '*Trial for Deanna – four in dock on Monday*', Laura decided to give Maxine a quick call. She had begun to get nervous about Monday herself and wanted to offer her support if possible.

Laura could tell Jess was worried, too, that her friend wouldn't come out of the secure unit. If there was one thing Jess would talk about, it was Katie.

She worried about Jess not coping. Everything hinged on this week, the trial and the judge. They couldn't sentence Katie – the evidence wasn't there. Laura was waiting for her to come out too.

She shuddered involuntarily. It could so easily have been Jess that was locked up, on trial for murder.

'How are you today?' she asked when Maxine answered the phone.

'I'm okay. I can't believe all the attention the case is getting already though. Have you seen the headlines in the *Stockleigh News* this morning?'

'Yes. Tensions are high I guess. How is Katie bearing up?'

She seems to have shut herself off, resigned herself to a guilty verdict.'

'It's just nerves as the trial comes closer.'

'She can't be found guilty of something she didn't do.'

Laura remained silent, knowing that Maxine wasn't after an answer.

'I just hope she holds it together,' Maxine added. 'She was so low the last time I saw her. I tried to hold back my tears while I was with her, but Katie had no tears this time. If the media see her showing no emotion, everyone will think that she doesn't seem sorry for what happened, but it isn't like that at all. She's blocked it all out. She's resigned to hearing her fate.'

'She'll be better when she sees you tomorrow,' Laura soothed.

'But I feel like I can't be there for her any more.'

'I don't think you've ever stopped.'

'I meant that she doesn't want me there for her.'

'Of course she does,' Laura insisted. 'She's just trying to cope, that's all. It's a terrible situation to be in.'

'That's just it. I don't know what to do, because I don't know how this will end. I don't even know if it will end after the trial. If we can't walk down the street, we'll have to move.'

'It sounds clichéd but try not to look too far ahead. Take each day as it comes.'

'But what will we do if she doesn't come home?'

Laura listened as if she was at work taking a call. What else could she do? The outcome of the trial could ruin the Trent family – lots of families if the verdicts were all guilty.

All of a sudden, Laura felt her skin flushing and was glad Maxine was on the phone and not here in person to see. She couldn't help but be glad that Jess had been ill that night.

'I pray it works out well for you,' she said when Maxine had finished talking.

'Yes. At least I get to see her tomorrow.'

Immediately Laura disconnected the call, she rang Jess. Maxine's pain had rubbed off on her.

# THIRTY-THREE

Eden sent Amy to interview Stacey Goodwin and Ruth Peters while she went to see Cayden Blackwell and Claire Mornington.

Even having been a regular visitor to The Cavendales when her sister had lived there, it still amazed her to see so many impressive houses all in one place. No two were alike on the same street. Most had been individually designed.

The Blackwells' house was on Peppermint Avenue. It was set over three floors with a larger than average two-car garage attached on its right and a garden manicured to within an inch of its life. Eden felt underdressed, as if she should take her boots off to walk up the driveway.

The heavy oak front door opened before she got to it. Cayden's mum, Andrea, ushered her into a large hallway. Eden knew her vaguely through Jess. She was a smart woman in her early forties. Cayden had her dark hair and brown eyes but was stocky to her small frame.

'Mrs Blackwell,' said Eden. 'How is Cayden?'

'He's still a bit shaken, but he's going to be fine.' Andrea pointed to a door and they went through into a living room that was the length of Eden's whole downstairs. Andrea's heels clicked on the cream marble tiles. Several white leather settees were scattered around a large television on the wall, complemented by black furniture. Vases of white lilies and roses sat on three tables in a row by a bank of windows overlooking a landscaped garden. It had the look of a show house, yet there was something homely about it.

Cayden was lying on a settee watching the television. His face was a riot of colour, and Eden could hear him sniffing, trying to breathe through his bruised nose. One eye was swollen almost shut, butterfly stitches above the other. Two fingers on his left hand were bandaged and taped together.

'Cayden, Eden is here to see you,' said Andrea, taking the remote control from him. She lowered the sound to almost nothing and turned back to Eden. 'Can I get you a drink?'

'No, thanks.' Eden sat down on an armchair and looked at Cayden. 'That's a mess, fella. I bet it's sore too. How long were you in A&E?'

'About six hours.'

'So you arrived there about. . .?'

'I think it was after six.'

'I was contacted at ten past seven,' said Andrea. 'Worst shock of my life when I had a call from a paramedic.'

'And you were there until just after midnight?' Eden continued.

As Cayden relayed what information he could recall, Eden took down some notes.

'You think it was definitely a man?' she asked afterwards.

'If it was a woman, she had a good punch.'

'Can you remember anything about how he looked?' She noted down his last sentence before her eyes flicked back up to his.

'I didn't really see him. He came from behind.'

'What was he wearing?'

'I don't know. Everything was dark, but he wore a balaclava.'

'Did he speak with a local accent?'

'I don't think he said anything. I thought he was after my phone. I was trying to find a good track to listen to while I made my way to Jess's house—'

'You were on your way to see Jess?' Eden's ears pricked up.

'Yeah, and I haven't seen her since. She must have got the huff with me for standing her up. She's in big trouble when I see her.' Cayden grinned then winced as his lip split a little.

'Go on,' Eden urged him.

'I had a whack across the back of my legs. I got up, turned round, pulled out my plugs and then he came at me again. I didn't have time to defend myself so I dropped to the floor and curled up in a ball until he stopped.'

Andrea whimpered. 'Sorry, just the image.' She reached for a tissue from the coffee table and dabbed at her eyes. 'It's so awful to see him like this. He's a good boy, not like some of the scum who go to his school.'

Eden decided to reserve judgement on that for now. 'What happened then?' she asked.

'I guess I must have passed out,' said Cayden. 'When I came round, I managed to get myself to the end of the path. I can't remember much after that, except arriving at the hospital.'

'He was given some strong painkillers,' Andrea explained. 'They knocked him out for most of the night.'

'Did Jess come?' Cayden asked, looking at his mum.

Andrea shook her head. 'Not while I was there.'

'So she might have called to see you?' asked Eden.

'I don't know,' said Cayden. 'I've tried ringing and texting her, but I've had no reply yet.'

Eden frowned. Like Casey, Jess never usually had her phone out of her hands. She stared at them for a moment before continuing. 'There were several attacks across the city last night. I'm sure they're all teenagers you'll know, Cayden. Stacey Goodwin, Ruby Peters and Claire Mornington.'

Cayden looked at the floor.

'All three girls often hang around with you and Jess of an evening. So far we know they were all attacked within an hour of each other, so it's possible it was the same people who were responsible. There have been four attacks that we know of now, with yours.'

'Wait.' Cayden sat up. 'What about Jess?'

'She's probably at home.' Eden raised a hand to calm him. 'Speaking to you is the first time I've heard about this, so I'll chase it up as soon as I leave.'

'Do you think it was one of Deanna Barker's brothers?' asked Andrea.

'You can't accuse just anyone, Mum!' Cayden shook his head then stopped abruptly, holding on to his cheek.

'I'm not accusing them,' said Andrea. 'I just want to rule them out. You're saying that three girls were attacked last night, and then this with Cayden?' She turned to Eden with folded arms. 'Your Jess isn't perfect, you know.'

'Mum!'

'It's true. Ever since she started going out with Cayden, Jess has been a law unto herself. I heard she did lots of things after Katie was locked up, but you did nothing to stop her, did you?'

'I'm sorry. I don't know what you mean,' Eden replied truthfully.

'Mum! Give over, will you?' said Cayden.

'I was told that she kicked in the glass at the bus shelter twice and spray-painted the side of the garage block over by the community centre.'

'Rumours, Mrs Blackwell,' said Eden, wondering why she hadn't heard this at the time.

'It isn't true,' insisted Cayden.

'And now you think Jess is missing?' Andrea continued.

'I didn't say that.' Eden hoped that Jess was tucked up safe in her bed. 'Why would you think the Barkers had something to do with this?'

'They were always going on about how Jess and Cayden had started all this mess, for some reason. It's such a coincidence that the trial starts on Monday, don't you think?'

'Wait.' Cayden held up his hand. 'I don't care about who did and said what. I want to know where Jess is.'

'I need to look into this further.' Eden stood up. 'I'll update you as soon as I can.'

As she walked back to her car, she ran through what Cayden had told her. The boy might be able to fool his mother into thinking that he couldn't remember much about the attack because he was concussed, but she had a gut feeling that he was lying. What she needed to work out was why.

She set off to see her sister. She needed to know if Jess was safe too.

# THIRTY-FOUR

There had still been no contact from Jess. Laura picked up the phone and rang Stacey Goodwin's mum. 'Hi, Sandra,' she said, 'it's Laura Mountford. How are you?'

'Oh, not so bad, thanks but our Stacey is in a terrible state. I can't believe anyone would do that to her. She's a complete and utter wreck. The paint has ruined her clothes, and it took a while to wash out of her hair.'

'Paint?' Laura questioned.

Sandra explained what had happened to Stacey. All the while Laura's hand covered her mouth. She couldn't believe what she was hearing.

'I'm just glad that it was emulsion,' said Sandra. 'If it was gloss, she'd more than likely have to have all her hair shaved off! But she got off lightly, I suppose, especially as there were other girls attacked as well.'

'There were more?' The hairs on the back of Laura's neck stood to attention.

'Ruby Peters had her hair hacked off and Claire Mornington was dumped a few miles from home, had her shoes and jeans removed and they took her phone. It's appalling. If I could get my hands on the—'

'And is Jess okay?' Laura interrupted. 'Only she's not answering her phone and obviously if she was with Stacey then I'm surprised she hasn't told me about this.'

A pause. 'I haven't seen Jess since earlier in the week.'

'But she sent me a message to say she was staying at your house last night.'

'She hasn't been here, Laura.'

Laura's blood began to boil. 'I'm so sorry to hear about Stacey, Sandra, but I – can I ring you back? I need to see where Jess is.'

'Of course. Let me know when you hear from her?'

'Oh I will. I'm sure it's nothing to worry about.'

Laura disconnected the call and went through to the kitchen. Andrea Blackwell's number was written on the noticeboard. If Jess wasn't with Stacey, then she must be with Cayden. And if she was, it meant that she must have lied and spent the night with him. She'd bloody swing for her when she got home.

But her phone went before she had chance to call Andrea. It was Eden.

'Hey, I'm just about to read the riot act to Jess,' Laura said. 'She's only told me that she was staying at Stacey's overnight, and it looks like she's been with Cayden. Oh, God, Eden. I hope she hasn't slept with him, you know, in that sense. She's only sixteen, and I know it will happen at some point, if it hasn't already, but I—'

'Laura – stop,' Eden broke in. 'Don't you know what happened to Cayden last night?'

'No, I haven't seen Jess this morning for her to tell me.'

'He was beaten up.'

'Oh no, is he okay?' Laura paled. 'What happened?'

'Someone set on him as he walked the cut-through from Railton Drive.'

'But Railton Drive is nowhere near our house. And Jess said she was seeing him last night but then sent me a text message to say she was staying over at Stacey's house. I just thought she and Cayden had had a tiff or something.' Laura caught her breath. 'Are you saying that Cayden hasn't seen Jess at all last night?'

'Yes. Do you—'

'But that can't be right.' Laura ran a hand through her hair. 'Sarah said Jess had a text from Cayden to meet her at Shop&Save. Oh God, I never thought to check that she wasn't there! And Stacey was attacked last night too.'

'There's something else you need to know.'

'What?' Laura snapped impatiently.

'Cayden sent Jess a message to say he'd been admitted to A&E. Apparently Jess replied to say she was on her way to see him.'

'She never arrived, did she?' Laura's voice came out as a half sob.

'I'm sorry, but neither Cayden nor his mum saw Jess last night.'

# THIRTY-FIVE

In a fit of panic, Laura rang Sarah asking her to come home. She paced the room as she waited for either her or Eden to arrive.

Why the hell hadn't she thought to speak to Jess directly to make sure she was okay? She should have tried the Goodwins' landline. All that talk about grounding her because she was being stroppy made her break out in a sweat. If anything had happened to her, and she had been hurt more because Laura hadn't acted sooner, she would never forgive herself.

Eden owned a white Mini Cooper with a black and white chequered roof. As soon as she spotted it pulling up outside the house, Laura raced to the door.

'She's missing and I didn't know,' she said. 'I tried to call her, but she sent me a text message, and I thought she was okay. I should have rang Sandra Goodwin and asked to speak to her, but it was late when I got home from work and—'

'Let's go inside,' said Eden, guiding her back to the front door. Her eyes were full of concern as they went through to the living room. 'When was the last time you saw her?'

'Yesterday evening before I went to work for six. We had a few words.'

'About anything in particular?'

'The usual teenage stuff. Watch her attitude mostly. She thinks she can act up whenever she likes, and I was just trying to knock her down a peg or two. You know she can be a bit fiery, especially when I'm at work and there's only Sarah at home.'

'What happened?' Eden moved her along.

'She stormed off upstairs. I did have a chat with her before I left, and I thought everything was okay between us.'

'So she has contacted you?'

'Yes.' Laura reached for her phone. 'I tried to ring her a couple of times, and she didn't answer. But she did send a few text messages. She seemed fine. And then she sent a message to say she was going to stay with Stacey. I thought nothing of it as it happens regularly.' She looked up at Eden again. 'I should have made certain that I spoke to her this morning. I was going to ground her because I told her not to stay out. I thought she was going to be with Cayden. I didn't think that she—'

Laura felt Eden's arms around her as she burst into tears.

'Can you remember what she was wearing?' Eden asked once Laura had stopped crying.

'Blue jeans, a black jacket and a black and white top. That's if she didn't get changed again after I left. Sarah's on her way home from shopping. She'll be able to tell us more.'

'Apart from the attack on Cayden,' said Eden, 'which was pretty brutal, the three girls seemed to have been attacked to be humiliated.'

Laura drew away from her. 'So you think whoever did that might have attacked Jess too?'

'It's something we need to look into.'

Laura began to cry again. Then she sat up. 'Is anyone else missing?'

'Not that we know of at the moment, but we obviously don't know for definite.'

Laura's heart sank. 'Why didn't I insist on speaking to her last night? At least then I would have known she was missing and I could have rung you.'

'You weren't to know.'

'But what kind of mother am I not to check?'

'I don't think you would have been the only one. As far as you were aware, Jess had told you she was staying at Stacey's. Did she send any more messages?'

'Yes, a few. And she said goodnight. But it wasn't her, was it?'

'We can't be sure yet,' said Eden.

'But the fact that Jess has been gone overnight and none of the others are missing doesn't look good.' Laura sat upright. 'Do you think it could be anything to do with the trial next week? Or has someone attacked her too? Then something went wrong?'

Eden held her hands. 'Try not to panic too much yet. Claire Mornington was dumped miles from her house and they took her money and phone so she had to walk home. *If* whoever took Claire has taken Jess, then she might be on her way home too.'

'But Jess is Katie Trent's best friend.' Laura ran a hand up and down her arm, as if trying to warm herself up. 'This can't just be a prank.'

'It can,' said Eden. 'You just have to sit tight. Either she will come home of her own accord, or we will find her.'

'Oh I have every faith in you,' said Laura. 'But I don't have faith in everyone else. These attacks must have something to do with the trial.'

'Can you give me a recent photo of Jess,' Eden brought her back to the job in hand. 'Do you have any printed out?'

Laura rushed off to find one, leaving Eden with her thoughts. Her niece was missing. She could be anywhere, but at least they might have a line of enquiry to work with. Jess could be another victim of the pranks from the night before.

# THIRTY-SIX

When Sarah arrived home, Eden checked the details with her. 'Can you confirm what Jess was wearing the last time you saw her?' she asked her eldest niece.

'She had her jeans on and a checked blue shirt under a navy blue V-necked jumper.' Sarah sat on the settee, Laura by her side. 'She had a black jacket on too,' she added, 'and black Chelsea boots.' She turned to Laura. 'The ones you bought her for her birthday.'

'And she told you she was going to see Cayden?' Eden took notes as she stood in front of the fire.

'Yes.'

'But when I got a text from her, she said she was staying over at Stacey's,' said Laura.

'So if she didn't go there and we know that she hasn't been with Cayden, then where is she now? She's been missing all this time and we didn't know?' Sarah turned to Laura. 'Why didn't you check up on her earlier?'

'There's no need to blame anyone, Sarah,' said Eden.

'But she should have—'

'I'm sorry, all right!' Laura shouted. 'I didn't know this would happen.'

'And you're sure that Cayden wouldn't do anything to harm Jess?' Eden ignored them both.

'I don't think so.' Laura shook her head.

'He is a bit full on at times,' said Sarah.

Eden and Laura looked at her.

'I like him, but sometimes he can be a bit cocksure, like he's God's gift to women, you know? Our Jess is a good-looking girl – she can have anyone. She told me he gets jealous of other boys looking at her.'

'You don't think he'd hurt her?' Laura questioned, her brow furrowing.

'And then beat himself up?' Eden raised her eyebrows. 'Anything is possible but those injuries weren't self-inflicted. Revenge is one line we will follow however. It could very well be someone getting even for something.'

'You mean the Barker family?' said Laura defiantly.

'I didn't say that!' Eden replied.

Sarah and Laura began to speak at the same time. Eden raised her hand. 'None of this makes sense to me at the moment.' She paused. 'I need to have a look around Jess's room.'

Laura stood up. 'I'll come with you.'

'I'd rather you didn't.'

'She's my daughter!'

'And she's my niece,' said Eden, 'and I'm going to do everything within my power to find out where she is as quickly as possible. But she might have things in that room that she doesn't want you to see, and I'd rather see them first and then warn you if I have to. Okay?'

Laura sat down again with a thump.

Eden took the stairs two at a time. On the landing, she flicked on a pair of latex gloves, left her feelings at the door of Jess's bedroom and went inside.

The room was decorated in silver and white, with the odd dash of lilac and magenta. The bed was made, three teddy bears sitting on the pillow at the headboard and there was a pile of clothes at the bottom.

Eden got down on her knees and looked underneath it. There was a pair of socks rolled into a ball, a festering mug of something sitting on top of a plate and several magazines. She pulled out a pair of slippers, checked inside them but found nothing. She lifted the mattress hoping to find a diary that might give her a clue but dreading doing so, because she didn't want to read about her niece's antics. But there was nothing there.

To her right there was a small set of drawers, its top littered with make-up, toiletries and perfume bottles. Hair straighteners were on the floor, the wire wrapped around them. A tall mirror rested on the wall beside the drawers, and a can of hairspray sat next to it.

Eden opened the drawers, searching through the contents one by one. She stood up to open the wardrobe, checking through pockets of clothes hanging on the rail. At the bottom there was a drawer full of flat shoes, shoved in haphazardly. She pulled them all out to feel around the top of the drawer above. There was nothing stuck to the inside of it.

As she put the shoes back, something dropped out of the toe of a trainer. It was a wad of notes wrapped tightly with an elastic band. Eden flipped off the band and counted out the money. Then she sat back and frowned. Satisfied there was nothing she had missed, she went downstairs again.

In the living room, she held up the bundle. 'Any idea how Jess came across this?' she asked.

Laura shook her head. 'How much is there?'

'Five hundred and forty pounds.'

'But. . .' Laura's eyes widened. 'She wouldn't be able to save that kind of money. She only ever has money for birthday and Christmas.'

'You do give her money, Mum,' said Sarah.

'Yes, occasionally, for doing jobs around the house, and you,' Laura looked at Eden, 'give her some every now and then, but it always burns a hole in her pocket. She could never save anything. She would be off to the shops to buy something new to wear.'

'She would never be able to save that much money,' agreed Sarah. 'Do you think it could be Cayden's?'

Laura shook her head. 'How would he have come across it?'

'We need to look into it,' said Eden.

'I suppose it must be,' Laura changed her mind, 'because it can't have anything to do with Jess.'

'We're not certain of that.'

'I am certain!' Laura shouted. 'Where would Jess get it from?'

Eden said nothing. She could suggest lots of ways but none of them would be legal, and she wasn't about to upset her sister any more than necessary.

'I'll see to it that we talk to Cayden about it,' she said finally, making another note in her pad. 'If it is his and she's keeping it for him, he's hardly going to cough up, because he knows we'd be on to something. But we will ask him if he knows where it came from.'

Laura looked at her with so much pain in her eyes that Eden almost heard her heart snap in two.

'Find her for me,' said Laura. 'She's out there somewhere! Please find her.'

'I will. Do you have a notepad? It will be useful to list everyone that Jess knows. And you, Laura. You too, Sarah – whatever information you have stored on your phone as well as anything else you can think of. I'll get Amy to list all the numbers and emails and go through your recent contacts, text messages, et cetera.'

'What do you need our contacts for?' Laura frowned.

'It's standard procedure. We need to find out the last person to see Jess and figure out her whereabouts in-between leaving the house and wherever she is now.'

Eden went outside to use her phone. Sean's line was engaged so she rang Amy while she waited for him to become free.

'I might need to come off my shift, for personal reasons,' she said after she had given her an update on the situation.

'Are you sure that's necessary, Sarge?'

'I want to work the case, but I might not be allowed, even if this is just a prank.'

'I think you'd be far better suited to stay close to it.'

Eden paused. Amy was right. She needed to speak to her DI.

# THIRTY-SEVEN

'Hi, sir,' said Eden when Sean answered his phone. 'I'm really sorry to interrupt your weekend, but I need some advice.'

'Fire away. You're saving me from a shopping trip. With any luck Lucy might go without me.'

Normally Eden would have laughed when she heard Lucy in the background giving Sean some lip. Sean and Lucy had the kind of marriage that she had shared with Danny in their earlier years. They were a dependable couple – one you would never dream would split. People had thought that of her and Danny too once.

'It's personal, sir,' she told him, trying to keep the emotion in her voice from erupting. 'I have a family matter to deal with.'

Sean had been laughing as he waited for her to continue but his tone became serious. 'What's wrong?'

Eden filled him in on what had happened overnight. 'I was wondering if I would be allowed to work on the case, sir? I'm hoping that Jess has been a victim of a prank and that she'll walk through the door any minute, and I can give whoever did it a bollocking. But until I know for sure what's happened to her, I suppose I have a personal interest to declare.'

'In a way, yes, although,' Sean replied, 'I hate to say this, but the case isn't serious enough for you to step down from yet. I really hope it doesn't escalate, and if it does we'd need to evaluate your position then, but for now you're fine.' He paused. 'Wait a minute, will you, while I have a word with Lucy?'

Eden did as she was told. She could hear muffled speech while he talked to his wife. There was none of the laughter from earlier but neither were there any raised voices.

'I'm coming in,' said Sean when he spoke to her again.

'But, sir, your weekend!'

'I've cleared it with Lucy. She'd never forgive me if I didn't help you out. Besides, I want to help. I can lead the investigation, and you can do what you always do best. Find out information.'

'Well, if you're sure.'

'I'll be there in half an hour.'

Eden disconnected the call, a huge weight off her shoulders. Having Sean looking into things would make it easier for them all. Even outside of the force everyone knew that people weren't reported missing until they had been off the radar for at least twenty-four hours – unless there was criminal involvement. Even though she wasn't quite certain of that yet, she was going to ignore that fact and get onto everything as soon as Sean came in.

Before she returned to the station, she called to see Cayden again. He was lying on the sofa where she had left him.

'Any news?' He sat up as soon as he saw her.

Eden was surprised to hear concern in his voice.

'Did Jess ring you or send you any messages?' she asked him. 'I assume she was waiting for you to turn up to meet her.'

'No,' he replied. 'I was on the way to call for her.'

'So you didn't send her a text message to say that you would meet her at the back of Shop&Save, in the car park?'

'No! Are you saying that someone else did?' Cayden stood up. 'Was it from my phone?'

'We're not sure,' said Eden. 'Sarah said that Jess received a text message from you to meet her in the car park at Shop&Save, and then she went out.'

'But I didn't send it.' Cayden reached for his phone. 'Look, if you don't believe me.'

Eden scrolled through his messages. She stopped at one in particular from Travis Barker, opened it up and closed it again quickly after scanning its contents. But there seemed to be nothing that he had sent to Jess since before he had been attacked.

'Could someone have sent the message and deleted it without you knowing?' she asked.

'I guess he could have sent it after he attacked me and then wiped it.'

'You're certain it was a he?'

'Yes. Do you think he has something to do with Jess going missing?'

'It seems possible. Have you any idea who we could start to question about it?' She looked at him pointedly.

Cayden suddenly went all quiet again.

'When was the last time that you saw her?' Eden wanted to know.

'I hope you're not suggesting Cayden had anything to do with her disappearance!' Andrea's tone was one of indignation.

Eden didn't reply to her. 'Cayden?' she asked.

'It was at school yesterday. We walked home together, and I said I'd see her later.'

'And you didn't go anywhere else before you were due to meet her?'

Cayden gulped.

'If you're afraid of getting into trouble, please don't be. Kidnapping someone will outweigh anything you tell me.'

'You think Jess has been kidnapped?' Cayden sat forward.

'We're not certain yet,' said Eden, still looking at him purposely.

'Do you know something?' Andrea looked at Cayden too.

'No! I swear,' he cried. 'I was going to meet her when someone attacked me. That's the truth.'

'So you had come straight from your house, on your way to Jess's?'

'Yes.'

'And you didn't go anywhere else?'

There was a slight pause that didn't go unnoticed.

'Cayden?' Eden pressed.

'No, I didn't go anywhere else.'

'You're sure about that? It could take a while but CCTV footage might show us your whereabouts if necessary. Where you were going to and where you were coming from. Plus text messages can give us lots of clues. . .'

'He's just told you all he knows.' Andrea's tone was sharp. 'He was seriously injured last night. You don't have to question him so vigorously, *Sergeant*.'

'Do you know what? I will have that cup of tea.'

Eden smiled at Andrea until she left the room. As soon as they were alone, she moved to stand above Cayden. She bent down to within inches of his face.

'I found over five hundred pounds in Jess's bedroom. Any idea what it's for?'

Cayden's eyes widened and he winced in pain. Eden stared at him, but he wouldn't look at her.

'Is it your money?' she asked.

'No.'

'So she's not keeping it for you?'

'No.'

'Do you know where it came from?'

'No.'

'Do you know if she is keeping it for anyone else?'

'No!'

Mindful of his injuries, Eden grabbed him by the chin. 'I know you're hiding something. And I know that our Jess must be involved in something to get that kind of money, whether it's hers or she's keeping it for someone. So if I find out this money has anything to do with you, you little shit, and that my niece has been hurt because of it, then I'm coming back for you. Do you understand?'

Cayden gave a quick nod.

Eden stood upright again, took out a card with her details on it and handed it to him. 'In case your conscience gets the better of you,' she said.

Andrea came back into the room.

'Sorry, I've been called back to the station.' Eden pointed to her radio. 'Could you show me out please?'

'Is there anything we can do – to help find Jess?' Andrea asked as she opened the front door.

Eden was about to speak when she spotted a photo on the wall behind her. It was of Cayden and another boy, a younger brother she assumed, sitting side by side in school uniform. Both boys were smiling. It spoke of family.

This was a member of her family who was at risk.

'You can ask Cayden what Jess is doing with over five hundred pounds in her possession that can't be accounted for right now,' she replied.

Andrea's mouth dropped open.

'Has Cayden been bringing in things lately, things you know he can't afford, maybe he's passing designer gear as knock-off?'

'I don't think so.'

'Have there been any visits to the house by people you don't know?'

'No! What are you suggesting?'

'I'm just doing my job.' Eden moved closer to her. 'My niece is missing, and I will do everything it takes to find her.'

'But this has nothing to do with Cayden!'

'No?' Eden huffed. 'Your son knows more than he's letting on, and I suggest you try and get him to talk. It will be much better if he admits to knowing something before I find anything out.'

Eden walked back towards her car. As she got to it, she took a glance at the house, wondering if anyone would be watching her from a window. But there was no one. Even so, she hoped that Cayden wasn't involved in some sick joke that had gone wrong. If he was, he would have her to answer to.

# THIRTY-EIGHT

Maxine picked up her magazine and flicked through the pages aimlessly. It was no good. She couldn't concentrate on anything. It seemed the nearer she got to the trial, the more anxious she was becoming.

She got up to make a cup of tea. In the kitchen, she squeezed the bridge of her nose. What must her girl be going through now? Katie had never been a glass-half-full type of girl, who would count down the days until the trial and hope that she would be free. She was a glass-half-empty type of girl, who would work herself up more and more the nearer the trial came. This weekend was going to be so hard for her. She would be going over and over everything again, hoping that she wouldn't slip up.

Maxine recalled the moment when she had first heard about Katie's involvement in Deanna Barker's murder. Phil had taken Matty with him to the shops. The bell had rung and she'd found four people there when she opened the door. A tall broad man and her friend's sister, Eden, a detective sergeant, were both wearing dark suits. Behind them were two male uniformed officers. In front of their house, she could see three police cars parked in a line. It had been a shock, to say the least. And a little worrying as she wondered if anyone in her family had been hurt.

'Mrs Trent?' The man nearest to her held up a warrant card. 'I'm DI Whittaker and this is DS Berrisford. Is your daughter, Katie, in?'

'She's in her room.' Maxine frowned. 'What's this about?'

'A member of the public was fatally stabbed last night. We have reason to believe your daughter was involved.'

Maxine paled. 'But she was in her room for half past nine. I heard her come in.'

'We need her to come to the station,' said DI Whittaker.

'What? I don't understand.'

'Mum?'

Maxine looked upstairs to see Katie was already on the landing. She was shaking violently, hair bedraggled, eyes raw from crying.

'I didn't do anything,' she sobbed. 'I was just there! She died in my arms.'

'Katie, you need to come downstairs,' said Eden.

When Katie hadn't moved, Maxine beckoned her down. As Katie hit the bottom step, she watched Eden step forward and take her arm.

'Katie Trent, I'm arresting you on suspicion of the murder of Deanna Barker on 17 April 2015. You do not have to say anything—'

'Wait!' Maxine interrupted.

'But it may harm your defence if you do not mention when questioned something that you later rely on in court,' Eden continued. 'Anything you do say may be given in evidence. Do you understand?'

'I haven't done anything wrong,' Katie said, stepping away from them.

'Please, you're making a mistake,' Maxine insisted. 'My daughter wouldn't have anything to do with a murder!'

'If she comes quietly, I won't need to use the handcuffs.' Eden looked at her for support.

'Tell them, Mum!'

Maxine reached out to touch her daughter's arm. 'Just do as they say until we can sort this mess out,' she said. 'I'll be with you.'

'I didn't do anything!' Katie said as they led her out of the house.

As she walked down the path behind her, Maxine saw several of the neighbours coming out to see what was going on. Katie was placed in the back seat of the first police car. Tears poured down her face.

'We'll have you home in no time,' Maxine told her, trying to contain hers. 'I'm sure this is all a misunderstanding. You haven't done anything wrong. . . have you?'

Katie shook her head.

'May I remind you that you are under arrest, Katie,' Eden turned to her. 'Anything you say may be given in evidence, including in this car.'

'Oh, for God's sake, Eden!' Maxine cried. 'She hasn't done anything wrong!'

'They must have seen us on camera,' said Katie.

'What?'

'CCTV – they must have—'

Maxine had put a finger to her lips, urging Katie to be quiet. Although she stopped talking, she'd wanted to ask Katie what she meant by that. If there was CCTV footage, then surely they would have seen who had stabbed Deanna Barker and they wouldn't be questioning her daughter?

The kettle flicked off and Maxine thought about the week ahead. She had bought Katie some new shoes to go with the clothes she'd chosen for her. A navy skirt suit that was fashionable but smart and a pale pink blouse to go underneath the jacket. When Katie had tried them on during her last visit, Maxine had looked at her with a mixture of pride and hurt. Pride because her daughter was growing up into a beautiful young woman. Hurt because she no longer had the world at her feet.

Matty rushed into the room, wearing his Manchester United strip and socks, boots in hand, gangly legs below his shorts. His hair stuck up in tufts, and she wondered as she did most mornings if he had brushed his teeth or not.

'Mum, can I go and play across the park? Sam and Aaron are there already and they want me in goal.'

'Not today, Matty,' said Maxine, remembering her confrontation with Travis the night before. 'I'd like you to stay close to home. It's cold out there too.'

'But everyone else is across the park.' He huffed loudly and folded his arms in protest.

'I know, but I'd rather have you here.'

'It's not my fault Katie is locked up and I have to be careful. I didn't do anything.'

'I know that too.' Maxine sighed. How could she explain to him that she'd prefer to have him near to home this weekend? Besides, look what had happened when Katie had gone to the park. One wrong move that night six months ago and a lot of people's lives had changed for ever.

'You can play in the garden.' She pointed to the window. 'It's hardly fit to play football anyway. The weather is atrocious still.'

'I don't care. I'm not scared of the rain.'

Maxine tried not to shake her head. Why couldn't he do as he was told just this once? Her phone rang and she picked it up.

'Oh, hi again, Laura. What? Oh no, when did this happen?'

As Laura filled her in with details of Jess, she turned around and saw that Matty had gone. She sighed loudly. Little bugger.

# THIRTY-NINE

Eden went straight across the traffic lights at the end of the road. A quick right followed by two left turns and she was outside Claire Mornington's home. It was in a row of terraced houses with small walled forecourts. Most had large bay windows upstairs and downstairs and the front gardens and walls removed. This one had a block-paved driveway and housed a car and a van advertising Mornington's DIY.

A woman about her age came to the door. She was short, with dark, curly hair, kind eyes and a welcoming smile, until she seemed to realise who Eden was. Eden vaguely recognised her too. She was sure she had seen her at a SWAPs meeting or a parents' evening, rather than arresting her for something in the past, as sometimes was the case.

'Mrs Mornington – it's Rachel, isn't it? I'm sorry to hear about Claire's attack. I know we need to see her to take a statement about what happened, but could I just have a quick word with her please?'

Eden was shown through into a large open-plan living room while Rachel shouted Claire downstairs. She appeared a few seconds later and sat at the edge of the settee, her hands inside the sleeves of an oversized red jumper.

Rachel switched off the television.

'I'm Detective Sergeant Berrisford. How are you feeling today?' Eden asked.

Claire shrugged. 'I'm okay.'

'Could you run me through what happened last night?'

Eden took down notes as Claire told her.

'And you have no idea who it was?' she asked once Claire had finished talking.

'No.'

It was said too quickly and sharply for Eden. When the girl's eyes brimmed with tears, Eden reached out to her, touching her gently on the forearm.

'I don't know what's been going on, but I do need your help. I know that you're scared. Your friends Stacey and Ruby are too. But Cayden Blackwell was beaten up. He ended up in A&E. He says he doesn't know who it was who attacked him.'

Claire looked at her mum, fear in her eyes. 'Mum, I don't feel very well,' she said.

'Are you scared of something?' Eden persisted. 'Because if you are, please try not to be. Any information that you have might help me too. Do you remember that I'm Jess Mountford's auntie?'

Claire nodded, her eyes going to the floor. Her knee began to jiggle up and down.

'What has this got to do with Jess?' Rachel asked.

'Jess is missing.' Eden looked at them both. 'She sent her mum a message last night to say she was staying at Stacey's house.'

'But Stacey was attacked too!' Claire shouted out. 'Jess didn't go to Stacey's house!' She stood up and tried to run out of the room. Eden grabbed hold of her arm.

'Please, Claire, tell me what's been going on. We can't reach Jess on her phone. I've searched her bedroom for clues of where she might be. Nothing seems to be missing, so we can assume she hasn't run away for any reason. But there was a lot of money found.'

Claire seemed to shrink a few inches.

'Money?' Rachel looked at her daughter. 'Claire?'

Claire sat down with a thump. 'They'll kill me if they find out I've said anything.'

'Who will?' asked Eden.

Claire remained quiet for a moment before looking up at Eden again. 'It was Damien Barker and his brother, Travis, who attacked me. We've been stealing mobile phones for them, and he doesn't want anyone to find out.'

'What?' Rachel stared at her daughter. 'But how?'

'From people's bags and on tables mostly, on a Saturday afternoon in the shopping centre. Outside we ride past on bikes while someone is texting on them and swipe them.'

Eden sat down again and took out her notebook.

'What have you been doing with the phones?' asked Rachel, her eyes wide with disbelief.

Claire wouldn't look at her mum now. She stared at the floor as she spoke. 'We get twenty pounds every time we take one to Damien.'

'How long has this been going on?' asked Eden.

'A few months.'

Rachel gasped.

'Exactly how many months?' Eden needed her to be more precise.

'Since the beginning of the year.'

'You'll need to make a statement.' Eden stood up. 'Seeing as you've been attacked, I'll get an officer to you if I can. I wouldn't normally, but these are serious allegations you're making and time is of the essence.'

'No!' Claire looked up at her. 'You can't tell anyone! I'll be in trouble.'

'You're already in trouble,' said Rachel. 'And you'll be in even more when your dad gets home. He's going to go ballistic.'

'Please don't tell him.' Claire broke down again. 'I'm sorry. I got dragged into it. I didn't want to do it, but they made me. They said I couldn't be part of their gang if I didn't join in.'

'Who did?' Eden wanted to know.

'Stacey and Ruby and—' She stopped short.

'Jess?' she questioned.

Claire nodded.

Eden had heard all she needed. Driving back to the station, she tried to work things out. The attack on Cayden Blackwell could very well be connected with Deanna Barker's murder trial the following week, but this threw up a whole new line of enquiry. It could have been one of the Barker brothers warning Cayden to keep his mouth shut about his part in the phone robberies. Which also meant that the money she had found in Jess's room more than likely belonged to her niece. She could be stealing phones to sell on too. How was she going to break that to Laura?

As well as Claire, they'd need to interview Stacey and Ruby and Cayden for statements. She'd have to get uniform to do that.

More importantly, they needed to speak to the Barker brothers. There were lots of questions to be asked of Damien and Travis. They could be holding Jess somewhere. Or they could have attacked her just like the other girls, and something had gone wrong.

# FORTY

Eden arrived back at the station and swiped herself into the building. She threw her car keys on her desk, sat forward and ran her hands through her hair while she waited for her nerves to settle. Sean's car was in the car park, so she knew he'd be out to see her soon.

She logged back on to her computer and pulled up the information on the girls who had been attacked last night, wondering again what the hell was going on. She knew Cayden Blackwell was lying about something, and she was determined to find out what.

'Eden.'

She felt a hand on her shoulder and looked up to see Sean. Seeing someone she had known since she'd started the job brought tears to her eyes. She wiped one away as it fell and tried not to cry again as he gave her shoulder a squeeze.

She filled him in about Jess, and Cayden, just as Amy arrived back. Behind her was Jordan.

'Look who I picked up on my travels, Sarge,' said Amy.

'You owe me one.' Jordan pointed at Eden with a grin. 'This one here just dragged me out of bed.'

'Not literally.' Amy swiped him as he went to sit at his desk. 'I rang him and he offered to help.'

Eden smiled her thanks, choked by their concern.

They made their way into the small meeting room along the corridor. There was only room for one table that seated six people so it was mostly used for one-to-one supervisory meetings or staff appraisals.

'What did you learn from the girls?' Sean asked Amy once they were all sitting down. 'Let's see if it tallies with what we know now about the mobile phones.'

'Stacey Goodwin,' said Amy. 'Number twenty-nine Hardman Road. She was pulled into bushes off a pathway at the side of Theodore House. A tin of paint was poured over her head. It's made her skin come out in a rash where she's had to scrub it away. She looks a right mess.'

'I picked her up on my way home last night,' said Eden. 'I saw her running down the high street and couldn't leave her in the state she was in. She was so traumatised that she wouldn't say anything. I just thought it was a one-off prank until this morning, so I sent Amy to interview her while I spoke to Claire Mornington.'

'I spoke to Stacey and her mum,' Amy continued. 'Stacey gave me the clothes she was wearing. She said one of her attackers held her down on her knees so there could have been prints on the shoulders of her coat, if forensics were able to get them off at all. But when we questioned her further, she thinks they were wearing gloves because as soon as she mentioned both were wearing balaclavas, she remembered them. Poor girl was traumatised – they all were actually, as they thought they were going to be sexually assaulted.

'Stacey was left a note that said *keep your mouth shut.*' Amy pulled an evidence bag out of her pocket and put it on the table.

'She never said.' Eden took it and held it up. It was handwritten in capitals, black ink on lined paper. 'Can she remember anything about what they looked like?'

Amy shook her head. 'Only that she thought they were male. And they spoke with a local accent. I asked her if she thought it was anyone she knew. She shook her head pretty quickly.'

'Too quickly?' asked Sean, taking the bag from Eden and peering at the note.

'I think so,' said Amy. 'Then there was Ruby Peters, seventy-two Diamond Avenue. She was the same. She wouldn't take off her hat to show me what they had done to her hair. Her mum is taking her to the hairdressers this afternoon. She's going to have it all chopped off. She was in such a state. Her mum kept saying that short hair was trendy and that they would spend as much money as it took to make it look great for her.

'She had a note too.' Amy pulled another evidence bag out of her pocket and gave it to Sean. 'The handwriting and the message are the same and the paper too. It looks like it's been torn from the bottom half of the first note.'

'Keep your mouth shut?' Eden frowned. 'Claire didn't have a note, but she had been told something similar. Did Ruby give any clue as to what about?'

'She didn't know.'

'She didn't know – or wouldn't say?'

'I think she wouldn't say.'

'Claire was less traumatised than I thought she'd be,' said Eden. 'I don't know how anyone can be so barbaric as to make someone walk home with no shoes and trousers on. She only thought to reverse the charges on a phone box as she passed it, and then her parents picked her up in their car. She ran past lots of people with phones, but she didn't feel able to stop and ask for help.'

'So Claire didn't have a note.' Sean frowned. 'But the other two did.'

'She was told to keep her mouth shut.' Eden reached for her notepad and read from the page. 'And "tell anyone what we've been up to and you're dead". She said he had a local accent but denied knowing who it was until I pushed her. Then she told me it was either Travis or Damien Barker.'

A collective sigh went around the room.

'Travis Barker was in Shop&Save having a go at Maxine Trent earlier too,' said Jordan. 'I called to see her, but she said she didn't want to make a complaint. Just wanted us to know what had happened. Travis made a threat to harm her son if her daughter got off with the murder of his sister.'

'Did it seem a viable threat?' asked Sean.

'I'm not sure.' Jordan cocked his head to one side. 'She was scared, but her husband said to leave things as they were. I think they're both concerned about repercussions. It could also mean that Travis is out of the picture time wise for the attacks.' Jordan paused. 'But perhaps he's in the right place for Jess.'

'Hmm. So each girl has been the victim of a humiliation attack allegedly by the Barker brothers.' Sean drummed his fingers on the table. 'Covered in paint, hair hacked off and returning home with no shoes and trousers. Pretty basic for those two, don't you think?'

Eden checked their addresses again. 'All three girls live within half an hour's walk of each other and they were all part of the gang of kids who hung around on the Mitchell Estate. These three were out on the night that Deanna Barker was murdered, but they weren't around when the murder took place. They were all questioned but had all seen nothing.'

'Yes, I can believe that,' said Sean. 'The area around the subway is vast. CCTV footage backed them all up eventually. These three had been with a gang of five boys who had gone to hang around down by the Butcher's Arms. Lucky for them. What about Mr Barker – is he around?'

Eden shook her head. 'Frank Barker left just after Deanna died apparently. He didn't take her death too well, blamed Lulu for not bringing the boys up right. Said if it wasn't for her, Deanna might still be alive.'

'But he's their father too?' asked Amy.

'Yes, but only the youngest two.'

'Then surely he should take some responsibility.'

Eden nodded and looked across at Sean. 'He could be a suspect we need to check out, sir? His whereabouts and what have you.'

'Yes, let's go and speak to the Barker family,' Sean agreed. 'Jordan, can you search out the CCTV footage from the supermarket and start going through that?'

'Yes, boss.'

'And, Amy, can you start going through the list of Jess's friends, and the contacts on Laura's and Sarah's phones?'

Amy nodded. 'Yes, sir.'

As they got up to leave, Eden felt Sean's hand on her arm and he urged her to stay seated until it was just the two of them. He closed the door behind Amy and Jordan before sitting next to her again.

'Is there anything I need to know about Jess?' he asked.

Eden shook her head. 'Not anything that I haven't already told you.'

'Does she associate with anyone who has form?'

'I don't have a clue, if I'm honest. I can ask Laura, but I think she would have told me everything she knows if it would help find Jess.'

'What about these phones?'

'I'll start looking into it.'

He nodded his acceptance. 'We have to play this carefully with the Barker brothers,' he added. 'Especially if we need to figure out who's further up the chain. They must be stealing the phones for some reason.'

'Yes, sir.'

'We also don't want to upset Travis or Damien, with what little evidence we have.' Sean paused for a moment. Eden watched as his Adam's apple bobbed up and then down. It was always a giveaway that he was nervous.

'And if we can't get anything out of them,' he continued, 'then we'll have to start looking for a missing person.'

Eden felt her stomach turn over.

Sean reached for her hand and gave it a squeeze. 'We'll find her, Eden. We'll bring her home.'

# FORTY-ONE

The Barkers lived in Bernard Place, a small but notorious cul-de-sac on the Mitchell Estate. Eden had had lots of dealings with its residents during her time in uniform, and some as a detective constable on the domestic violence team. Lulu Barker, however, was more known for the trouble that her four sons caused.

Eden got out of Sean's car as he parked outside the house. A van had come too, to pick up Travis and Damien Barker for questioning.

'Fills me with dread and pleasure in equal measure coming here.' Eden followed Sean up the path to the front door with the peeling paint. The fence was down in places, the gate had gone walkabout and the hedges were unkempt. Eden felt the wet of the grass seep through the bottom of her trousers. It was October so it was dying off, but it must have been a foot in height. She pressed through it as Sean avoided the hedge on the other side of the path.

The door was opened by a middle-aged woman who gave out an exaggerated sigh when she saw who it was. Lulu Barker was only a couple of years older than Eden, but life hadn't been kind to her. She'd been left with the four boys and the gossip when Deanna had been murdered, and husband number two had walked out on her.

'Lulu.' Sean didn't bother to get out his warrant card. 'Your boys in?'

Lulu left the door open and turned to go back inside. 'I don't know what you want with them. They haven't done anything wrong.' She shuffled back down the narrow hallway.

Lulu Barker hadn't let herself go – she just hadn't been there to start with. Unpainted nails, unwashed black permed hair and clothes that had clearly been worn more than a day were her staple uniform. Eden closed the door behind her, just catching a glimpse of Lulu's black leggings, short, tight T-shirt and cracked feet in flip-flops as she stepped into the living room.

The smell assaulted her first: teenage boy and unwashed clothes. Something similar to cat pee too. She followed Sean into the room. The smell was marginally better, but the colour of the walls was a faded nicotine yellow. A black leather settee was shoved up against the back wall and a large television screen stood next to the fire, Xbox and PlayStation consoles plugged in permanently by the look of the grubby fingerprints all over them. A tabby cat was curled up on a fluffy yellow hearth rug, two kittens tearing after each other nearby.

'I need to talk to both Damien and Travis,' said Sean. 'About some trouble around the city last night.'

'Nothing to do with them.' Lulu folded her ample arms. 'My boys were here all night.' She stared. 'Both of them.'

'Both of them stayed in?' Eden came into the room.

'Yeah. We watched a film – *American Sniper* – it was good.'

'Neither of them went out all evening?' added Sean, asking the same question another way.

'No, we wanted some family time together before the trial next week.' Lulu sat down. A huge sigh escaped her as Eden wondered if the settee might collapse under her weight.

'You know, it's going to be tough for us all,' Lulu added. 'It will bring back bad memories.'

Sean nodded. 'How are you bearing up?'

'I'm not,' she said matter-of-factly. 'But my boys won't ever know that. I miss Deanna every day. She was my little girl. And those – those bastards took her away in one second.' Her eyes filled with tears. 'But they'll pay for it next week. As long as you lot have got all the evidence to convict them.'

A hush came over the room.

'I know you think it's wrong to charge them all,' Lulu turned on them, 'but I don't care if they rot in hell. My girl is dead. They were each to blame.'

'We're not here to discuss the case, Lulu,' said Sean. 'We're here to ask the boys some questions.'

'About what?' Lulu stared at them before her eyes shifted to the doorway.

'Are they in?' Sean wouldn't be drawn.

'They might be.'

'And Frank, where's he residing nowadays?'

'He's been gone for months now, since Deanna was murdered.'

'Do you have an address for him?'

'Why?'

'Do you?' Sean sighed.

'He lives on the Hopwood Estate. But you won't find him there. He's—'

'What's going on?' a voice came from behind them.

Eden and Sean turned to see a young man. Damien Barker had a shaved head and a face full of spots, making him more distinctive yet uglier than his younger brother, Travis. He was always a little scruffier than Travis, always a little mouthier. He looked as if he had just got out of bed, although he wore jeans and a white shirt.

'It's Damien, isn't it?' asked Sean.

Damien shrugged. 'Might be – what's it to you?'

'Manners, Damien,' Lulu remonstrated.

Eden sniggered under her breath. Sean knew exactly who Damien was and so did she. She'd arrested him on several occasions, each one so far ending up with no charge or a small fine. She had hoped he'd stay out of trouble, but with a family like his, with his two older brothers in and out of prison, there was no one to set a good example for him.

'They want to know where you and Travis were last night.' Lulu reached for a cigarette and lit it. She blew out smoke before speaking again. 'I said we were all in. That's right, isn't it, son?'

Damien folded his arms and leaned on the doorway. 'Yeah, that's right. All three of us.'

'Great,' said Eden. 'Then I won't catch any of you, or that banger of a car you have parked outside, on any street cameras anywhere, will I?'

Damien said nothing, but Eden saw his eyes flitting around everywhere to avoid looking at her.

'There were several attacks across the city last night.'

'And?'

'Where were you between the hours of five thirty p.m. and ten p.m. last night?'

'I told you,' said Lulu. 'He was here, and so was Travis.'

'If we have to go through every single minute of footage around the city, we will,' said Sean. 'The attacks last night happen to have been very brutal and very demoralising. I wonder why that would be.'

'I wonder.' Damien shrugged.

'So are neither of you going to ask what's happened?' said Sean, looking at them both.

'No need.' Lulu took another drag on her cigarette. 'The jungle drums have been banging since early morning. I know what's happened to them girls and it's—'

'Three females were attacked and a male seriously beaten up to be exact,' said Eden. 'And another female is still missing.'

'That's got nothing to do with us!' Damien frowned before backtracking. 'I only heard about the three girls.'

He knew more than he was letting on, Eden was convinced. 'Can I look at your phone?' she asked him.

'What for?'

'Got something to hide?' she challenged.

Damien disappeared for a few seconds and came back with his mobile. He handed it to her.

Eden scrolled through his messages. There were none from Cayden yesterday evening and none sent to him either. It was possible that they had been deleted though.

'You don't know Cayden Blackwell then?' she asked, staring at him pointedly.

'Not much,' he replied.

'Is Travis in, Lulu?' Sean asked.

'He's in bed. If you want to speak to him, you should come after lunch. He'll be up then.'

'Not to worry.' Sean pointed to the door. 'I'll get him up myself. You don't mind, do you?'

'You can't just go upstairs!' Lulu shuffled to the edge of the settee.

'We need you both down at the station to help with enquiries,' Eden said to Damien.

Damien protested as Eden held on to his arm and read him his rights.

In minutes, Sean came back downstairs with a sleepy-looking Travis, handcuffed.

'Mum, this is harassment,' he cried. 'Make a note of when they came. I'm not having this all the time.'

'Yeah, yeah.' Sean shook his head. 'My heart bleeds for you.'

The two brothers were bundled into the waiting van. Lulu was still shouting as it moved off. She barged past Sean and Eden and into the house with a slam of the front door.

Sean rolled his eyes.

'Can I be in the interview with you, boss?' Eden asked. She wanted to help, but she knew it might not be ethical. Sean could get what he needed from them and relay the information to her.

But she wanted to know if they knew Jess's whereabouts. She had to hear what they said.

'As long as you leave your emotions at the door,' he told her.

Eden couldn't promise that, but she nodded to him all the same.

# FORTY-TWO

Jess had been waiting and worrying all morning. She'd been on full alert, listening for the man downstairs. She'd heard a door open and close every now and then and a toilet flush but no footsteps on the stairs.

But now she could hear him outside the door. She gulped. Was she strong enough to go through with her plan?

The door was unlocked and opened, and she pressed herself into the wall again, making sure to keep her hands hidden under the covers. Although she was terrified, she didn't want him to know that.

'I've brought you something to eat and drink.' He held a tray with a mug of something steaming hot and two slices of buttered toast on a plate.

He came towards her. As he put down the tray, she produced the can of hairspray and pressed the button down, aiming at his eyes.

'Argh!' The tray clattered to the floor as he put his hands up to his face.

Jess shuffled off the bed and ran towards the bucket. She picked it up and flung the contents at him. She flew down the stairs, not daring to look behind to see if he was following her.

He shouted as she got to the front door. Looking behind her now, she could see him at the top of the stairs. She grappled with the door lock, but she couldn't open it.

'No, no, no!' A sob escaped her as she realised it needed a key, which wasn't there. Not having time to look around, she ran through to the kitchen.

'Wait!'

A hand reached down from the stairs as she raced along the narrow hallway, and she screamed. She slammed the kitchen door and reached out for the saucepan she had seen the day before. The kitchen door opened. She raised the pan in the air as he came towards her and yelled as she brought it down on the side of his head.

He staggered a step backwards at the impact. 'You mad bitch,' he cried, pressing a palm to his ear.

For a few seconds, they stood still in the room. Then he ran at her, taking hold of both her arms.

The pressure that he put on Jess's wrist made her drop the saucepan, and it clattered to the floor. His creased-up features scared her, but she brought up her knee and aimed it where she knew it would hurt. He turned his body to the side and it missed its target. Jess tried to break free from his grasp, but he was too strong for her. She screamed again and he turned her around and pulled her into his chest, covering her mouth with his hand.

'I told you no one could hear you, and I said that you can't get out,' he seethed.

Jess still struggled to escape his grip. She wasn't giving up until she knew she was beat. She couldn't let him take her back to that room again. She had been so close. Her hand reached out as they shuffled across the room. She could almost touch the handle to the door that she had first come through, the one that went into the garage.

He said nothing as she continued to try and free herself. She knew he was thinking she would give up eventually. Behind his hand she opened her mouth as wide as she could, causing his fingers to come nearer to her teeth. Then she bit down hard. In that split second, she kicked behind at his shin.

He cried out again, this time releasing his grip slightly. And she was away, stepping towards the door and into the garage.

'Help! Help me!' She banged on the garage door. 'Can anyone hear me?'

He grabbed her round the waist and pulled her off her feet, his hand across her mouth again.

'If you don't be quiet, I will shut you up. Do you hear?'

Jess's body went limp and she began to cry. It was useless. She was so near to freedom yet so far. He pulled her through, back to the kitchen, pushing her to the floor.

His face was inches away from hers. He reached for the duct tape, ripped some off and pressed it over her mouth. She tried to resist, but he stood firm. Then he turned her round and did the same to her hands, wrapping the tape round and round so that she knew she wouldn't be able to bite through it again. He hurled her to her feet, seized a kitchen chair and pushed her through into the living room. He placed the chair in the middle of the room and shoved her down into it, making sure her hands were behind its back.

'If you can't behave yourself, I'll have to keep you where I can see you.' He wrapped the tape around each of her ankles and firmly to each chair leg so she couldn't kick out.

Her eyes flitted around the room. It was sparse, just the minimum of the kind of old furniture that she would never have if she owned a house. A dusky pink Dralon three-piece suite, a rectangular pine coffee table and a small flat-screen television on a stand. Over on the back wall she could see a photo of a small girl, about three years old. There were more photos above the fireplace and some standing up in frames on the shelf.

He left her in the living room with the kitchen door ajar, and she watched him pace up and down the small kitchen. He wasn't a repulsive man, but he looked rough because of his appearance. She reckoned he hadn't shaved in a week; his clothes were a bit whiffy when he was close up and his eyes were bloodshot.

He turned to her. She knew he would see the fear in her eyes, but she tried to hide it. He wiped at his shirt where her urine had splashed. Most of it had missed him and gone over the carpet as she had run.

Then he opened a bottle of lager and came back into the living room. With every step he took, Jess tried to press her body further into the chair.

'You'll have to stay there now,' he told her as she moved her head to one side, as far away from him as possible. 'Somewhere I can keep my eye on you.'

Tears dripped down her face. She was trapped in this room now.

She was never going to get away.

# FORTY-THREE

Laura sat down on the settee. All around her was activity, yet she didn't feel like doing anything. All she wanted to do was curl up in a ball until someone brought Jess home safe and sound.

It was the not knowing that was the worst thing. What might be happening to her? She squeezed her eyes shut to stop the graphic images from appearing and piling up one after the other.

Maxine had arrived fifteen minutes after Laura had called her and explained that Jess was missing. After comforting Laura and hearing all the details, she asked what she needed to do.

'You take everyone in this address book, and I'll ring everyone I know at the same time,' said Laura. 'Some of the mothers from SWAPs are on their way too.'

'Would you like me to handle them? We can arrange a search party. Get some of the local kids looking for her. If anyone has her, they might get scared if they know the police are on to them.'

Laura nodded vehemently. 'Thank you so much.'

'She could be anywhere, but she might be close too. You remember the case of Shannon Matthews when the family hid her in a flat nearby?'

Laura covered her hand with her mouth as tears slipped down her face. She would hang those Barker brothers if she found out they had anything to do with this.

'We might be better going to the park, trying the kids there first.' Maxine broke into her thoughts. 'What do you think?'

'Yes, good idea. Anything to start people looking for her.'

Sarah came downstairs with her coat on. Before zipping it up, she gave Laura a hug. 'We'll find her, Mum. She hasn't been gone long.'

'It's ten a.m. She's been missing since last night.'

'We'll bring her home.' Sarah drew away. 'Anything from Eden yet?'

'She's on her way back now.'

'I hope she has some news.'

There was a knock on the door.

'I'll go,' said Maxine. She came back with two women. Carol Drayton lived across the way at number seventeen. She had her daughter, Judith, with her. Carol was in her mid-sixties with the look of a young grandmother. Her hair was in a short, sharp bob, her Burberry jacket the latest style of classic. Judith wore her hair long, hidden mostly under a woollen hat, and had a multi coloured scarf wrapped around her neck. Both had concern on their faces.

Part of the Neighbourhood Watch group, Carol had been badgering Laura to get involved, but she hadn't been too keen. Even though she seemed the type of woman who wouldn't hold that against her, she was still grateful when she offered to help find Jess.

'We've just heard on the radio,' said Carol. She placed a gloved hand on Laura's arm and gave it a squeeze. 'She'll turn up soon. I'm sure.'

'It was on the hourly news,' Judith clarified when Laura frowned. 'Is there anything we can do?'

'I was going across to the park,' said Sarah. 'I thought I could start asking some of the kids if they saw anything.'

'Do you have a notebook we can use?' asked Maxine. 'So we can jot down anything important and pass it on.'

'I'm sure there'll be one somewhere,' said Sarah, disappearing into the kitchen.

'Are you coming, Laura?' asked Carol. 'Or are you staying here?'

'I don't want to leave just yet. I'm going to wait for my sister, Eden. She's a detective sergeant. She told me that one of the other girls reversed the charges at a phone box and her parents went to fetch her. Jess might do that too.'

'I bet it was Eden who contacted the radio station,' said Sarah, coming back with a small lined notepad. 'I bet she'll contact the *Stockleigh News* too.'

Laura ran a hand through her hair, unsure what to do with herself. 'And you've done what you need to on Facebook and Twitter? And that Snapchat thing?'

Sarah nodded. 'The message has been shared a lot already. People will know about her soon.'

Laura gave her daughter a hug, a special one for two people. She wanted Jess home so much.

'We'll be back in an hour or so,' said Maxine. She waggled her mobile phone in the air. 'Sarah can ring you if we find out anything.'

# FORTY-FOUR

He left the girl in the living room, with the kitchen door ajar so he could see what she was up to.

Stupid bitch. She had taken him completely by surprise. He hadn't expected her to get free. How the hell had she got that tape off? More to the point, he was angry with himself for not checking the room first to see if it was clear of everything. He thought he'd got it all – he'd removed the clutter from the dressing table.

He looked at her sitting in the chair, staring back at him. He could see fear in her eyes, but she seemed defiant. Maybe that was the adrenaline kicking in because she had been so scared. Or maybe she was afraid and trying not to show it.

He wiped at his shirt where her urine had splashed. Despite his doubts, he couldn't back down now. He was doing this for his daughter – it was justice for her. No one could take away his pain, so someone had to pay.

He reached for another bottle of lager and knocked back a mouthful. But he kept it in his mouth; he wouldn't swallow it. He turned and spat it out into the sink. He had to stay sober or else this could go very wrong. He had to teach her a lesson before the weekend was out.

He walked through into the living room, watching her press her body into the back of the chair.

'You'll have to stay there now,' he said as she moved her head to one side, as far away from him as possible.

He couldn't blame her for not trusting him. He didn't trust himself right now.

The drink called out to him again. But he stayed put for a moment. If he kept looking at her, he would be reminded of his daughter, and why he was doing this. For her.

In frustration, he went back into the kitchen, reached for the bottle and gulped down the last inch. Standing hands wide, leaning on the worktop, he looked out over the mess of a garden. It was a tip, just like the rest of the house. With his job gone now, the bailiffs would be at the door next month to get him out of the house. Every which way he turned he was screwed. Life didn't seem worth living. Which was fine by him.

He picked the bottle up and threw it against the wall.

# FORTY-FIVE

Jess jumped when she heard the bottle exploding. He was getting more volatile, but she wanted to stay calm. She was uncomfortable on the chair, sitting in the middle of the room like she was at a child's birthday party and the last one left in a game of musical chairs. Except there was no prize, no birthday tea.

Even though her plan to escape had completely backfired she still had to believe that she would get out of here alive. If she had bad thoughts, she wouldn't be able to think straight. Instead she tried to think happy thoughts.

Jess was a popular girl at school, with lots of friends. Katie had come to her school when she was nine. Jess had loved hanging around with her. Despite a lot of people thinking Katie was boring and quiet, she wasn't. She had the most wicked sense of humour, and they'd often get into trouble at school because she'd come up with some one-liner in class that had made Jess get a bout of the giggles.

Thick as thieves, they were always together. When Katie had been sent to the secure unit until the trial, Jess's life had changed too. She'd had no one to confide in. Some said she'd lost her shadow, but to Jess it was more than that. It was as if she had lost her second skin.

Katie would be as nervous as hell about next week. Jess thought back to her last visit. It was about a month ago, and Katie hadn't looked so good. Jess had been surprised at some of the things that Katie had told her happened at the home, recalling the conversation they'd had.

'You have to ask for your toiletries?' She'd baulked when Katie had told her.

Katie had nodded. 'Anything that can be used as a weapon. A canister, toothbrush. Hairbrush. You can put shampoo in coffee, you know, and make someone sick. So everything has to be monitored.'

'Jeez, it does sound bad.'

'It's not like that in prison. My key worker says you get more trust. It's because we're younger, they have a duty of care or something.'

'But you're not going to prison, are you?' Jess shook her head.

'I shouldn't even be here!' Katie whined. 'I didn't have anything to do with what happened to Deanna. You do believe me, don't you?'

'Of course I do!'

'And you haven't said anything about,' Katie took a quick glance around to see if anyone was in hearing range before continuing, 'you know.'

'About the photos?' Jess shook her head. 'I can't tell anyone. It'll get me into trouble too.'

'Not that – I meant about working for Damien Barker.'

'Oh. No, I haven't said anything about that either.'

'Are you still doing it?'

Jess nodded. 'Me and Cayden are getting quite good at it now. We're a team.'

'We used to be a team.' Katie's tone was sullen.

'We still will be, once you get out.'

Katie huffed. 'I'm going to be stuck in here and then go to prison for years because of Nathan. I hate him – and what he did. He's an animal.'

'The judge will be lenient with you, though, for a first-time offence.'

'For murder?'

'Well, that's what my mum says.'

'Like your mum knows anything,' Katie said, her tone spiteful.

Jess turned to her sharply. 'What's that supposed to mean?'

Katie lowered her eyes and ran her toes in a line in front of her. 'I didn't mean anything,' she replied. 'Just that my key worker keeps telling me I need to think of both decisions. What will happen if I'm found guilty?'

'You won't be,' insisted Jess.

'And also what will happen if I'm acquitted. She says it will be hard for me to reintegrate into a community that blames me anyway. I'm scared of what Deanna's brothers will do to me, and everyone knows that Travis Barker is a nutter. He threw Caleb Morrison down the stairs, didn't he, when he looked at his girlfriend the wrong way?'

'I doubt it,' said Jess. 'Most of what we hear is rumour. Don't get too wound up about it.'

Katie had thrown her a filthy look. 'You don't know what it's like to be locked up.'

Jess could empathise with her words right now. How heartless she had been at the time. She made a promise to herself that she was going to be at court to see her friend next week. If she kept Katie in her mind, along with Cayden and her mum, she'd survive.

He came into the room. Just the sight of him was enough to set her into a panic. He could do anything to her, and no one would know. Where was everyone? She needed them here right now.

She sat as quiet as she could, hoping not to antagonise the man any further. Her plan had backfired, but she wouldn't show him how scared she was now. She could see the cut on his eye, the swelling of his cheekbone after she had whacked him with the saucepan, but she knew he had her exactly where he wanted her, and she could do nothing about it. Her hands were tied so tight that she was sure her circulation would be cut off. She could feel the bruising already, every time she moved.

The man walked towards the fireplace. He picked up one of the photos in a frame, of the girl about her age.

'This is my daughter,' he told her, but he didn't show her the image. 'It was taken last year at school. She was fifteen then – she didn't make it to her sixteenth birthday.'

Jess frowned. What did he mean she didn't make it? Where was she? And then a horrible thought dawned on her. It was her room she was in, wasn't it? She'd been sleeping in the room of a dead girl. Had he killed her? Had he brought her here to kill her too? If he could kill his daughter, he would have no problem killing her.

He huffed as he caught the look on her face.

'Don't worry – I didn't kill her. I know who did though.'

Katie – June 2015

Dear Mum,

I hate being here. I wish I could stay in my room until it's all over. There are nine teenagers at the moment, four boys and five girls including me. I'm having trouble with a new girl who's just arrived. She doesn't like me. I haven't told anyone, but she's been trying to turn the other kids against me. They're all scared of her so they do what she says.

I don't know why she doesn't like me. I guess she wants to be top dog around here. I've never been interested in that, have I? So really there shouldn't have been a problem with Charlie – that's her name. But she's a bully. She wants people who she can control, so she can make their life hell and get away with things because others are too scared to speak out.

The staff have tried hard to make things better. Things change for a few days, but then Charlie is soon back to her ways. There doesn't seem anything anyone can do about it.

Charlie has to serve three months. She's been here twice before, so if she does leave, she'll probably come back again.

Mary-Anne says she's a serial offender, beaten down by the system, so she's kicking back.

I tried to square up to her once, but she didn't like it. Charlie has a spirit that won't be broken. She's had a tough life. But I know if I don't stand up for myself now, my life will be over. I can cope with being away from you and Dad and Matty if I'm left alone. But Charlie can change all this in a few minutes.

This is what I need to tell you before your next visit. She'd been ripping into me, punching me when I'm walking past. I took it for a while, but then I snapped. I was the one who ended up in trouble. I don't want you to see me in the state I'm in. My eye is bruised where Charlie punched me, and I have four scratch marks down my cheek where she dug in her nails. They're really sore and they look awful too. The other kids keep calling me scar face. That hurts more than the scratches.

And now no one is allowed to talk to me when Charlie is around. She's extra nice to me in front of the key workers and the rest of the staff, but whenever they're out of ear range, she starts again. I hoped it would die down, but it's just got worse over the past few weeks. Charlie might get fed up after a while, and maybe she'll settle down. But by that time, there could be someone new and the whole thing could start again.

Anyway, I wonder what you're doing now, Mum. Tell Dad he needs to keep your spirits up. He can make you laugh. You need to laugh, as four months is a long time before I'll be home again.

How's Matty? Tell him I'm missing him. I miss you too, Mum, and Dad. So, so much.

Love Katie x

# FORTY-SIX

As soon as all four women had left to go to the park, the house dropped into silence again. Laura sat down on the bottom stair and hugged herself, resting her chin on her knees. She couldn't contemplate what was happening. They had gone to look for her daughter, who was missing. Eden was looking for her too. She hoped this was just a practical joke.

*Where are you, Jess?*

Was she somewhere that she couldn't escape from? Laura tried not to think of all the crime dramas she had watched where young girls had been abducted, raped and murdered.

Then she sat up. She needed some answers, and she knew just where to start. She searched out her car keys and ran out of the house. Ten minutes later, after a deep breath, she strode down the path of 22 Bernard Place and banged on the front door.

'Where is she?' she said as soon as it opened.

'Where is who?' Lulu Barker folded her arms.

'My daughter is missing, and I know your boys have something to do with it. Let me speak to them.' Laura tried to get a foot inside the house.

Lulu stopped her.

'I want to talk to them!'

'They had nothing to do with those attacks as they were with me, here, all evening.'

'You would say that.' She stood her ground. 'Have the police been to see you?'

Lulu glared at her.

'Jess is missing. I need to know if they've seen her.'

'Why?'

'I think your boys might know what's happened to her. There were a few girls attacked last night. One of them didn't get back until late. She was left to walk home miles because her phone was stolen.' Laura wanted to take hold of Lulu's arms and give her a good shake, but she knew it would do more harm than good. She tried to keep calm. 'Now if your boys have played a trick on Jess, then okay, I get that, but I need to know, because if they haven't then she's missing and—'

'Whoa!' Lulu held up a hand. 'I don't want any more police at my door. I've had enough of them to last me a lifetime.'

'Tell me!' Laura pleaded. 'I need to know where she is.'

'When did you last see her?'

'About half past five last night.'

'So when did she go missing?'

'I thought she was at Stacey's house – Stacey Goodwin – but when I checked this morning she wasn't there.'

'You never checked on her for a whole night?' Lulu shook her head and whistled through her teeth.

'I was working,' Laura explained. 'Jess sent me a message to say she was staying at Stacey's. I've just told you that.'

'You've also told me that you're a bad mother,' Lulu replied. 'Who in their right mind wouldn't ring their child to see where they were until the next day?'

'I did try. . .' Laura faltered, 'but her phone went to voicemail.'

'And you ignored that?'

'No! She sent me a few messages so I—'

'Did you speak to her?'

'No.' Laura hung her head. 'I thought she had sent the messages. That was enough.'

'That was enough?' Lulu tutted.

'I trusted her!' Laura cried.

'You didn't think to ring Stacey's mum?'

'Not until this morning.'

'Some mother you are.'

'How would I know that it wasn't her?' Laura saw red. 'Do you always know where your boys are?'

'Of course I do!'

'Yes, that's right. Two of them are in prison, aren't they? I suppose they're easy to keep track of.' She sounded antagonistic, but she needed answers.

'Now listen here.' Lulu prodded Laura's shoulder, enough to make her take a step back. 'Don't come round to *my* house and have a dig at *my* sons when you can't even look after your own daughter. For your information, I'm not the bad mother here.'

Laura didn't believe her for a second. 'It seems a coincidence that Deanna's trial starts on Monday and—'

Lulu pushed Laura away with all her might.

Laura landed on her backside. She scrambled away as the woman came towards her, almost baring her teeth.

'You have no right to mention her name,' Lulu spat. 'It's going to be a tough few weeks for us.' She pointed to the window of her home where there was a poster of Deanna, the word 'justice' printed at the bottom in large white capital letters. 'That's my girl there. I miss her so much.'

'Then you'll know how much I need to see Jess,' said Laura. 'There were people attacked last night, and I don't know where she is. I just need to know if you, or anyone else, knows her whereabouts – that's all.'

Lulu paused for a moment. Then she seemed to drop her attitude. 'My boys are at the police station answering questions,' she said.

Laura stood up quickly. As she turned to leave, Lulu grabbed her arm.

'I don't know where Jess is, but I do know that my boys have nothing to do with her disappearance. They would have told me when the cops came calling. They said they knew nothing about Jess or Cayden, and I believe them. I can tell when they're lying.'

'And the other girls?'

Lulu shrugged. 'They're not perfect. But my boys wouldn't do anyone any harm unless they had it coming to them.'

'But my daughter is missing!'

'At least she's still alive.'

Her words cut Laura to the core. She was beginning to feel the anguish of losing a child, just an inkling of what Lulu and her family might have gone through. And she couldn't even be sure if Jess *was* alive. She couldn't be sure of anything.

With people out on their steps taking in everything, Lulu marched back into her house with a slam of the door.

Laura went to her car. There were no new messages on her phone so she started the engine and drove away. As she stopped at a junction, she banged a fist on the steering wheel. She would have been better staying at home for all the information she had gleaned. And what if Jess had tried to call her on the landline? She pressed her foot to the accelerator.

She had to get home.

# FORTY-SEVEN

Eden and Sean had just come out of interview room one after talking to Travis Barker. Travis had claimed to know nothing about the attacks on the three girls and was strongly denying any involvement with Cayden Blackwell and Jess too. They'd left him to stew while they caught a breath before going to speak to his brother.

'What do you think, sir?' asked Eden as they walked up the stairs together, back to their office on the first floor.

'I'll pass judgment when we've spoken to Damien too,' said Sean. 'One of them will slip up.'

'I hope so.'

'Or else they really don't have anything to do with Jess's disappearance. You need to brace yourself for that.'

'I don't even want to think about it.' Eden went cold again.

Sean opened the door to the office and she stepped in first as he held it for her. A buzz of activity greeted them as people around them worked on the case. Amy was at her desk, Jordan was on the phone and there was a group of officers sitting around the desks nearby.

'So we're talking to staff at the supermarket, hoping for sightings of Jess from yesterday,' said Sean as they walked. 'Maybe someone saw her on her way to the supposed meet-up with Cayden. I'm going to organise a press conference – just routine but necessary I think. Okay, Eden?'

'Yes. I'll let Laura know.'

Sean nodded. 'For now we're still going along the lines of a practical joke gone wrong, but if we can't get one of the Barker brothers to confess to anything then someone might have seen Jess somewhere last night. Keep checking in with press and radio, and social media.'

'Yes, sir.'

Eden sat down. Amy looked across at her.

'Anything good on that list?' Eden asked, knowing full well that there wouldn't be. Amy was looking through Laura's contacts on her phone.

'Well, yes and no,' Amy replied. 'I'll email you what I have first rather than print it out.'

Eden frowned but opened her email inbox and waited for an envelope to appear. She clicked on it when it did. A spreadsheet full of names and telephone numbers appeared on her screen.

'Anything pop out at you?' she asked Amy, as she scrolled down the boxes.

'Not necessarily, but you check.'

Eden glanced down the list of names, reading them slowly, one by one, to see if any of them meant anything to her. They seemed to be mostly female, friends of Jess's she guessed, a few that she knew and some she didn't. Then she checked through the lists that Laura and Sarah had given.

She froze as she spotted a familiar number. That's why Amy hadn't wanted to print it out straightaway. It was her husband, Danny's.

Why would it be on this list? But before she had time to panic, she realised it could have been on there for years. After all, she had kept it on her phone. Whereas she hadn't deleted his number because she'd wanted to keep it, perhaps Laura had kept it and not even known she still had it stored.

It took Eden by surprise when a rush of feelings washed over her at the thought of Danny. She looked along the line that held his details to see if any messages or calls had been recorded between them recently. Thankfully there were none. And Danny hadn't answered any messages or emails that she had sent to him since he had gone.

She continued to look through the list, chastising herself for allowing Danny to infiltrate her thoughts again.

# FORTY-EIGHT

Before they went in to interview Damien Barker, Eden picked up her phone and rang *Stockleigh News* crime reporter Ryan Copestake to give him an update. He'd left her a voice message earlier, and she'd tried to ring him a few minutes later, but he'd been engaged. Ryan had reported on a few serious cases since she had met him, but more often than not you'd find him in Stockleigh Magistrates Court reporting on benefit frauds and shoplifters, burglaries and anti-social behaviour, mostly from either the Hopwood or the Mitchell Estate. He was always moaning that it was rare he could get his teeth into something – he always seemed to be reporting after the event.

Eden had known him for many years, and even though they didn't see eye to eye when he let out a little more information than she would have liked every now and then, most of the time they got on well. Ryan would often call in to the station, along with several housing officers, to glean information or intelligence on certain people. She'd share what she could and sometimes a little of what she couldn't and vice versa. The housing officers, police and press needed to get on. They were on the same team, serving the general public.

'I know we've been retweeting tweets, but do you have a higher resolution version of her photo that you can send to me for the print edition?' Ryan asked once she had told him more about Jess. 'Obviously I'll still keep sharing it across our social media channels too. We have nearly 50,000 followers on Facebook and

Twitter. You'd be surprised how many times locals will retweet this type of appeal. They like to look out for their own.'

Eden had seen this several times. Mostly she disliked social media because difficult situations were shared online quicker than it took to blink an eye. Lots of people wanted to film the police hoping that injustice would be done. Their job was hard enough without people interfering.

But to her knowledge there had only been one occasion when a person hadn't been found alive after a campaign like this. He had been a man in his eighties with dementia who had taken himself for a walk along the canal. They'd found his body in a lock a few weeks after.

'Yes, I'll get it to you as soon as possible,' Eden replied. 'Jess's sister, Sarah, has been rallying all their friends and sharing it too.'

'Can I see your sister?' Ryan wanted to know. 'Is she up for it?'

'We don't want to blow this out of proportion.' Eden wanted to protect Laura for as long as she could from media intrusion. 'Jess has only been missing for a few hours, and we don't want to cause any controversy and have people link it to the case of Deanna Barker.' There. She had given him something.

'Ah, understood,' Ryan replied. 'Although I'll be the first to know when anything is happening?'

'Yes,' Eden told him. 'But please keep this to yourself until then.'

She heard him snigger. 'You don't expect *me* to sabotage anything? It's the Barker brothers I want, and you know that.'

Eden knew only too well. She disconnected the call and stood up. Time to see if Damien Barker would give them anything. But she'd barely taken a few steps when her phone rang again. It was one of the housing officers, Josie Mellor.

'I've just heard on the two o'clock news, Eden. I'm so sorry.'

Eden pinched the bridge of her nose.

'I'm on my way in.'

'You don't have—'

'You think I can sit at home now I know what's going on?'

Eden didn't know what to say. It was so brilliant to have a group of people who wanted to support her, do their little bit in the search for her niece.

'Are you sure?'

'I'm here to help,' Josie continued. 'Just tell me what you need me to do.'

# FORTY-NINE

Eden went in to interview room one behind Sean. Damien Barker and the duty solicitor, Martin Dinnen, were already seated at a desk. Dinnen was a reed of a man, with long hands and fingers, a head of thick dark hair, and red socks showing beneath his grey and white pinstripe trousers, part of a three-piece suit. Round frameless glasses made his blue eyes much larger. Eden didn't much care for him, having gone into battle with him on several occasions now. He was a ruthless character and far too smarmy for her liking.

She set everything up for the interview and pressed record on the player. She went through the usual requirements and asked Damien to confirm his name. Once that was done, she sat back and let Sean start the questioning.

Damien Barker was slightly taller than his brother, Travis, and two years older at nineteen. His hair was sludge brown, and he wore a ring through his right eyebrow. With dark and moody eyes, he had the demeanour of a rat, the persona of a snake. But if he thought he could live off his older brothers' reputation, he was wrong.

'Damien,' Sean started, 'where were you during the hours of 5.30 p.m. and 10 p.m. last night?'

'I told you, innit. Me and my bro were at home with our ma. We watched *American Sniper*.'

'Good, isn't he, Christian Bale?'

'You trying to trip me up? Christian Bale isn't in *American Sniper*.' Damien sat back and folded his arms. 'That's *American Psycho*.'

'Ah, yes.' Sean nodded. 'My mistake.'

Martin Dinnen flicked his pen on and off at great speed.

Eden glared at him when it became annoying. Dinnen caught her eye and stopped for a few seconds before starting up again. She wondered if it was a habit he wasn't aware he had.

'So we won't find your car on CCTV footage anywhere in the city?' Sean continued.

'Not unless someone else was driving it,' said Damien.

'And were they?'

Damien shrugged. 'Not sure. I can't remember it going from outside of the house.'

'Do you always drive it?'

'Yeah, because I'm insured, innit.'

'Innit?' snapped Eden. 'How old are you, Damien? Ten?'

Dinnen stopped flicking his pen enough to glare at her this time.

'I was in all night,' Damien repeated. 'So you have nothing on me – or my brother. If you had, you'd be dealing your cards.'

'If you thought we had, you'd be saying no comment, wouldn't you?'

Damien smirked at her. 'I would.'

'So tell me, how did it feel to tip paint over someone's head?' she asked. 'Make you feel like a man, did it?'

Damien sniggered. 'It weren't me, but I bet it was funny.'

'Damien, can you write me something down?' Sean pushed a piece of paper and a pen across the desk to him.

He looked at Dinnen. 'Do I have to?'

'Humour us,' said Eden.

He picked up the pen with a sigh. 'What do you want me to write?'

'How about. . . keep your mouth shut.'

Damien looked up and shook his head.

Sean leaned forward. 'Not to worry. If you sit here for a few hours longer, we'll be back with the CCTV footage that puts you in the frame for the kidnap of Jessica Mountford.'

'Wait!' They had his attention now as he sat upright. 'I don't know anything about that!'

'It's plain and simple, Damien. If you're saying you were at home and didn't attack Stacey Goodwin, Claire Mornington or Ruby Peters last night, then you would have been free around the time that Jess Mountford went missing. If I find out that you're lying then I'll want to know why.'

'But surely if my client was home when those girls were attacked,' said Dinnen, 'then he would have been at home when Jessica Mountford was taken.'

'Yeah, that's right,' smirked Damien. 'I don't know owt about no kidnap.'

'You're denying being anywhere near Jess Mountford last night between the hours of six p.m. and ten p.m.?'

'Yes.'

'How about Cayden Blackwell? Do you know what happened to him?'

Damien shook his head.

'He was beaten up. When was the last time you saw him?'

'I haven't attacked him either!' He looked at Martin Dinnen again.

Eden could see desperation in Damien's eyes as he began to squirm. He was going to wrap himself up in knots if he didn't think about what he was saying. She loved Sean's interviewing techniques. She had seen him do this so many times. He'd get the suspect to deny something and then ask them where they were instead. It often put them in the frame for something without them realising it.

'So you're still denying attacking anyone last night?' asked Sean.

Damien nodded.

'One of the three girls says she's been stealing mobile phones to order for you, and you give her twenty pounds a piece for them.'

'Whoever it is, she's lying,' said Damien.

'She says that's why you attacked her and why you told her to keep her mouth shut. Know anything about that either?'

Damien physically shrank in his chair. He shook his head.

'Is that no comment?' asked Eden, her voice dripping with sarcasm.

'No comment,' he replied.

'Fine. We're interviewing all three girls plus Cayden at the moment, so I trust you won't mind waiting until we're done. I'm sure some of their details will overlap.'

'More importantly,' added Sean, 'if it's proved that you're involved with the abduction of Jess Mountford, then you and your brother are going to be looking at jail time. She's only sixteen.'

'I told you I don't know anything about that!' said Damien.

'If we can't corroborate anything then it will be up to the judge to work it out. It will mean both of you going on remand until the case comes to trial, I guess.'

'Do you have anything to charge my client with?' asked Dinnen.

Sean shook his head. 'But we're working on it. It will just take time.'

Damien leaned over and whispered something into Dinnen's ear. After a few moments, Dinnen nodded.

'I'd like some time alone with my client please,' he said.

Eden announced the interview had been paused and Sean got to his feet.

'Coffee break, I think.' He looked at Eden and then Damien. 'We'll join you later once you've had time to think about how much trouble you'll be in if you continue wrapping yourself up in knots. In the meantime, we'll keep checking through all the CCTV footage.'

'But that could take hours,' Damien protested.

'Indeed it could. But if you won't help us out and you prefer to get yourself and your brother into a whole heap of trouble. . .'

Back in their office, Eden gave a huge sigh before dropping into her chair.

'So far both Barker brothers have denied attacking all three girls now,' she told Jordan, who was across from her. 'They're also strongly denying having anything to do with either Cayden's assault or Jess's disappearance.'

'But it doesn't add up!' Jordan slammed down his pen. 'What did they say about the phones?'

'Strongly denied that too. Although that's not our main priority right now. We need to find Jess.'

'Do you believe them?'

Eden shook her head. 'Damien is talking to Martin Dinnen. I reckon he'll confess after Sean put the fear of God into him about the consequences of lying. We have no evidence either way yet. Besides, they both told us where they were—'

'But they were lying?' Jordan broke in.

'That's why we're scouring CCTV now.'

'We're checking to see if she went into A&E too,' he added, 'after the message was sent to say she was on her way.'

Eden visibly shuddered at the thought.

'Sorry,' said Jordan. 'I didn't think.'

'It has to be said.' Eden shook her head. 'If Jess is on camera then we know she went missing later in the evening, so it could be the Barker brothers.' She looked up to see Amy walking towards her. She looked none too happy about something.

'What's wrong?' Eden asked as she drew near.

'I – I think you might need to see this.' Amy's face was a mixture of dismay and anxiety.

'What is it?' Eden urged.

'I've spotted someone pushing a person I believe to be Jess into the back of a white van.'

Eden felt her legs turn to jelly, but she forced herself to follow Amy to the other end of the room. Jordan was right behind them.

'Is it one of the Barker brothers?' she asked.

'I don't think so.' Amy pressed play on the monitor, and they watched as the scene unfolded. They saw Jess run under the shelter that held the supermarket trolleys and a lone male walking past her. He stopped, said something to her and continued on his way. Then he doubled back and Jess followed him.

'Why did she walk off after him?' said Eden.

'I'm not sure.' After a moment, Amy pressed pause. 'Are you sure you want to see this?' she asked.

Eden nodded, dread creeping through her veins.

Amy pressed play again.

Eden covered her mouth with her hand as she watched the man punch Jess full in the face. She felt tears sting her eyes as he bundled her niece into the back of a small white van. There was a kerfuffle as Jess put up a fight, but he managed to get the door shut. Shortly afterwards the van moved away.

Eden banged her hand on the desk and groaned. 'If I ever get my hands on him, I'll swing for the bastard. He could be anyone, could have taken her anywhere!' She looked at Amy. 'Do we have the plates?'

Amy shook her head. 'Only partials. They've been smeared with mud or something so we can't see them. But we're working on all the images now, as well as hoping to pick up a good one of his face that we can put out to the media.'

'Which means he planned this?' Eden gulped. 'Is she anywhere else on CCTV?'

'I'm still going through it,' said Amy.

'Me too,' said Jordan. 'We'll find her.'

Eden breathed deeply. She had watched Jess being born sixteen years ago, held her soon after she had taken her first breaths. She had fed her, changed her and looked after her on numerous occasions. They couldn't lose her, not after Laura had lost Neil too. It would be too much to bear.

She wiped a stray tear away before she looked up again.

'This is looking like it will go much deeper than a group of kids stealing mobile phones and playing tricks, Eden,' said Sean, who had joined them. 'Dinnen says that Damien Barker is ready to talk. I'm going in there now.'

'What did he mean by that?' asked Amy once Sean had gone. 'Surely everything has to be connected?'

'It means that Jess could have been taken by someone further up who's out to prove a point. Or it might even mean this has nothing to do with the mobile phones.' Eden got up quickly. 'I'm going to join Sean. Oh God, and then I'll have to let Laura know what we've found out so far.'

# FIFTY

Eden glanced at herself in the rear-view mirror as she parked up outside Laura's house. Her hair was a mess where she had run her hands through it; her face looked pale, worried eyes staring back at her. She seemed to have aged ten years in as many hours.

How could she tell her sister what she knew? That she had seen her niece being punched and then dragged into a van before it drove off to Lord knows where. She'd have to put on a brave face. It wouldn't do for her to crack too, no matter how hard it was to deal with.

During the second part of the interview, Damien Barker had finally admitted that he and Travis had played the tricks on the girls, and Sean had given him a dressing down, saying there was having a laugh and causing offence with threatening intent, and what they had done was clearly the latter. They had assaulted each girl and would be charged and bailed pending further enquiries. Yet Damien, and subsequently Travis, categorically denied any involvement in the attack on Cayden – nor were they aware of Jess going missing until she and Sean had told them.

She'd collected Casey on her way over to her sister's house. Eden had wanted to tell her in person what had happened. She couldn't let Casey hear from anyone else – it wouldn't be fair to keep her out of the loop. Besides, Eden had wanted to see her, hug her, reassure her as well as know that she was safe.

Sarah opened the door. In the hallway there were hugs all round before anyone spoke.

'Casey, will you help Sarah make drinks while I have a chat with Laura?' Eden asked.

Casey nodded and followed her cousin into the kitchen.

Eden and Laura went into the living room. Eden took a deep breath, but before she could say anything, Laura looked at her sheepishly. Her cheeks were tinged with red.

'I went to see Lulu Barker,' she admitted.

'You had no right to do that!' Eden looked at her sister with wide eyes.

'I only wanted to know if anyone had seen Jess!'

'And we're looking into that. You have to let us do our jobs. We have the Barker brothers in custody. I don't want you making matters worse.' Eden wondered if she would have to go and see Lulu again, limit the damage that might have been done. 'What happened?'

'We had words. Lulu told me her boys had nothing to do with Jess being missing. But she did tell me you were talking to them.'

Eden pointed to the settee. They sat together as, with a heavy heart, she updated Laura with everything she had found out over the past two hours about the Barker brothers. She watched her sister drop her head into her hands.

'But if you know it's not those two, then who has her?' Laura wanted to know. 'You're sure it's not them?'

'Damien said they wouldn't do anything like that with the trial coming up on Monday. He said there was going to be enough media looking at them and that they just wanted to warn the girls off.'

'Warn the girls off what?'

'The money that Jess had?' There was no easy way for Eden to tell Laura about it. 'It looks like she's been in a gang that's been stealing mobile phones and selling them on for cash.'

'But I don't understand.'

'The three girls who were attacked were all warned to keep their mouths shut. At first we thought it was something to do with the trial, but now we know the Barker brothers were warning them off saying anything about their sideline business.'

Laura shook her head, tears running down her face. 'Jess would never be involved with anything like that. Would she?'

'I'm sorry.' Eden squeezed her sister's hand again. 'We're going to charge them and then bail them for now.' When Laura began to protest, she stopped her. 'We don't have enough evidence yet, but we will.'

'Maybe it's someone who the Barker brothers have upset,' Laura whispered, almost pleading with Eden to say differently.

Eden bit her lip, cursing herself inwardly. She'd put off this moment, talking about the brothers because she didn't know how to put everything else into words. She should have told Laura what she knew as soon as she'd arrived.

She didn't want to cause her sister any more distress, but she had to tell her everything they had found out.

'Laura,' she swallowed, 'we've seen someone pushing Jess into the back of a white van.'

Laura stood up quickly. 'When? What do you mean?'

Eden couldn't speak for a moment. She almost felt like she would choke if she said the words.

'What do you mean?' Laura cried, looking down at her. 'Who has her?'

'We don't know.' Eden stood up and told her sister what she knew. Held her while she broke down in her arms. Told her they would get the bastard who had taken Jess.

'Can you see the man's face in the picture?' Laura asked through her sobs.

'We're getting the images enhanced.'

Eden felt helpless as Laura cried. She didn't need to say that since this wasn't connected with the pranks, everything had turned a lot darker now.

Katie – August 2015

Dear Mum,

It's been four months now, and I miss you so much. The way you always make me feel loved and protected. The way you always know how to cheer me up. The way you can always make me smile. I miss you so much it hurts.

I miss Dad laughing and joking. The way he'd try to flick my ears whenever I walked past. The way he always burns cheese on toast and then blames me. The way he'd try and hug me to embarrass me.

I miss Matty, even though he's a pain at times. I miss his smile, his laughter and his goofy ways. I even miss both of us bickering and arguing between ourselves, usually over something silly.

I miss my room. I miss my clothes and all my shoes. I know I have some to wear here, but I have so many more at home. I miss having my own TV in my room. I miss being able to go to bed when I want, unless it's a school night obviously. I miss being able to eat what I want for breakfast. And school – I even miss going there. It's not the same here. I miss my friends.

I really miss hanging around with Jess. We used to swap clothes and magazines and messages – anything. I miss talking to her over FaceTime and as you would say, Mum, being in each other's pockets. Me and Jess are more like sisters – you always called us the terrible twins.

I don't have anyone to confide in here. I miss being able to talk to her when I'm feeling low, when I want to share a joke with her or when I hear a new song on the tinny radio in the kitchen. I want to share it with her or dance around *our* kitchen with her.

Will she even want to be my friend if I'm found guilty? I hope she comes and sees me again soon. Jess will know how to cheer me up. She can make me smile and laugh. She'll tell me what's going on with the old gang, and keep me up with the gossip until I come home.

Because I will come home. I have to come home, Mum.

But then I feel guilty. Because even though I miss all these things, at least I'm still alive. Deanna isn't. She's never coming back. She's never going to wear nice clothes and fancy shoes ever again. She's never going to see her mum and dad and all her brothers.

And all I keep seeing is her face as she lay dying in my arms. I see it when I wake up. I see it before I go to bed. Sometimes I see one of the kids running towards me and I see her. It's like her ghost is with me.

All the blood – how could someone do that to another human being? I hope Nathan gets what he deserves. He's evil to do that.

I wish I could have saved her, Mum. She shouldn't have died. It wasn't fair.

Love Katie x

# FIFTY-ONE

Laura was in the bathroom upstairs. It was the only way she could get a bit of peace and quiet to think. Over the last half hour, her kitchen had been taken over as more people had turned up to help with the search. Maxine and Carol were back from the park and were making drinks for everyone as they came and went. The police were out doing house-to-house, so they were taking trays of tea outside as well.

She was so grateful for everything being done, for it all to be happening so quickly, but it terrified her too. Who was the man who had her daughter? Eden wouldn't let her see the images of him pushing Jess into the van, but she had promised to let her see pictures of his face close up if they could get any.

Her biggest fear was that she would know him. Not that she had made any enemies over the years, but it was common knowledge that most victims of crime knew their assailants. But worse, what would happen if she didn't know him and couldn't give the police any help?

She glanced at her reflection as she splashed her face with cold water. Puffy eyes, blotchy face and neck. Her hair was greasy where she had run her fingers through it constantly. But she didn't care what she looked like any more. All she cared about was finding Jess.

It was 4.30 p.m. Why couldn't Jess just come walking through the front door? Or even ring home so that Laura could go and pick her up? Unharmed, a little shocked but innocent of all the things that were running through her head right now.

It was the not knowing that was torture. Not knowing where she was, not knowing who she was with. Not knowing. . .

No, she would never think anything less than that Jess was alive. If she did, she'd crumble – and she wouldn't do that. She would stay strong.

When her phone rang, she reached for it out of her pocket. The name flashing up on the screen made her swipe at it quickly.

'Jess!' she cried. 'Where are you? Are you okay?'

'It's not Jess.'

Laura gasped. The voice was male.

'Who are you?' she cried. 'Where is my daughter? Why do you have her phone?'

'Because I have your daughter.'

Laura grasped the edge of the sink before sitting down on the side of the bath. All her specialist counselling training went out of the window in a split second. But she remembered to speak calmly and quietly, hoping not to antagonise him.

'Please don't hurt her,' she said.

'It's too late for that.'

His accent was local. Laura bunched her fingers into a fist.

'Look, I'll pay you back the money. Five hundred and forty pounds.'

'What are you talking about?'

'If you leave her somewhere to make her own way home, just tell me and I'll go and collect her. The police don't need to know anything else. You can give—'

'You've told the police?'

'My sister is a detective sergeant. She was coming to see me when I realised Jess was missing.' Laura lost her cool. 'What have you done to her, you bastard? If you've hurt her, I'll—'

'You shouldn't have involved the police! This was between me and you. I didn't want anyone else to know!'

'She's my sister! And did you think no one was going to find out what you've done?'

'It doesn't matter about that. What you need to know is this has got nothing to do with money. No one owes me anything except you.'

Laura wasn't listening to him properly. 'Please,' her voice faltered. 'Just let her go.'

'You owe me an explanation first. It's your fault I have her.'

'Me? I don't understand!'

'My name is Jason Proctor. My daughter was Ashleigh Proctor. Does her name ring a bell?'

# FIFTY-TWO

## April 2015

*Laura: How are you feeling today, Ashleigh?*

*Ashleigh: I'm fine.*

*Laura: Just fine?*

*Ashleigh: Yes, just fine.*

A pause.

*Laura: So what do you want to talk about?*

*Ashleigh: Have you ever wanted to kill yourself?*

*Laura: No. Do you feel like you want to do that?*

*Ashleigh: In the past yes. But I don't want to now.*

*Laura: That's good to hear.*

*Ashleigh: I want my mum to be proud of me.*

*Laura: That's good.*

*Ashleigh: You remember I was thirteen when my mum died?*

*Laura: Yes, I remember.*

*Ashleigh: She died of cancer. My dad went to pieces. He lost his job through bad timekeeping.*

*Laura: That's a shame.*

*Ashleigh: Is it?*

*Laura: What do you mean?*

*Ashleigh: It was his fault. He was drunk all the time. Once Mum died he began drinking even more. It was as if he was trying to blot out his pain. I tried that too. Not with alcohol though.*

*Laura: Oh?*

*Ashleigh: I like to take control in other ways.*

The line was quiet.

*Laura: How have you been at school?*

*Ashleigh: I haven't been this week.*

*Laura: Why's that?*

*Ashleigh: School is boring.*

*Laura: I suppose I thought the same when I was your age. But it really is worth sticking at it. You'll be surprised how many people wish they had in their later years.*

*Ashleigh: All the girls want to talk about boys. All the boys want to talk about football. I can't stand small talk, can you?*

*Laura: I suppose not. Don't you have friends at school?*

*Ashleigh: No.*

*Laura: No one to talk to at all?*

*Ashleigh: No. They all hate me.*

*Laura: What makes you say that?*

*Ashleigh: I just know.*

Silence.

*Laura: So what do you like to do when you're at home?*

*Ashleigh: I read. I like psychological thrillers.*

*Laura: Read any good ones lately?*

*Ashleigh: I'm reading* Gone Girl *at the moment.*

*Laura: Isn't that a little old for you?*

*Ashleigh: Not really. Have you read it?*

*Laura: No, I don't get much time for reading.*

*Ashleigh: It's okay, a bit slow until the middle, but I'm told it gets better then. I'll have to wait and see. I've read* The Girl on the Train *too. Have you read that?*

*Laura: No.*

*Ashleigh: I didn't like that one because it reminded me too much of my dad.*

*Laura: Does he still drink a lot?*

There was silence down the line.

*Ashleigh: He drinks way too much.*

*Laura: Does he know it upsets you? Have you talked to him about it?*

*Ashleigh: You can't talk to him. If he's sober, he doesn't think he's in the wrong. If he's drunk, he doesn't think there's anything wrong either.*

*Laura: Does he talk to you?*

*Ashleigh: No, he shouts all the time. Either that or he's sleeping off a hangover.*

*Laura: What about when he goes to work?*

*Ashleigh: I told you. He lost his job a few months ago. We lost our house too.*

*Laura: So he's in all the time?*

*Ashleigh: If he isn't down the pub. He won't be able to go there soon.*

*Laura: Why not?*

*Ashleigh: I've seen letters. Threatening to take the house from us. He's in debt. I don't want to move from this house as well. We live down by the park. It's a shithole though.*

*Laura: I don't need to know those details, Ashleigh.*

*Ashleigh: Sorry.*

Another pause.

*Laura: So you really have no one to talk to?*

*Ashleigh: No. Everyone hates me.*

*Laura: Of course they don't.*

*Ashleigh: Children can be so cruel.*

A pause.

*Ashleigh: I had my phone stolen.*

*Laura: Oh no, have you managed to get it back?*

*Ashleigh: No. There were lots of photos of me on it.*

*Laura: It's a shame when you lose them. Have you got them backed up anywhere?*

*Ashleigh: No, but everyone has seen them.*

*Laura: What do you mean?*

*Ashleigh: They were shared.*

*Laura: At school?*

*Ashleigh: Online. Facebook. Snapchat.*

*Laura: Were the photos special to you?*

*Ashleigh: You don't understand. The photos were private. Of me. Naked.*

*Laura: That's against the law, Ashleigh. Can you tell a teacher if you can't talk to your dad?*

*Ashleigh: They were photos of me in my underwear. I wasn't doing anything dirty. People said I looked like a skeleton, but I was so fat and disgusting.*

*Laura: That's terrible, Ashleigh. Have you reported it to the police?*

*Ashleigh: What's the point? It's too late. Everyone knows how fat I am now. I've had to close my Facebook and Twitter accounts. But the photos are still out there. I had to get a new phone.*

*Laura: Ashleigh, don't cry.*

Silence.

*Laura: Ashleigh, talk to your dad. Tell him what happened, and he could go to the school and sort it out.*

*Ashleigh: I can't.*

Silence.

*Ashleigh: Even you don't want to talk to me now.*

*Laura: Of course I do. I was just adjusting my headset. Ashleigh. . . Ashleigh?*

# FIFTY-THREE

Eden was in the kitchen when she heard a scream.

'Laura?' She took the stairs two at a time, only to see her sister standing in the bathroom doorway.

'He has Jess,' Laura cried. 'This isn't anything to do with the Barker family or the phones. He's got my daughter.'

'Who has?'

'He – he—'

'Who?' Eden put a hand on each of Laura's shoulders to stop her from pacing the room. 'Tell me everything.'

'His name is Jason Proctor.' Laura began to shake. 'His daughter used to be a regular caller to our helpline until about six months ago. I thought she had moved on – sometimes these kids do, find another friend or a boyfriend or confide in someone face to face and they don't need us any longer.'

'So she stopped ringing CrisisChat?'

'He's just told me that she killed herself. He says it was shortly after she was talking to me.'

'What?'

'He must think I had something to do with her death, that I could have done more to prevent it. Eden, I couldn't. I couldn't!'

Eden tried to get her head around what Laura was saying. 'You mean he's taken Jess as some kind of punishment?'

'I don't know what he'll do to her! She's just a child – my child.'

'Is he thinking that she's his daughter? What was her name?'

'Ashleigh.'

'Is he grieving for her and mixed up?'

'I don't know.' Laura shook her head. 'He sounded angry. He says he's keeping Jess to teach me a lesson.'

'What for?' Eden frowned. 'You did all you could to help Ashleigh.'

'I think I did. He's grieving for his daughter, and his wife died too. I'd have to check my notes, but if I remember right, Ashleigh said it was three years ago. I think she said she was thirteen.'

'Did he ask for anything? Money? Did he say why he took her?'

'No, he just said he had her and then mentioned Ashleigh.'

Eden reached for her radio. 'I need to call this in.'

'You can't!' Laura exclaimed. 'He went mad because the police know. He could hurt Jess if you get any more involved.'

'He could have hurt Jess already!' Eden cursed as she saw her sister's face crumble at her bluntness. 'What did he say?'

'He put the phone down after he told me who he was. He said it had nothing to do with money.'

'Let me look at it.' Eden took it from her and dialled Jess's number. They should be able to put a trace on it. She closed her eyes momentarily when it wouldn't connect. 'It's been switched off.'

'So what do we do now? We don't know where she is. We don't know anything about him. He might hurt her – he's told me that. How do we get her back, Eden? What do we DO?'

Eden knew she was out of her depth right now. As well as alerting the control room to update everyone, she had to speak to Sean.

'I need to call it in.'

'You don't understand. A man is holding Jess to punish me.'

'Of course he isn't trying to punish you. Sometimes people react when they're angry.'

'He told me he'd taken Jess because of Ashleigh. How can that not be punishment?'

'Let's try to think rationally.'

'I can't fucking think rationally!' Laura screamed.

'I need you to—'

'If this was Casey you'd be doing more.'

Eden stared at her. Of course Laura was wrong, but she was only trying to ease the situation for her sister. Her reply was stern but firm.

'Nothing puts fear into me more than when something like this happens,' she replied. 'So don't play the "you wouldn't understand" card with me. I have known Jess since she was a baby, and I want her home too. So let me, and my team, do our jobs.'

'But—'

'I need to know that I have your full cooperation. The whole focus of this investigation has changed.' Eden stopped because she didn't want to say the words. 'We're looking at a kidnap situation.'

'Kidnap?' Casey and Sarah said in unison. The girls stood in the bathroom doorway behind them. Several people stood at the bottom of the stairs, anxious looks on their faces.

'Mum, what's going on?' said Sarah.

But Laura couldn't speak for crying.

Eden's bottom lip trembled as she got on the phone to Sean.

# FIFTY-FOUR

Jess watched as the man, whom she now knew to be named Jason, disconnected the call and switched off her phone.

He'd been talking to her mum! How could she be so close yet so far? Tears poured down her face and she groaned, pulling at the tape around her wrists and ankles. She had to get away from him. But how?

It was hopeless. She sobbed uncontrollably.

Seeing her distress, he came towards her. She turned her face from him, squeezing her eyes shut. But he stopped short in front of her.

'Your mum, she works in a call centre for teenagers, right?'

Jess opened her eyes and nodded fervently.

'Is she a good mum to you?'

She nodded again.

'She wasn't good to my Ashleigh. She let her down.'

Jess frowned. She didn't know anyone named Ashleigh – was that the girl in the photographs?

'Did she always listen to you?' Jason asked.

Jess shook her head this time but regretted it the moment she had and tried to nod. Her mum didn't listen to her at times because she gave her cause not to. Moaning and whining to get her own way. No wonder she never wanted to listen. But she couldn't explain this with the tape covering her mouth.

'Ashleigh was my only child,' he went on, 'and I have nothing now. Your mum needs to know how painful it is to be without her daughter.'

Jess's eyes met his as she tried not to show the shiver that was running through her at his words. What did he mean by that? What the hell was he going to do with her?

'So I'm going to teach her a lesson, show her what it is to lose control and not to be able to communicate with her child.' Jason reached beneath a cushion on the settee and pulled out a knife with a five-inch blade.

Jess screamed behind the tape and thrashed about in the chair again.

'This is plan B,' he said, pushing it back to where it had been. 'I don't have a plan C.'

Jess knew it was imperative that she stayed calm, but she couldn't help herself. Why would he have a knife if he wasn't going to hurt her? She sobbed so hard that she couldn't catch her breath. She began to cough, her eyes watering and her face going red.

He reached for the tape on her mouth and pulled it away. She gasped in pain.

'Calm down,' he said.

'Please let me go,' she said, her voice croaky. 'I won't say anything, I promise.'

He looked at her with such loathing that she wanted to retch. She held in more tears as she calmed down. A few minutes passed and she wondered if it was worth attempting a scream. But for some reason, she stayed quiet. Even when he placed a fresh strip of tape across her mouth.

Then he picked up the photo he'd been staring at and held it in front of her.

'This was Ashleigh.'

Jess saw a girl, a teenager like herself. She had long dark hair, hollowed out cheekbones and a chin full of angry spots. Dark eyes were almost sunk into her skull. She didn't look very happy, hardly a smile on her thin lips.

But Jess couldn't look for very long without getting upset. She knew who the girl in the photo was.

# FIFTY-FIVE

Eden stayed with Laura for an hour before returning to the station. Sean had set up a team brief for 6.30 p.m. before he went to do a press conference on camera.

Everyone working on the case was in the main conference room. There was chatter in the air until she walked in. A hush descended as people threw her half smiles and sympathetic looks. Then they all spoke at once. 'We'll get the bastard,' said one colleague, Pete Davidson, whom she had known since she'd joined the force.

But her eyes fell on the image of Jess attached to the whiteboard on the far wall. It was the one that she had taken from Laura earlier. A head shot of a bright and bubbly smiling teenager in her school uniform.

Eden counted eleven people as she sat down at the table, concentrating on the wall ahead as she felt tears welling in her eyes. She couldn't cry now, not in front of everyone. But then again, she was only human. Sean had been good to keep her on the case after she had seen footage of the man who had taken Jess. It had become personal now, and she had to be careful not to show too much emotion.

'Just a recap for a couple of you who weren't on shift yesterday,' said Sean, standing up and pointing at the board. 'Jess Mountford. Sixteen years old and Eden's niece.' He glanced at her quickly. 'Last seen by her sister, Sarah, leaving the house at 6 p.m. last night. On her way to meet her boyfriend, Cayden Blackwell. He was beaten up and taken to A&E just before he was due to meet her. Three other girls were attacked, and we now have footage to show Jess being taken by a lone male in a white van. We think the man attacked Cayden and sent a text message to Jess to meet him at the back of Shop&Save supermarket. He also replied to a message from the boyfriend to say that Jess was heading up to A&E to see him, but we've checked on CCTV and she hasn't been seen going into the main entrance.

'There was mud obscuring the number plate on the van, which we've now had enhanced and been able to pick up. However the van belonged to Mrs Maria Candish, who lives over in Knutsford. She sold it on as scrap a few months ago, so we don't know who owns it yet, but we're still looking into it. Amy followed it on the CCTV for about half a mile until it went off screen.

'At 4.35 p.m. today, a call came in from a Jason Proctor to say he has Jess. He rang her mum, Laura Mountford, and said that he had taken her. Can you enlighten us on that, Eden? That okay?'

Eden cleared her throat before speaking. 'My sister seems to think he blames her for the death of his daughter, Ashleigh. Laura works at CrisisChat, a helpline for teenagers. Ashleigh had been ringing her a couple of times a week, talking about problems she was having after her mum died. She then took her own life in April last year.'

There was a collective hum around the room as everyone absorbed what she was saying.

'We haven't got any intelligence on him yet,' Amy enlightened them. 'He's not known on our system. Council tax and electoral roll records have been asked for, along with checking to see if he is in receipt of any benefits, which would give us an address.'

'We need to locate him,' said Sean, looking around the room. 'As you know, I've set up a TV press conference this evening and we have the local press and social media channels involved. We're checking everything we can to find him. House-to-house started this afternoon and the SWAPS have been out and about with the local community. Anything they have found out has been filtered through or actioned.'

'What about the Barker brothers?' someone asked.

Eden looked to see that it was a PC drafted in to help. She'd seen him around but couldn't place him. He was young, mid-twenties, and keen and eager to impress whenever she saw him. He wanted in to CID, and she was sure he would get there soon.

'They admitted to the attacks on the three girls but not to Jess and Cayden.' Sean explained all he knew about the mobile phones.

'Any known associates?' asked another PC. Eden didn't know him at all.

'Not yet.'

'We have caught up with their father, Frank Barker,' said Jordan, sitting forward. 'Uniform went to his house, but he wasn't home. Further investigations revealed that he's in Cyprus and won't get back to the UK until late this evening, in time for the trial on Monday morning.'

Ruling out all the Barker family had taken a lot of time, but it had been necessary to get to the bottom of things. At least Eden could be thankful that Jess hadn't been taken by someone further up the chain, way higher than Damien and Travis, in a mobile phone racket that they could now look into further.

'The kids must be stealing the phones for some reason,' added Jordan. 'Someone will be making more than a few quid on each one. Or maybe they're being used to smuggle something else inside their casing?'

'Good point. Make a note to check that out,' said Sean. Jordan nodded.

Eden closed her eyes momentarily as images of Proctor pushing Jess into the back of the van assaulted her: Jess waiting, the man approaching her the first time and leaving her, then coming back, her following him. She'd cringed when she'd seen him punch her in the face, gasped when he had dragged her to the van and shoved her inside. Felt her own fists clenching when she'd watched him hit her again before closing the door and driving off. She wondered how he had managed to coerce Jess into following him. Jess was street savvy. He must have been very clever.

'Even Storm Monica was against us last night,' said Sean. 'The wind was noisy and not as many people would have been out. Those that were would have had their heads down, going home as quickly as possible, unable to notice things they might have seen had the weather been calmer.' He checked his watch. 'Let's see how we go over the next couple of hours. I want all hands on deck once the press conference is done, see if we can find any leads.' He looked at Eden then the group as a whole.

'Let's bring Jess home, people.'

# FIFTY-SIX

Although she wanted to go back to be with her family, Eden knew she'd be more use to the investigation if she was close to it, and as Casey was with Laura, she didn't have to worry about her.

The door to Sean's office was open, but she knocked anyway before walking in. 'Can I join you at the press conference?' she asked.

'Of course. I'll also speak to DCI Benton,' said Sean, referring to his superior officer, 'but we need to take this up another level. You know that, don't you?'

Eden could barely bring herself to nod her acceptance. How had it come to this: her niece being kidnapped because of her sister?

'Do we have any idea what the connection is between his daughter and your sister?' Sean sat with steepled fingers.

'Nothing that Laura can think of, apart from that she used to talk to her on the chatline.' Eden shook her head. 'She told me she keeps the notepads that she uses at work in a locked cupboard. It might be worth going through those to see if there's anything useful anywhere, a mention of something that might lead us to Jason Proctor. We're also chasing phone records for the charity, to see if we can pinpoint his address through Ashleigh's phone records. I'm going to get in touch with Josie Mellor too. See if she can find out anything on her system. He must be known to someone, somewhere.'

'And in the meantime we wait for him to contact Laura again.'

Eden gulped. She felt so helpless.

'Do you want to stay with Laura, after the conference? I can assign you to her house, like an unofficial family liaison officer, if it would make you feel better about being the first to give her updates.'

Eden sat back in her chair, her body flopping. 'I can't do that, sir. I want to be with her, of course, but I need to be doing something. I need to be working with my team to find this. . . this bastard.' Her voice broke, but she regained her composure quickly. 'Find out why he has Jess. Find him so we can bring her home.'

'We'll piece it together soon.' Sean sat quietly for a moment. 'Why don't you take Amy and nip across to have a look in the offices of CrisisChat?'

'Yes, sir.'

CrisisChat was three streets away from the police station, so she and Amy headed out on foot. Laura had given her the key and access to the alarm code, so getting in the building didn't take long. Eden almost ran up the three flights of stairs, taking a moment to catch her breath at the top before going into the office.

She flicked on the lights and glanced around the drab room. The charity had done its best, but it was an old building and it showed. High ceilings made it feel cold, along with cream-painted walls and high skirting boards and, she guessed, draughty windows. Eden thought how depressing it must be to come to work there every evening. Again she felt proud of her sister and what she did.

Laura had told her to look in the second cupboard on the right. She unlocked it with a small key. There were five shelves inside, each full of notepads dating back to 2000. Laura's shelf was one from the bottom, so she bent down and picked up a pile of notepads. When she had found the few dating back six months to around the time Ashleigh Proctor had committed suicide, she passed two to Amy, took the other two and sat down at a desk.

'Laura says she probably uses a notepad on average every month, so if we look around April 2015 first and then we can move earlier than that to see if there are any clues around Ashleigh. She says they don't take down many details as everything needs to be confidential, but they do keep these notebooks for a couple of years.'

Eden opened the first one.

'Do we know what we might be looking for?' asked Amy, leafing through the pages.

Eden shrugged. 'Laura said she doodles a lot. See if you can find the word "Ashleigh" written anywhere.'

They sat in silence as they flicked through the books. 'Here's one, dated 7 April,' said Eden, her heart skipping a beat as she read over the page. But then she blew out her breath. 'There's nothing we can use. Just notes about how she's feeling.'

'Here's another, 14 April.' Amy passed it to Eden, who shook her head and threw it to the floor.

Several minutes later after the first few had been discarded, Amy looked at Eden as she sighed.

'Nothing?' she queried.

'Nothing. It's all so fucking useless!'

'It isn't,' said Amy. 'You know how we piece together every tiny item until they join up. We might find a tidbit of info and crack the case.'

'But Jess is missing – she might never be seen again.'

'It's not like you to be so defeatist.'

'You don't know the half of my life.' She opened her mouth to speak but decided better of it. She'd already said too much.

'Do you mind if I ask you something, Sarge?'

Eden had managed to keep the details around Danny to herself since he had disappeared. She knew people had talked about his swift exit when it had filtered through the station eventually – and the fact that she had remained close-lipped about it for a long time since.

'You want to know more about Danny?' Eden bristled. 'Office gossip not enough for you?'

Amy blushed. 'I – I didn't mean to pry. It's just that you and your sister seem so close. I was wondering if this was because you could empathise with her over losing someone you loved.'

Eden concentrated on the page she was flicking over for a moment before looking up again. 'Danny left of his own accord. One morning he was there, and when I got home in the evening he had gone. At least when my brother-in-law, Neil, was killed there was closure for Laura. I'm left wondering all the time.'

Eden felt a sense of betrayal as she talked about Danny, especially after seeing his telephone number stored on Laura's phone. But she also felt the need to talk, to tell someone who wasn't family a few things that kept her awake at night.

'Danny disappeared two years ago now, and yes, it still hangs over me. He sold his car, cleared out our bank account, and I haven't seen or heard from him since.'

It had been hard for Eden to tell the people close to her that Danny had upped and left, but the longer it went on, the more she realised he wouldn't be coming back. For months she had tried to track him down, but there had been nothing. There was still nothing, which was frustrating to say the least given her role. Except for the pile of debt that he had landed her with. Things she hadn't known anything about, like the online gambling, which had only come to light when bills had come in for him. Twice she'd had bailiffs at the door – luckily she'd been able to prove that her name wasn't on the debt, but she lived in fear of every visit.

It had been quiet now for six months. Yet it still irked her that he would walk out on his wife and child without saying a word, disappearing more or less into thin air.

'He was a shit to just up and leave.' She waved a hand for dismissal.

'I'm sorry,' said Amy.

Eden shrugged. 'It's okay. It never really goes away. I do wonder where he is and what he's doing. Why he felt the need to leave without an explanation.' She stopped this time before she really did say too much. She didn't want anyone to know the exact reason why Danny had left.

They sat in silence while they flicked through the rest of the entries in the notepads for April, but there was nothing. They tried a few more, back to the start of 2015 but still nothing.

With a sigh, Eden locked up the offices and they went back to the station. The press conference would be starting shortly. Maybe that would bring in more clues, sightings, whatever it took.

# FIFTY-SEVEN

The press conference was set up in a room downstairs in the main belly of the station. It was a small square room with a long table on one side and two rows of chairs for journalists and press officers. A camera was set up at the back of the room.

Eden was apprehensive about the outcome of the gathering. She had been involved in many press conferences but had never been in the situation before where she knew the victim so well. Never been in a position where she had known a victim at all. Her heart pounded in her chest. All she wanted was for someone to ring in with information that would lead them straight to Jess.

Sean cleared his throat and looked into the camera. The buzz around the room silenced.

'My name is DI Sean Whittaker and my team are looking into the disappearance of sixteen-year-old Jessica Mountford. She was taken last night, Friday, 15 October at approximately 1800 hours. She was last seen on CCTV footage being bundled into the back of a white Volkswagen van against her will, registration number V39 ETA. If you know of this van's whereabouts or you think you might have seen it recently, please contact the number that will be flashing across the bottom of your screen. Anything big or small could be vital.

'Jessica Mountford is approximately five foot seven inches tall, slim with long blonde hair. She was wearing jeans, a black jacket and boots. Her hair would more than likely have been tucked under a black woollen hat. The weather was pretty atrocious last night, but if you were out near to Shop&Save, the large superstore on the high street, please cast your mind back. Did you see anything suspicious?

'I also urge everyone to check any outbuildings – sheds, garages, outhouses – in case Jessica managed to get free and is hiding out. We're obviously not certain why she has been taken at this stage, but we do know that the man who has her claims to be Jason Proctor. We are unable to confirm his address at this moment in time, so any help from the public about his whereabouts would be appreciated. If you do know Jason, please be warned that he may be unstable, so again I urge you to contact the police. Do not approach him.

'Jason Proctor is of medium build and appears to be in his early forties. Our enquiries are continuing today, and I would urge anybody with any information about the incident who has not already spoken to officers to contact us. We would be grateful to the public for any information they can provide to help bring Jessica back safe and well and reunite her with her family. Thank you.'

Once the conference was over, Eden followed Sean back to the room to help man the phones. Her phone would have been switched to the helpline number. Others were already ringing and three officers were taking down notes from calls. It was always like this during the first hour after a live press conference, with people wanting their two minutes of glory, hoping to have spotted something that would lead to an arrest. Most of the calls amounted to nothing, and they would slow down eventually, but for now they all had to be treated as if they could hold vital clues. In all fairness, they could do.

Eden took her mobile phone off silent and checked to see if she had any messages. There was one from Laura to say that she had seen the press conference but nothing else connected to the investigation. Same with her emails – everyone was waiting on information from other people.

A couple of hours manning the lines while the calls came in thick and fast would keep her mind from working overtime and imagining the worst.

Across the city, Jason Proctor stood up and paced the room. He'd sat open mouthed as he'd watched the press conference. The girl had begun to cry again when she had seen her photo and the police talking about her.

'Fuck!'

This was never meant to happen. Damn the police. Things shouldn't have escalated so quickly.

He needed to speak to the girl's mother, but it had to be tomorrow. Then he could follow through with the rest of his plan on Monday – on Ashleigh's birthday.

He'd better start to think of an alternative backup plan, just in case he had to move the girl quickly.

# FIFTY-EIGHT

After an hour hearing nothing but time-wasters and no leads, Eden left the other officers to it. A few things had come up that they had actioned for the morning, but other than that things had gone quiet. She decided to go and see Laura, give her an update on everything so far.

Casey opened the door. 'Any news, Mum?' she asked as she hugged her.

Eden ran a hand over her daughter's hair. 'Nothing yet, princess. But we're working on it.'

'I saw you on the television.' Casey couldn't help but beam. 'You look so trendy in your Doc Martens and parka.'

Eden gave her a half smile. Casey never missed commenting on what her mum was wearing whenever she caught her on television. Although she'd made her sound like a teenager, in actual fact her parka had come from French Connection and had cost a small fortune.

She could hear noise in the kitchen so she went through. There were five women in there, three sitting round the table and two washing and drying mugs at the sink.

'Hi, Eden,' said Josie, as she pulled out a chair. 'Any news yet?'

Eden shook her head.

'Want a cup of tea?'

'Yes please.'

Josie flicked on the kettle as another woman pressed a piece of paper into Eden's hands.

'We've compiled another list for you, but we're about done for the day now it's gone dark. Is there anything else you'd like us to do?'

'Not for now, but thanks, Maxine. You've all been such a great help. I'll have a look through this and then get my team onto it in the morning. There could be vital information in there somewhere.'

Eden wanted to raise the women's spirits even though she knew most of it would come to nothing.

'I'll come back in the morning,' said Josie. 'We can start off where we finished. I'm sure there will be lots for us to do.'

'But it's Sunday.'

'And?'

Eden nodded her thanks. Josie had been such a help, organising the women, getting any information to her team straightaway, jotting down anything that needed following up.

She was just about to speak when there was a voice from behind.

'For God's sake, it's eight o'clock in the evening. Jess has been missing since six o'clock last night!'

Eden turned to see Laura standing in the doorway. Her eyes were raw from crying, her face gaunt as she hugged herself.

'I've had a house full of people all day and now you're coming back and telling me everything and nothing in one breath?'

'We're doing all we can to help you,' Eden replied, frustrated by her tone. 'The least you can do is show your gratitude that people have put themselves out to help you.'

'I *am* grateful,' said Laura. 'But I need some space. What would happen if it was Casey that had gone missing? You'd be the same, Eden, and don't you dare tell me different.' She stared at her sister before addressing the room. 'Out, please. All of you.'

'But, Laura, we can—' Maxine started.

Laura picked up the nearest coffee mug and slung it across the room at the wall. It smashed into smithereens, the last remnants of the coffee dripping down the wallpaper. She sank to the floor at the same time.

'I just want to see Jess home,' she whispered.

Eden rushed across to her, took her in her arms and ushered everyone out of the kitchen.

'Mum?' Sarah wavered in the doorway. Eden shook her head, and she left to sit with Casey in the living room.

Once the door was closed and they were alone, Eden let a few of her own tears fall as her sister sobbed. Jess was such a huge part of their family, and she loved her as if she were her own daughter. She couldn't let Jason Proctor get away with this. He wouldn't tear her family apart.

Even though they were doing all they could, she knew to Laura it wouldn't be enough. It didn't seem enough to her, but she knew that every officer available in the area would be working on this case. They would be looking out for Jess.

She sniffed long and hard, trying to compose herself. She needed to keep up a brave facade to help her sister. Crying with her would show solidarity, but it wouldn't do Laura any good. She would go to pieces if she knew how scared Eden was. How terrified she was that Proctor would harm Jess. He seemed hell-bent on revenge. Revenge was different than grief. Revenge was built of more than anger. Revenge was meant to hurt, maim – kill even.

She closed her eyes for a moment, trying to rid herself of the image of her niece lying dead somewhere that they hadn't looked yet. Even though everyone locally had been asked to check their sheds and outbuildings and garages, not everyone read or listened to the news. The police couldn't cover all the city, and they had wasted a lot of time chasing after Deanna Barker's family on a dead-end lead.

She shut the thought out of her mind and returned to police mode. She could cry later when she was on her own – and when they had Jess back safe and sound.

'Where is she, Eden?' Laura said, a few minutes later.

'I don't know.' Eden placed her hand on her sister's head, rubbing at her hair the way Laura used to try and soothe her as a child.

'Why can't you do more?'

'We're doing everything we can.'

'But you haven't found her, and you're the police. If the police can't—'

'We'll find her.'

'But what if you can't?'

Eden pulled away from her sister and took her face in her hands. 'You've always been there for me, Laura, and I'll always be there for you. When have I ever let you down?'

Laura stared at Eden before bursting into tears again. 'I want to believe you, but I can see in your eyes that you have doubt.'

Eden didn't know what to say to that. Laura was right. She couldn't hide her uncertainty that Jess would come home. But she did have faith in her colleagues.

She held her sister's hands in her own this time. 'We will find her, Laura. We will bring Jess home.'

# FIFTY-NINE

Sitting in the living room, Maxine tried to read that evening's newspaper so that she could stop stressing about the last visit to Katie in the morning. The 10 p.m. news had just finished. Across the room, Phil lay on the settee, gently snoring. She wished she could switch off as easily as he did. He could go to sleep on a washing line, whereas she could take hours to drift off. Especially when something was on her mind.

All day, the rest of the volunteers had been out and about trying to locate Jess. With Josie Mellor's help, and the police that had been drafted in during the day, they must have covered most of Stockleigh. Social media had worked a treat to share new details as they emerged, but although there had been several possible sightings after the press conference, all of them had led to nothing. Still, the police said a lot could happen in a few hours, and they would keep working on it until something came up.

It had been dreadful thinking that Jess's disappearance might have something to do with the trial for Deanna Barker, and part of her had been grateful when it had been proved that it wasn't. But for the police to have reason to believe that Jess had been kidnapped, well that was even worse. It had made her feel guilty too.

Jess and the investigation were spread over the first few pages. Her disappearance had really got to Maxine that afternoon, especially when she was helping some of the other mums and volunteers with Josie. It had been strange to go to the park, to see the subway where Deanna Barker had been murdered on the night that changed her daughter's life for ever. But gradually she'd started chatting to some of the local teenagers about Jess and then the conversation had turned to Deanna, and then someone had started to ask about Katie. For the first time in a long while, people had listened to her rather than condemning her before they got to know her.

But it had been terribly upsetting to see Laura collapse when they had gone back to her house. They'd left quickly, but now she felt really guilty. She should have stayed behind and comforted her, even if Laura hadn't wanted her to. Laura had always been there for her, and she had no way of thanking her for that. Lots of people had ignored her since April – the phone had stopped ringing after Katie's arrest. There had been some nosy friends after gossip, but once they realised they weren't going to get any, they hadn't called again. Her circle of friends had turned into something resembling a hula hoop.

So she should have shown more support for Laura. She would do as much as she could tomorrow instead, once she'd been to visit Katie. She hoped Jess would be found safe and well long before that though. That poor child. Wherever she was, she hoped that man wasn't hurting her.

Phil snored and woke himself up. Staring around as if he had lost where he was, he grinned at her before closing his eyes again.

Unable to relax, she got out Katie's letters. Last week she had received several all together that Katie had written over the months she had been at the secure unit but had never sent. At the time, Maxine had been really upset that she hadn't known anything of how she was feeling. Katie had kept a lot of it hidden.

The last letter had all but broken her heart:

*Dear Mum,*

*I can't believe the trial is only two days away now. I can't wait to see you on Sunday.*

*I'm sorry that I was miserable when you came last weekend. But it's getting so near to the trial that it's all I'm thinking about. I just wanted to come home with you. I hope I didn't make you angry, because I know how hard you try to get to see me every week. Some of the kids here don't have any visitors at all, and I know I'm lucky.*

*Like you said to me, it is hard in here, but please don't stop coming to see me if I don't get out because I'm sad. I get low all the time. It's not my choice to be here. And I really want your support.*

*I know you need to remember that smile of mine, and my face lighting up when I see you, but it's when you leave that I go to pieces. I just want to come home, and every time I see you leave it makes me sad that I can't go with you.*

*You're right – I do have to look after myself while I'm here. I'll try and eat more regularly, even though I have no appetite. I do need to keep my strength up. It's hard to think past the trial at the moment. All I can think about is if I get a long sentence and I'm brought back here. And then when I'm eighteen, I'll go to a proper women's prison. I won't be put in with normal people either – I'll be put in with the bad ones. The ones who really did murder someone or killed their babies.*

*It was good to see you though. To have a hug and have your arms wrapped around me. You've always been there to protect me. I couldn't wish for a better mum. I'm really sorry you have to go through this too. I can just imagine how everyone will be, staring at you and Dad and Matty. Condemning me before I have time to say what happened. My side of the story.*

*I know I should plead not guilty, despite my solicitor saying I should plead guilty to get away with a lesser sentence, but I shouldn't really be sentenced at all. I haven't done anything. If I say I'm guilty, then I am guilty. But I'm not guilty. I tried to help Deanna when the boys ran off.*

*All the memories have been rushing back to me over the past week. The blood on my hands as I tried to cover up the wounds in her stomach and chest. I tried to press on them, stop the blood from oozing out, but it didn't work. The blood kept on coming, all over Deanna's stomach and on the ground. It was on the knees of my jeans. I'm sorry I hid them away from you, Mum. I didn't know what else to do. The police got to them before I had a chance to wash it away anyway, and the blood was all over my boots.*

*But I didn't kill her, Mum. And everyone needs to know that, because I just want to come home. I love you, and I miss you all. I want to be with my family again. Please don't let them keep me away from you.*

*Love Katie x*

Maxine hoped tomorrow morning would be the last time she had to visit the secure unit. If Katie was found not guilty after the trial, she could come straight home. If she was convicted, she would go back to the unit and be sent to God only knows where in later years. She would be without a daughter for a very long time. And, although she kept telling Katie to remember Deanna and her mum, Lulu, and how the family would be feeling, she didn't want to think of them right now. All she wanted was her own family to be one again. Life could be so cruel at times.

After reading the final letter in the order that Katie had written them over the past six months, Maxine picked up her pen and began to write a reply. It wasn't the one Katie would want, but she had to make sure it was ready if it was needed.

It was the letter she had been dreading writing most, and yet she had to write it just in case. If Katie was convicted and given a long sentence, then she hoped her words would be soothing, hoped that in time she would be able to find comfort in them.

*Dearest Katie,*

*This breaks my heart to write. They found you guilty of manslaughter, but it doesn't change anything for me. I feel very sorry that Deanna is no longer with us, and Lulu Barker has my sympathies, but I've lost my daughter too, for the time being, and I'm hurting as well.*

*I want you to know that you and Matty are the most precious things in my life, and I love you both so much. I can't believe I won't get to see your smiling face every day. But these years will go quite quickly. I'm sure you will think they could have been the best years of your life, but as young as you are, you will be able to start again and put all this behind you.*

*Your dad and I will still fight on your behalf to bring you home. Just because the jury found you guilty doesn't mean they're right. We'll help you to appeal, and we'll get you home as soon as we can.*

*Please don't worry about anything. I will take care of whatever needs to be done. I want you to concentrate on getting over the shock.*

*I'd also like you to remember that Deanna Barker died. I know you won't want reminding, but she was someone's daughter too and you mustn't forget that. Just as much as I love you, Lulu loved Deanna.*

*Please don't let this ruin you. You have your whole life ahead of you. Your dad, Matty and I love you very much. We miss you and we want you to come home. Until then, chin up, young lady, and let's do this. Believe me when I say you are brave and strong. Hang on in there.*

*We'll fight this, Katie.*

*Love always,*

*Mum x*

Maxine put down her pen, trying desperately to stop her tears from falling but failing miserably. Really, she hoped Katie would never get to read it. But what mother would have let her daughter get in so much of a mess? Guilt consumed her, yet surely it couldn't be down to her and Phil? They hadn't taught her to be violent. It was just a matter of being in the wrong place at the wrong time. If only Jess had been out with her on that night, it might have been her then.

Even as she thought it, she despised herself. How could she even look Laura in the eye again as she thought such things about their daughters? She knew it was only grief talking. Grief that she had lost her daughter for at least six months, maybe years if she was found guilty, for something she hadn't done. Grief and worry about Jess still being missing.

But at least at the end of the trial she would still be able to see her daughter. She hoped that Jess would be found soon and returned to Laura. But Lulu Barker would never see Deanna again.

Somehow, no matter how bad things were for her, Maxine should never forget that.

# SIXTY

After Laura's breakdown, Eden returned to the station, hoping for any kind of lead from the press conference. But there was nothing, and she wished she'd stayed with her sister. The weather was still atrocious and she'd need to collect Casey anyway.

There was nothing more that could be done until the morning. She and Sean had put in every possible request to agencies to find out as much as they could about Jason Proctor. Every call after the press conference had been logged and any follow-up actions had been listed.

Amy and Jordan had gone home, but Sean was still in his office. She knocked on the door and walked into the room.

'You should be at home, Eden,' he said, looking up quickly and then back to his screen.

'So should you. It's your weekend off.'

'There'll be others.' He looked at her again. 'Go and get some rest. I won't be far behind you. There's not a lot we can do until the morning.'

Eden didn't want to hear that. Not from him. It sounded defeatist. It must have shown on her face.

'We're doing all we can,' he said. 'But it's tough without any intelligence to go on. Usually by now we've had a ransom demand or a phone call asking for something to let us know what it's about. He seems only to want to speak to your sister.'

Eden sighed in frustration.

'Let's hope tomorrow brings more leads. My mobile will stay on. I'm here for you, if you need to chat about anything. I can't begin to imagine how you feel.'

She left quickly with the weight of the investigation on her shoulders.

When she arrived back at Laura's house, Casey was asleep in the armchair, a single quilt tucked around her. Eden didn't want to wake her – she'd had a traumatic day too – but it wasn't fair to leave her there. Besides, she needed to go home and grab a bit of sleep so that she could push on through the following day. It would be all hands on deck again until they found Jess. She nudged her gently.

'Mum.' Casey stirred. 'Have you found her?'

'Not yet,' said Eden. 'But we're working on it. Come on, let's get you home.'

In the hallway, she hugged Laura fiercely. 'I'll be back about six, unless I'm called out sooner. Are you sure you'll be okay? I can stay if you prefer.'

Laura shook her head.

'I'm only on the end of the phone if you need me.'

'Go and get some sleep. I know I won't be able to, but I need you alert tomorrow.'

'I'll be back soon, I promise.'

'And you'll let me know anything you find out the minute it comes through?'

Eden nodded. Casey gave Laura a hug before opening the front door.

As they walked outside, Laura reached for Eden's arm. 'If anything bad has happened to her, I only want to hear from you,' she whispered.

Eden swallowed. She had done plenty of death knocks in her time. Telling relatives bad news was always harrowing, no matter who it was or the circumstances. So it was a cruel thing to ask, but she respected Laura for it. And she would have it no other way.

'Always,' she told her.

She drove slowly through the streets, the wind howling around them, buffeting the car as it went along the main road. There was hardly a soul on the pavements, but still she kept her eyes peeled, looking for Jess. The rain was still lashing down, the wipers on full finding it hard to deal with. She and Casey had been quiet with their own thoughts until Eden pulled into the drive. Casey seemed wide awake now.

'Will Jess come home, Mum?' she asked as Eden pulled up the handbrake.

Eden switched off the engine and turned to her daughter. By the light of the street lamp, she could see tears glistening on Casey's cheek. She wiped at them gently with her thumb.

'I don't know, sweetheart,' she replied. 'I can't lie and say everything is going to be okay, because there are some nasty bastards out there. Until we hear from him again, and see if we can figure out where she is in the meantime, we won't know.'

'Why can't you find him?'

'We're doing our best to locate him. He doesn't have a criminal record, nor does it seem he is at a place of work, so it just takes longer.'

'How long?'

'I don't know that either.' She sat quiet for a moment. 'Casey, is there anything you can tell me about Jess that might be worth me knowing?'

Casey shook her head quickly.

'Not even about why you haven't seen too much of her lately?'

Casey and Jess had been really close as children. Spending a lot of time together as cousins, they had formed a bond that both her and Laura had thought would be unbreakable. But they had fallen out about something recently and no matter how much each mother had talked to them, tried to coerce them into making up, the girls hadn't bothered with each other. Eden and Laura often talked about it, wondering if they had rowed over some boy and hoping that once the troublesome teen years were behind them, they might become as close as they had been before.

'Jess changed when she started to go out with Cayden,' said Casey. 'It was like she became this big show-off, like she was untouchable. She said they were like Bonnie and Clyde – she was almost proud of the fact. I didn't want to be around her much after that.'

'Did you know about the phones?'

The look on Casey's face told Eden that she did.

'I wasn't involved, Mum! I swear. That's why I've been avoiding her. I was hoping she would see what a prick – sorry – Cayden is, but she didn't. She just adores him.'

The outside light came on and the front door opened. Joe stood on the step, his face sombre, but Eden almost smiled with relief at seeing it. How thoughtful of him to be waiting for her to come home.

'I didn't know what to do with myself,' he said. 'I hope you don't mind me coming over.'

Eden shook her head. 'Not at all.'

The wind blew them into the house and the kitchen door slammed, making them jump. Joe closed the front door and they went through to the living room.

'Would you like a mug of hot chocolate, Casey?' Eden asked.

Casey shook her head. 'I just want to go to bed. There might be news in the morning.'

Eden nodded. 'Let's hope so.'

Casey ran into her arms. 'I love you, Mum.'

Eden put her arms around her daughter and squeezed her tightly. 'I love you too. So very much.'

She kept in the tears until Casey had left the room and she'd heard her pad up the stairs. But when Joe wrapped his arms around her, she sank into his chest and finally let them fall freely. Rasping sobs escaped her as she fought to get her breath. It was all too much. She felt so disappointed.

'Where is she, Joe?' she asked over and over. 'Where is she?'

# SIXTY-ONE

Laura flopped down onto the settee. The news channel had covered Jess's story for most of the day, since her photo had first gone online. Now it was telling of the aftermath of Storm Monica as it had torn across the West Midlands, showing shocking images of the damage and despair it had left in its wake. Two people had died, killed by falling trees, and there was a man who had been walking his dog who had gone missing. Silly idiot, she thought. Why would you go out in those conditions, put your life in danger, unless you had to? He should be at home, safe with his family. She knew the pain that they would be going through.

It was close to midnight, and it had been nearly thirty hours since she had last seen her daughter. The longest time of her life. She was glad she had Sarah, and Eden, but she missed Neil. She didn't want to do this alone.

She sat quietly for a few moments before her eyes returned to the television. A photo of Jess flashed up on the screen and she gasped. Even with the storm raging, Jess was still headline news. The photo was her last one to be taken at school, at the beginning of the autumn term. Jess wore her hair down, a cheeky smile and her school uniform. A tear dripped from Laura's nose as she wondered where she was.

After the noise and commotion of the day, she was glad to sit in silence. But thoughts of Ashleigh Proctor soon infiltrated her mind. Why did her father think she could have done any more for Ashleigh? It wasn't her fault that she had died. She had tried her best. She had only been there to listen, to be someone to talk to. But then again, maybe she could have listened more. Guilt pulsed through her as she thought of the night in question.

At least they had a name for him now, although why he would give out his details was beyond her. They might be able to trace him quicker for sure, so it was good for Jess. Eden said they would find him soon. It was all she could think about. Josie Mellor and her friends had been fantastic today, and she was ashamed of breaking down in front of them and telling them all to leave. Her house had been full of people wanting to help. Everyone had been so generous with their time. Maxine had been out talking to people in the park, as well as making endless cups of tea, despite worrying about Katie. She had been a huge support to Laura. Maxine had far too much to think about with Katie and the trial to be thinking of her family too. Laura must thank her properly soon.

She glanced at the television again, the image of her daughter smiling back at her. She felt numb, sick, shocked, fearful all at the same time. She couldn't even cry any more.

Laura needed to rest too. She had a long day ahead of her and hoped it would be a good outcome. She wrapped her arms around herself. The police would find Jess. She wouldn't allow herself to think anything else.

Eden wouldn't let her down.

# SUNDAY

11 October 2015

# SIXTY-TWO

It was 6 a.m. Jason Proctor stared at the girl as she slept, the light of the small lamp next to her illuminating her face. Her head lolled to one side, but he didn't feel any guilt for making her sit in the chair. He wasn't going to take any chances that she would try and escape again. Not until he had done what he'd set out to do.

Her mother needed to know what she had done. She had taken Ashleigh away from him. She had no right to do that. She'd let her down. She wasn't doing her job properly. It was all her fault.

He groaned loudly. Who was he trying to kid? He'd tried to talk himself into this state of mind several times since Friday night, since he had taken the girl. But still it didn't sit right with him. He wondered if he should just let her go. Drive her to somewhere and dump her. But she would be able to identify him.

Maybe he should just do a runner. There wasn't anything here for him any more. No wife, no daughter, no beautiful home he'd cherished. Everything he held precious had gone within a matter of three years.

It was Ashleigh's sixteenth birthday tomorrow. He looked at the image of her on the wall. She had been three in the photo. Vanessa had insisted on taking them all to one of the photographers in the city to have a portrait done. He hadn't been keen at the time, but it was his most treasured possession now.

The three of them were lying on their stomachs, cradling their heads in their hands. Ashleigh's face was a riot of happiness, the biggest smile, and it was captured forever in that photo. Now all he had was the images he carried around in his head. He tried to remember the girl she had been rather than the one she had turned into. Lively, bubbly, smiley.

No, he had to go through with his plan. He needed to see the mother, tell her she'd taken away the only thing that had been precious to him. Made his life incomplete, not worth living. She had ruined everything. She hadn't given him time to make amends with Ashleigh. Until he'd read her diary, he had been sure it was grief that had made her do it, but it was more than that. Some of it had shamed him as it was about him, being drunk all the time, not there for her. He'd had no idea she'd been so unhappy and had been saddened that she hadn't been able to confide in him. But it was too late for that now.

The girl mumbled in her sleep, her head jerking as if she was having a dream. He stayed silent, hoping she wouldn't wake yet. He couldn't stand to see the fear in her eyes. He wondered what she thought he was going to do to her. Did she think he would abuse her?

Everything had escalated so quickly. He'd thought he'd be able to keep the girl, talk to the mother and then let her go. What had he been thinking? Actually, he hadn't been thinking at all.

He'd planned to ring her later today, but now that the police were involved, maybe he should think about bringing things forward. The less time for anyone to find them, the better. Despite all his panic, he had to speak to the girl's mother. Ashleigh would have wanted that. He wanted to make his daughter proud.

# SIXTY-THREE

Eden was up and dressed and going over things from the day before. She'd had an email from Sean to say he would be taking the team briefing to update everyone on what had come in overnight. It was good of him to give up all his weekend. Time spent with families was so precious.

Eden was well respected and knew that had gone a long way to people wanting to help her. Several officers had come in on their day off yesterday to help with the house-to-house enquiries. It was the simplest of tasks, and the most tiring and often frustrating, but putting tiny pieces of information together from snippets of conversation, an odd sighting of someone here, a weird coincidence there, often solved the case. Amy was right – something would trigger a reaction, a thought, and the police would have a lead. She hoped this would be the case today. She worked with some of the best people she had ever known.

Her mission for the day as a police officer was to find her niece alive and well and bring her home. She wouldn't stop thinking that. The alternative would be damaging to her state of mind. She had to believe in herself, in the people she worked with, in the general public. People wanted to help in situations like this.

The community spirit was phenomenal. The mums from SWAP were doing an incredible job. Josie Mellor had been putting her organisational and persuasive skills to great use, getting them all working together in some kind of order. Until they'd received the phone call from Proctor, Josie had been in the team asking the kids down at the park if they had seen anything and then relaying the information back to her. Amy had kept a spreadsheet and passed it on to her to action.

She pushed open Casey's door. Casey was asleep, the duvet tucked under her chin as she wrapped herself in it like a cocoon. Eden gazed at her daughter. Knowing she was safe and secure was a double-edged sword. She wanted to reach out, touch her, stroke her hair, her face, but she didn't want to wake her.

She didn't want to leave her either, but it was only for a while. Once she was up, Casey was going to Laura's. Joe would be here for her until then. Right now, Eden needed to be at work and Casey would respect that, despite her thoughts about Joe.

She went back into her own bedroom. She'd spent the night with Joe's body wrapped around hers, even though she hadn't had much sleep. Knowing that her niece was out there somewhere and not tucked up in her own bed, like Casey, hurt too much for her to switch off. She knew she would be better if she got some rest, able to work harder in the morning, but it had proved near impossible.

Joe yawned and she went to sit beside him on the bed.

'Sorry, was I restless?' she asked.

'Only to be expected.' A hand came out of the duvet, stretched into the air and then rested on her thigh. 'Are you leaving now?'

'Soon.' At that moment, Eden just wanted to climb under the covers with him and pretend everything was okay. Pretend that Jess was asleep in her bed, that she wasn't going to work to look into her kidnap. Pretend that she could love Joe as much as he loved her, like she knew he deserved.

He sat up and pulled her into his arms. 'I have every faith you will find her,' he said.

She squeezed her eyes tight. She needed to keep a level head, no matter how hard it would be.

He reached for her hand as she was leaving. 'I love you, Eden. Be careful.'

She smiled to acknowledge his sentiment, but she didn't say anything. Joe was a dependable man, but she didn't know if she wanted to settle down with him. She'd thought she'd be with Danny for ever. She had felt safe with him until he'd walked out.

She hadn't told him she loved him yet because she wasn't sure she did. And right now, she just wanted to get her niece back.

# SIXTY-FOUR

Maxine arrived at Ashcroft House just after 8.30 a.m. As she went through the usual routine before she could visit, she wondered if Katie would have heard about Jess and if she hadn't, whether she should tell her. Katie had enough to contend with this weekend, thinking about tomorrow. She must be worried stiff about what was to come. She'd lost so much weight these past few weeks.

But as soon as she saw her, Katie ran into her arms.

'What's happened to Jess, Mum?' she said, teary eyed. 'Do the police know who has her?'

'Yes, but they don't know where she is yet.' Maxine hugged her tightly. She marvelled at how good it was to feel her daughter's arms around her. 'I'm sure Eden will do her best to bring her home.'

A look of shock crossed Katie's face. 'I thought the police would have somewhere surrounded and be working on getting her free. She can't be that far away, can she?'

'I don't know,' Maxine replied truthfully. They sat silent with their thoughts for a moment. It was strange talking about Jess. It hadn't been something anyone could have anticipated. But she also needed to talk to Katie about the trial starting in the morning.

'I hope you're not too nervous about going to court.'

'I'm petrified. I'll have to see Nathan and Tom and Craig again, and I don't want to do that. I hate Nathan Lucas.'

'I know it will be tough, but just think about what might happen by the end of it.'

Katie burst into tears. 'I don't want to go to prison,' she sobbed.

Maxine held on to her again. 'I know, I know,' she soothed.

Katie gazed at her, tears in her eyes. 'Mum, I did something terrible.'

'What do you mean?' Maxine went cold.

'I've been wanting to tell you for ages, but I just couldn't find the right words.' She swallowed. 'Me and Jess were stealing mobile phones.'

'What?'

'We were getting twenty pounds each for them. That's why I was going out with Nathan. We were stealing phones, and he was giving us money for them.'

'Oh, Katie,' said Maxine, furious that she'd always thought her daughter was one of the better girls. But if it was peer pressure and done only the once or twice. . .

'How many times did you do it?' she asked.

'I lost count, but it was lots.'

'But why? You've never gone short. Haven't we always given you everything we could afford?'

'It wasn't like that. And that's not the worst of it.' Katie looked shamefaced. 'Cayden, Jess's boyfriend, stole this one phone. Sometimes we'd have a look through the photos before we sold them on. This phone had photos of a girl.' Her skin began to turn red. 'She was really pretty but she was so thin. She'd taken photos of herself in her undies.'

Maxine could imagine where this was heading as she tried to keep her temper. This wasn't what she had been expecting today at all.

'Cayden kept looking at them, showing them to all the boys. Jess got really jealous so she shared the photos. The girl got a lot of stick for it on Facebook. Everyone was laughing at them and making horrible comments.'

'Did you know the girl?' asked Maxine.

Katie shook her head and burst into tears again. 'But I read online that she died. I saw a photo of her on the *Stockleigh News* website. It said she committed suicide.'

Katie looked at her with so much self-loathing that Maxine fought the urge to hug her again.

'It was because of those photos that she killed herself, wasn't it?' she said. 'I didn't want Jess to share them. She can be so cruel at times. I should have stopped her. I think that girl would still be alive today.'

'You don't know that,' said Maxine, 'but it wasn't a very nice thing for Jess to do. She's probably breaking the law too. You can't just post photos of people without their consent.'

'But don't you see, that's why the judge can't acquit me. I've been sent here for payback because of those photos and that girl dying. I've been involved in the deaths of *two* people.'

'Only indirectly.' Maxine shook her head. 'You were easily led, especially over the phones. I thought we'd brought you up better than that.'

'You have! And now I'm never getting out of here, am I?' she sobbed. 'I deserve to be locked up here for ever for what I did, but I don't want to be. I want to come home.'

Once the visit was over, Maxine went back to her car. The tears that she'd held in fell fast and furious. She sat in the driver's seat, waiting for her temper to subside. Banging her fists on the steering wheel, she screamed. It didn't release much tension, but it made her feel better.

Why had this happened to her daughter? She'd thought Katie wouldn't do anyone any harm. Before she had been locked up, Maxine had thought she was just timid, but now it seemed she had been easily led. Maxine had always thought that Jess was a good influence on Katie, bringing her out of her shell, but now she was beginning to think that if the two of them hadn't become close friends then maybe it would be Jess who was in the secure unit and Katie would be home with her. She'd thought about it several times since the murder. What would have happened if they'd both been there?

Then she admonished herself. She wished she could stop thinking that! What an awful thing, especially when Jess was still missing. Still, she would keep what Katie had told her to herself. It wouldn't do any good if anyone was to know anyway. She would always protect her daughter.

# SIXTY-FIVE

Eden was back at her desk after the early morning team brief. Sean had tasked her and her team with several jobs, the first of which was for her to go over to Laura's with Amy to set up the volunteers who wanted to help look for Jess.

Her mobile rang. It was Josie Mellor.

'Josie! Thank you so much for giving up your Saturday,' she said before letting her speak. 'It was very kind of you, and your organisational skills came in really handy. I owe you a curry when this is over.' She stopped, wondering if this would ever be over. Her stomach flipped as she thought of the one outcome that she was dreading. 'How—'

'Never mind curry, Eden, I have an address for Jason Proctor.'

'What?' Eden shot out of her chair, her face draining of colour as she stood up.

'Look, I'm not supposed to do this, so you haven't heard it from me. I couldn't sleep last night knowing I could access the information you might need. So I went in to the office this morning to look on our system. I know if I'm checked they can tell it was me that logged on, but I'll sort that out as and when. I'll just say I got an email from your intelligence unit and wanted to help out. He's registered on the electoral roll at number twenty-two Shaftesbury Avenue. It's from last year so I'm not sure how relevant it will be. It's only two streets away from me, here in Warbury.'

Eden waved her hand to get Sean's attention. Several officers had already stopped what they were doing to listen in. Jordan was watching her intently.

Suddenly the door burst open and Amy came running up the corridor towards them.

'I've just had a call from Intel. Ashleigh Proctor's phone records have come through,' she cried as Eden disconnected the call. 'I have an address.'

They both spoke together. 'Number twenty-two Shaftesbury Avenue.'

'I'll radio through to the control room,' said Jordan, as Sean came rushing from his room, shrugging on his coat.

'We have an address,' Eden told him breathlessly, grabbing her parka.

'Stay close to me,' he told her. 'Jordan, Amy – you two take another car and meet us there.'

They ran downstairs and out into the car park. Seconds later, they were racing down the A road, sirens flashing. Shaftesbury Avenue was in the north of the city and part of a patch that Eden had covered with Sean years ago, so they both knew the area well. It was in an affluent area of Stockleigh, consisting mostly of large houses that would look good in any country magazine.

Eden fought back tears, hoping to hide her emotions, and wondered if Jess was there and what state of mind she would be in.

'If that bastard has harmed her in any way. . .' She took a deep breath, trying to remain calm.

'He must have used force to get her into the house.'

She knew Sean was trying to prepare her just in case. 'Other than that he must have drugged her,' she replied.

Voices came over the radio. 'Uniform are at the house, DI Whittaker.'

'Received,' said Sean.

When they rounded the corner into Shaftesbury Avenue, there was already a marked police car parked horizontally across the street, two more in front of it, lights flashing, blocking off access.

Above her, Eden could see an ambulance. 'No.'

Sean parked and reached for the door handle. 'I know I should have left you back at the station. You need to stay here until I find out what's happening.'

Eden nodded and sat on her hands to stop them from reaching for the door handle. Grateful to him for allowing her to come along, she didn't want to let him down.

'Please let her be okay,' she whispered.

She watched Sean go into the house and come back out moments later. But she couldn't see Jess. Where was she?

She couldn't stay there any longer. Getting out of the car, she ran up the pavement, past the rows of detached houses, family cars and well-kept gardens. Sean was walking back towards her.

'Where is she?' she shouted.

People turned to look, but she didn't care – and she didn't stop running. The front door to the property was open, but everyone seemed to be coming out. Still she couldn't see Jess.

'Where *is* she?' As he drew level with her, she tried to get past him, but he blocked her way.

'She isn't here,' he said.

Eden couldn't contemplate that. She had been so sure on the ride over that she would find her niece, unharmed, and she would take her home. Now all her hopes had been dashed.

'What do you mean? She must be!'

'The house belongs to Mr and Mrs Malcolm. They moved in three months ago. It was repossessed from Jason Proctor. They must have bought it shortly after his daughter died.'

'But why didn't they get in touch with us and tell us that he used to live here? We've wasted valuable time.' Eden glanced at the house again, still expecting to see her niece. 'And Jess's face was everywhere on the television.'

'They've been staying with family in Australia for the past month. The plane didn't touch down until late last night and they went straight to bed. When we woke them up asking for Jason Proctor, it was the first they had heard about it.'

'And you believe them?' Eden pressed. 'They could be involved in this. They could—'

'You know all this is easy to check out.' Sean stopped her. 'They have suitcases standing up in the hallway, luggage tags on them and flight stickers around the handles. They got in at midnight and went straight to bed.'

'So we're no further forward than yesterday?' Her tone sounded accusatory but Sean didn't respond. It was then she noticed the media vans pulling up, the cameraman filming their every move. 'Oh, no.' She pointed to them in exasperation.

They went inside the house. A young woman wearing pyjamas and a dressing gown was rifling through a box of paperwork. Eden sank into the settee. Sean sat down next to her.

'Do they know where he moved to?' she asked.

Sean shook her head. 'He didn't leave a forwarding address.'

'I think he rented a property from a firm called Properties Direct,' said the woman, who continued looking through the box. 'I remember a letter coming here for him after he had moved out.'

'Thanks. We'll look into it,' said Sean.

Eden glanced at the television screen to see Jess's image. Then she saw the house, and a few officers entering the property, including herself. The yellow tape below was showing breaking news that there may be a lead on the missing girl. She couldn't begin to imagine how Laura would feel once she told her the lead had led to nothing.

Out of the window, she could see more news reporters. She jumped to her feet. 'I have to go and see my sister.'

'Would you like me to come with you?'

Eden looked at Sean with a pained expression. 'I can't go home without her. I can't go back to the house and face the neighbours, see her empty bed. What happens if we don't ever find her? Or if we find her but she's dead and we didn't do enough to save her? What do I—'

'Eden, this is not your fault.' He placed a hand on her arm. 'Go back to the station and get your car. You need to be with your sister.'

# SIXTY-SIX

Last night, Laura had insisted that Sarah go to bed when Brad had left just after midnight, but she herself had stayed downstairs. She'd lain on the settee, the house phone and her mobile next to her, waiting for another call. She wasn't sure she'd had more than an hour's sleep. She had dozed because her body had made her, but she didn't want to rest. Every time she closed her eyes, she would see images of Jess. Lying beaten, bound and gagged on the floor of a disused warehouse. At the bottom of a ditch covered in leaves and detritus. Eyes dead. Body hurt. Soul gone.

It was past 9 a.m. Eden said he would call again and that they would have to wait. He'd want to let them know what his intentions were, what he was going to do next. Now she pushed open the door to Jess's bedroom, feeling the need to be close to her daughter.

It was exactly as she had left it. No one had touched anything since Eden had searched it. She sniffed, smelling her daughter's deodorant in the air. Just the lingering tang made her eyes brim with tears. Jess was into her perfumes and make-up the same as most teenagers. It was something to make them stand out from each other rather than end up looking like clones.

She opened the wardrobe, ran a hand over the clothes. Why hadn't she noticed a few new ones creeping in? Jess had told her they were from some cheap high street shops in Stockleigh where everything was marked as five pounds, and she had believed her. Why wouldn't she? Even seeing the labels on them now, why would she have doubted her? There had been no reason to until she had found out from Eden what had been going on with the mobile phones.

When Jess came back – because she had to believe she would come back – she would make sure there were no secrets between them. She wouldn't give her the benefit of the doubt for a long time.

She sat down on the bed, reaching for Jess's pyjamas and holding them against her face. Her smell was there too, fresh and clean. She gulped.

'Where are you, Jess?' she whispered.

'Mum?'

Laura looked up to see Sarah. Her eyes were swollen, her cheeks blotchy and her hair, although brushed, hadn't been straightened to its usual perfection. She patted the bed and Sarah sat down beside her. Laura drew her into her arms.

'I didn't sleep much,' Sarah said, 'but I didn't want to get up either. How are you?'

'Numb, I guess.' Laura gave a half smile.

'Everything seems strange without Jess here.' Sarah's thoughts echoed her mum's. 'Where is she, Mum? Do you think she'll be okay with that man?'

'I hope so.' Laura tried not to look at the photo on the noticeboard by the side of the wardrobe. It was of the three of them on holiday last year in Spain. Happy, smiling faces. Arms around each other.

'Do you know why he took her? It can't be because you spoke to this Ashleigh on the phone and he says you let her down.'

'You mean did I do anything wrong?' Laura bristled. 'Anything to antagonise him?'

'No, I didn't mean that at all!' Sarah looked at her in disapproval. 'I was just wondering if you could maybe think back to when you last spoke to Ashleigh. Did she mention anything that could give you a clue about why her dad has done this to Jess?'

'I've been doing that for most of the night.' Laura gnawed at her bottom lip. 'Ashleigh was a mixed-up child. Her mum died when she was thirteen, and neither she nor her dad came to terms with it, I don't think. I guess they couldn't cope without her and instead of coming together they grew more and more apart, unable to connect.'

'Did she tell you all that?' Sarah raised her eyebrows in incredulity.

'In a roundabout way, yes.' Laura nodded.

'Then you are definitely in the right job, Mum.'

Despite herself, Laura felt proud to hear her daughter say that. But at the same time, she disagreed.

'If I was in the right job, she wouldn't have died,' she said.

'You can't know that.'

'Perhaps not, but I will always think it. Ashleigh was hurting. She couldn't get any support from her dad, so she was unable to speak to anyone but me. And I'm only there to listen, really.'

'Didn't she ever talk to Nicola, or Marian?'

'No, but that's not unusual. That's what most of the teens do. They see us as support figures, someone who they don't know so they can talk freely without judgement. Ashleigh latched on to me. Maybe if I had listened to her more during that last call, shown more sympathy. . . I don't know.'

Sarah shook her head fervently. 'You don't know if she killed herself right after a call to you. It could have been after a row with her dad. Maybe *he* tipped her over the edge.'

Laura wasn't so certain about that, and it still wouldn't stop her from feeling guilty. 'Either way, it's such a shame that a teenager felt the need to take her own life. In this day and age we should be able to refer them to other organisations.'

'Why don't you do that?' Sarah's brow furrowed. 'I never understood why.'

'Because to the caller it might seem like you're passing the buck. Like you don't want to listen to them so you're trying to get rid of them.'

'But that's ridiculous!'

'It is, I suppose,' Laura agreed. 'But my job is to listen to them.'

'And you do it so well. So don't go beating yourself up that any of this is your fault,' Sarah added. 'It isn't. It's just that sick bastard who has our Jess. He's the psycho.'

But Laura had stopped listening as her phone began to ring. It was Cayden's mum, Andrea. As she listened, she stood up quickly. 'There's breaking news on the television,' she relayed to Sarah. 'The police have a house surrounded.'

Sarah reached for the remote control to Jess's small TV and switched on a news channel.

Laura gasped as images came up of a house in a suburban street, police cars blocking it off, lights flashing. She looked closer: was it in Stockleigh? She read the ticker tape beneath the images.

*Lead in hunt for missing schoolgirl Jessica Mountford.*

'Have they found her, Mum?' Sarah asked, eyes wide with excitement. She pointed to the screen 'There's Eden!'

'I'm not sure.' Laura reached for her phone. 'Eden would have told us if they had.'

# SIXTY-SEVEN

Jess sat in the middle of the room. The curtains were drawn, but she knew it was light outside. The clock on the back wall said it was nearing 9.30 a.m. The television was showing Sky News, but the sound was muted. Amongst the shadows, she could see him lying sleeping in the armchair. His loud snores had kept her awake most of the night, but now they were gentle. She knew he would wake soon, so she kept still in the chair. She didn't want another day to start.

She tried to swallow behind the tape. She'd been sitting in the chair for near on twenty-four hours. He'd let her off to go to the toilet, only removing the tape from her hands long enough for her to do what she had to and then replacing it with some more. She'd had to leave the toilet door ajar so he could hear what she was up to. It meant he could hear her pee too. She had been so embarrassed.

As soon as she'd finished, he'd made her go back to sit in the chair. Her bottom was stiff, but she hadn't complained. She'd wanted him to think she was complying. Because when she got the chance, she was going to grab for the knife under the cushion and try to escape again. He would slip up. She would never give up.

She just wanted to go home. She wanted her mum, because she needed to hear what she had to say about Ashleigh. Her mum had always been there for her, so she didn't believe what he was saying.

She remembered when she had broken her arm when she was seven and how Mum had looked after her then. She remembered how she had held her hand when she'd had a tooth removed after having a painful abscess. She remembered the times she had sat with her and Sarah on the sofa, snuggled up together to watch a video.

If her mum found out that she had been stealing mobile phones to make some cash, she would be so disappointed. Her mum hadn't brought her up to do that type of thing, she would say. She knew she'd say that her dad would have been disappointed too. That would sting the most.

Jess was eight when he had been killed in a car accident, and her mum had brought them up single-handedly, but they had never gone short of love and affection.

She looked at him again. No matter what he said, it wasn't all down to her mum. He was at fault too. He should have listened. Her mum hadn't gone to pieces when her dad had died.

When she got out of here she would give her mum and sister the biggest hugs ever. Even though they argued, it was only because they were so close. Sarah had always been there for her too. Her sister and her mum could get her through anything, and she needed to be more appreciative.

A flash of red and blue caught her eye. A breaking news sign was showing on the television and a house came into view, surrounded by police cars. There were police officers going in and out of the property. As the camera zoomed in, Jess spotted Eden among them. She groaned loudly. The ticker tape was saying they had a lead on the missing girl. That was her!

But they were at the wrong house.

Her groan woke Jason. He followed her eyes to the television screen. Sitting up quickly, he reached for the remote control and switched up the sound.

'Mmmm!' A tear escaped and trickled down her cheek.

'Fuck! This wasn't supposed to happen.' He turned to her. 'I only wanted to speak to your mother. Now it's all going wrong. It's escalating into something horrific.'

Jess sat, eyes wide, groaning every now and then.

Jason took Jess's phone out of his pocket and switched it on again. He glanced at her, pain in his eyes.

'If your mum had done her job properly, none of this would have happened.'

Then he began to type out a message.

# SIXTY-EIGHT

Eden had collected Amy, as well as her car, and was on her way back to her sister's house when her phone rang.

'Shit. It's Laura,' said Eden, glancing at the screen lighting up in the holder on the dashboard. 'I can't answer this. I need to speak to her in person. I'll switch it to silent until she disconnects.'

Laura tried her twice more before she arrived outside the house a few minutes later. Eden threw off her seat belt and raced in.

'Where is she?' said Laura, disappointment clear in her expression.

'She wasn't there,' Eden explained. 'It was his previous address.'

'So they must have a forwarding address! Why aren't you going there?'

'There's nothing. He didn't leave one.' Eden didn't tell her they had a lead to look into. She wouldn't tell any other member of the public for fear of escalating hope, so she wouldn't tell Laura for the same reasons.

'You can't find her, can you?' Laura gave Eden such a sharp look she almost gasped.

'We're doing our best,' she started.

'Your best isn't good enough! I can't—'

Eden's phone alerted her to an incoming message. At the same time, Laura's phone went off too.

Eden read the message.

*Help me. 17 Lewistock Lane. He's locked me up. I can't get away.*

'Jess!' cried Laura.

Before she could respond, Eden heard footsteps thundering down the stairs.

'I have a message from Jess,' said Sarah, running into the room. 'It says she's at seventeen Lewistock Lane! That's not far from here!'

'Me too,' cried Laura. 'This means she's alive, doesn't it, Eden?'

Eden held up her hand. She wouldn't confirm that. It was too soon. For all they knew, Jess might not have sent the message.

Laura's phone rang. 'Yes, we've had the same message. We're on to it, thanks. I'm putting the phone down. Yes, speak soon.' She looked at Eden. 'That was Rachel Goodwin, Stacey's mum.'

Laura's phone went again. It was from another of Jess's friends.

'She must have sent the message to everyone on her contacts list,' Laura said after she had spoken to her.

'No, that's the last thing we need!' Eden looked at Amy, who was radioing in the details. She rang Sean to update him and then turned to Laura as she finished another phone call.

'We need to go,' she said, heading for the door. 'I'll be in touch as soon as I know anything.'

'I'm not staying here.' Laura was behind her. She tried to push past Eden.

'We can't put your life in danger too.' Eden held her back. 'For all we know we could be walking into a trap.'

'You can't tell me what to do. She's MY daughter!'

'Mum.' Sarah touched her gently on the arm. 'Let them do their job. Eden will find her.'

'Like she did this morning?' Laura snapped. 'You went to the wrong house!'

'We were following a valid lead!'

Laura's phone rang again. 'It's Cayden,' she said, answering it. 'Yes, we know. The police are on their way. No! You stay away, do you hear?'

Eden didn't stop to hear any more of the conversation. If Cayden was going to the address, he could mess things up. She was out of the street within a minute and on her way to Lewistock Lane.

# SIXTY-NINE

As Eden left the house, Laura's phone rang. It was from an unknown number.

'Hello?'

'Do not alert anyone to the fact that I've rung you. Do you hear me? Anyone.'

Laura gasped. It was him again. Jason Proctor.

Sarah was on her phone talking to someone about the text message she'd received. Laura went into the living room and closed the door quietly.

'What do you want?' Her voice came out sharper than she had intended. 'Is Jess okay?'

'She's fine. I'm just letting you know that she isn't at Lewistock Lane.'

'What?' A strangled sob escaped Laura. 'You bastard! Where is she?'

'Don't worry – she's with me.'

'I want to speak to her!'

'You don't get to say what happens.'

Goosebumps prickled all over her skin.

'You need to come and get her. But you don't tell anyone you're coming. You certainly don't tell that sister of yours.'

'I—' Her mind went blank as she thought about what he might do if she didn't go right now. 'Please don't hurt her,' Laura whispered.

'You're wasting precious time.'

'Where is she?'

'Number 269 Davy Road. It's on the Mitchell Estate. You have fifteen minutes.'

The phone went dead.

'Who was that?' asked Sarah as she came into the room.

'Someone else she's sent a message to.' Laura wiped at her eyes. 'I feel so helpless here.'

'Me too, but you heard Eden. They don't want you turning up and distressing Jess, or making things worse for him. If he reacts when he sees you, things could go very wrong.'

'But—' Laura protested.

'Eden can't be worrying about you while she's looking out for Jess.'

'But she's my daughter and I need to be—'

'And she's my sister! I'm frightened too.'

'I'm sorry.' Laura sat down quickly. 'I didn't think.'

'It's okay.' Sarah sat down beside her. 'I know you've always had enough love for two of us.'

Laura's heart almost broke. Sarah was trying to make her feel better, but all she felt was dishonest. She needed to get out of the house as quickly as possible. The clock was ticking. What could she do?

She put a hand to her forehead. 'I feel quite faint.'

'You do look pale.' Sarah moved towards her. 'Put your head between your knees.'

Laura did as she was told.

'Would you like a glass of water?'

'Yes, please.'

'Stay right there.' Sarah rushed out of the room.

As soon as she heard the water running from the tap in the kitchen, Laura sat up. She picked up her car keys and ran outside.

'Mum?' Sarah shouted after her. 'Mum!'

But Laura was already in the car with the engine started. As she saw Sarah running out of the house towards her, she put her foot down. She felt so deceitful, but she had to go to Jess.

# SEVENTY

Laura drove to Davy Road, all the time trying to think everything through, wondering why he wanted to see her. He hadn't suggested she brought money, so Jess wasn't being held for ransom. Her head said she needed to tell Eden, as she would know what to do. Her heart told her to tell no one where she was going, because she might put Jess in danger. Her sister would be mad at her, but she couldn't think about that now. He'd told her to come alone. He'd told her not to inform the police. She didn't care how much danger or trouble she would be in. She couldn't leave Jess with that man a minute longer.

As she tore down the road faster than she should, her mind went into overdrive at the possible danger she could be going into. It might be a trap. For all she knew, there could be more than one man there. Maybe this was nothing to do with Ashleigh Proctor at all. Maybe she had stumbled upon a gang who had been getting away with kidnapping young girls until they abducted one with a cop for an aunt. Maybe she was going to be beaten and attacked when she got there too.

She gulped down a sob. It could be that none of that was true, but she still expected the worst. He must want her to come and get Jess for some reason, especially without the police knowing. If Laura was walking into danger, maybe she could persuade him to let Jess go and take her instead.

She checked the clock. Five minutes to go.

Laura had never visited anyone in Davy Road before, but she knew where it was. Although the Mitchell Estate had a notorious reputation, they had an enterprise centre, The Workshop, that had been set up five years ago. It provided all kinds of training courses, and she had completed an extra counselling course there the year before last. Knowing a few of the estate mums through SWAPs, and having met some of the girls from the estate, who Jess had brought home on occasion, she really didn't think it was as bad as people made out.

She parked across the way from number 269. The street was quiet, perhaps due to the weather. It had been blustery for near on forty-eight hours now, but the rain had died down a little. The house was semi-detached with an adjoining garage. It was a little scruffier, with overgrown hedges, but otherwise it was indistinguishable from any one of many she could see.

She looked at the front window downstairs and swallowed. The curtains were closed. Was Jess in there? Or was she upstairs? Or even worse, was she locked up in a shed or a cellar? Her breathing escalated. She'd better not think about what she was about to do too much or else she wouldn't go through with it.

Instead she flicked on her phone. The screen came up with the image of Sarah and Jess. Her heart went out to her youngest daughter as she ran a finger over Jess's face. 'I won't let you down,' she whispered, swiping the phone to wake it up.

Quickly she typed out a message. Her finger hovered over the send button. Eden was going to be so mad at her. But she wasn't stupid. She couldn't go into the property without letting someone know where she was.

Without another second's hesitation, she pressed send.

As soon as she saw that the message had gone, she deleted it and switched the phone off. She pushed it into the pocket of her jeans, took a deep breath and opened the car door. A man and woman ahead of her were getting into a car. She waited for them to drive off before crossing the road.

She might get a caution from the police for withholding vital information, but she had to do what Jason said. Getting Jess back was her main priority. They could lock her up later, but no one was keeping her from going after her daughter.

# SEVENTY-ONE

Eden drove in the direction of Lewistock Lane. 'Tell uniform to meet us there,' she cried over Amy's voice as she updated the control room.

Eden's phone rang.

'It's Sarah,' said Amy.

'Answer it and put it on loudspeaker for me.'

'Eden?'

'What's wrong?' Eden could hear the panic in her voice.

'It's Mum – she's gone. I think she's coming after you.'

'What?'

'She said she felt faint so I went to fetch her some water, and when I left the room she ran out of the house and drove off in the car. I tried to stop her, but she was too quick.'

Eden banged a palm on the steering wheel. 'Okay, Sarah.' Eden changed her voice to a tone of reassurance. 'Stay where you are and wait for any calls to come in. If your mum comes home, be sure to let me know?'

'O-Okay.'

Amy disconnected the call and Eden put her foot down. They were only minutes from Lewistock Lane now. If she was first on scene, she wasn't hanging around this time, despite the trouble she would be in.

A minute later, her phone went again. This time it was a message.

*I'm sorry but he asked me to come alone. He's at 269 Davy Road. He says he has Jess there and that there should be no police. I'm outside now. You must only be fifteen minutes behind me.*

'No, no, no!' Eden indicated and pulled in to the kerb. She rang her sister's phone to find it switched off. She handed hers to Amy and pulled out into the traffic again. 'Read the message. I know where she is. Call it in.'

'Shit.' Amy was on the radio before she sped off. 'All units – urgent assistance required. Suspect in the case of missing Jessica Mountford is at 269 Davy Road, on the Mitchell Estate. I repeat 269 Davy Road. Anyone in the vicinity please respond.' She glanced at Eden. 'Are you sure you believe this message? He could already have Laura there and be sending it from her phone, like he did with Jess.'

'It could be another wild goose chase, but I can't chance it. Ring Sean and put him on loudspeaker for me,' she barked. 'Please.'

'I'm not prepared to call them off until I know she isn't there,' he told them. 'We've already had one false lead this morning. I have to make sure this is false too. But officers are on their way to Davy Road. If you get there before they do, don't go in.'

'Try Laura again,' Eden told Amy once he was off the line. 'Tell her to stay away!'

She took a corner a little too fast and slowed down slightly. She needed to get them both there in one piece. They were on the main road that would take them to the Mitchell Estate. A row of terraced houses flashed past either side, one parked car after another, but the road was wide enough for two cars to pass. Still drivers didn't seem to move quickly enough. She waved her hand in front of the steering wheel when a bus indicated to pull out a good way in front of her.

'Get out of my way!' Eden yelled.

'There's still no reply,' Amy said seconds later.

'I told her to stay put! I'm trained to deal with shits like him, not Laura. She doesn't have a hard bone in her body.'

'You'll be surprised how strong she'll be when it comes to one of her girls.'

Eden glanced at her. Amy was right. Of course Laura would be strong. If it were Casey, Eden would be doing exactly the same as her sister.

In the passenger seat, Amy relayed details to and from the control room. Eden felt lucky to have her. Even in a moment of stress Amy was thinking on her feet. Eden would be buying several packets of Jaffa Cakes once they were back in the office.

But first she was bringing her niece home. She wouldn't let that bastard win.

It would take them about two minutes to get to the Mitchell Estate from where they were now. Proctor had played them well. Most of the team were at the other end of the city. Everyone else would be heading the other way.

She couldn't help thinking that he would have realised that too. Her sister could have walked into a trap. She pressed her foot to the pedal a little more. She needed to get there in time to talk him down or he could take another member of her family hostage.

Amy's phone rang and she took a call from Jordan. 'It's been confirmed, Sarge,' she said afterwards. 'The owner of Properties Direct has just got back with the same address for J Proctor: 269 Davy Road on the Mitchell Estate. He's been there for a few weeks now, waiting for a claim for housing benefits to go through. It doesn't look like he's found work again.'

Eden banged a hand on the steering wheel. 'If he's hurt either of them, I'll rip every hair from his balls, one by one. I'll make him pay in ways he never knew existed. I'll— What?'

Amy had put a hand on her arm. 'Let's get there in one piece, Sarge.'

Eden threw her a look, but she didn't slow down. 'I just want to see they're all right.'

'But you heard the DI. We need to wait for backup if we do get there before anyone else. If he's holding them both then it's a hostage situation and there'll have to be a trained negotiator called.'

'Stuff that.' Eden floored the pedal this time. 'I'll do my own negotiating with my baton if I have to. I'm not waiting to see if my family is safe.'

# SEVENTY-TWO

Laura looked up and down Davy Road, houses either way for as far as her eye could see. It was 10.30 a.m. Most curtains were open but a few were still closed. Everyone would be going about their morning weekend routine, unaware of the drama unfolding nearby.

She wondered what they'd all think when this was over and they heard the news that everything had happened on their doorstep. Whether Jess was here or not, pretty soon the place would be swarming with police and press. This was one Sunday that wasn't going to be a quiet one for the neighbours.

Urging one foot in front of the other, she walked down the path of 269. She pressed through the fear when she saw the door was open slightly. But Jess was in there with that – that man, and she had to stay calm, despite her rising anxiety.

She pushed the door open and gingerly stepped inside.

'Hello?'

She heard a loud groan. Knowing it was Jess propelled her through the door. She entered a hallway, wallpaper peeling down in the nearest corner, carpet threadbare beneath her feet. She took another step forward.

The door slammed shut behind her. She gasped as she was grabbed around the neck.

'Don't say a word.'

It was a man's voice. The same one she had heard on the telephone. Her hands went to his arm, but he held on to her.

Ahead she could see a small kitchen. Adrenaline pumped through her as she grappled with him, but his grip didn't lessen. Then she felt the tip of a knife pushed against her stomach. She gasped again and it came out as a strangled sob.

'Please don't hurt me,' she whispered.

He said nothing but urged her forward. They inched along the narrow hallway as if they were slow dancing. A door came up on her right and he pushed her through it. Still he kept his grip on her tight.

A television appeared in her view first, its sound muted. Her daughter's face was freeze-framed on the screen. She saw an armchair, then she caught a glimpse of Jess's feet – and then her daughter.

'Jess!'

She was sitting on a chair in the middle of the room, her hands behind her back. She had tape across her mouth and wound around each shin and wrist, keeping her bound to the chair.

Jess groaned loudly when she saw her. Her eyes reflected the fright in Laura's own, tears escaping. Laura skimmed quickly over her. Jess didn't seem hurt, apart from a bruised face, and both eyes looked sore from crying. Thankfully, her clothes were still intact.

Laura could see Jess's panic building as she thrashed about in the chair. She stared at her, urging her to stay calm. Hopelessness washed over her. She wanted to help her child so much, and she couldn't do a thing. One false move and he could thrust the knife into her stomach, and who knows what would happen to Jess then.

'I know you'll have told that sister of yours my address.' He spoke in her ear, making her jump. His breath smelled of stale ale. 'That's why I sent a text message from your girl's phone to say she was in Lewistock Lane. It gives me enough time to do what I have to before the police arrive.'

Laura swallowed. The last thing she needed was for Jess to jerk around in the chair and fall over. Any reaction would startle him, and he might just respond rashly.

'You let her down, didn't you?' said Jason.

Laura tried to see him from the corner of her eye, but all she got was a glimpse of his hair. 'Please don't blame my daughter for something I did,' she said.

'I lost *my* daughter because of you!'

He screeched so loud that she scrunched up her eyes fleetingly. She could almost feel the anger seeping out of him. Laura hoped she could keep him calm by talking to him. It was up to her until the police arrived. Maybe she could talk him down and get them both out of the situation.

'What do you want with us?' she asked, her voice croaky from the pressure of his arm around her throat.

'I want to know what Ashleigh was like when you spoke to her.'

It took Laura by surprise. 'What do you mean?'

'Was she happy or was she sad?'

'She was happy sometimes and sad others,' she told him truthfully. 'She was a lovely girl to talk to when she was in a good mood. She used to talk about you and her mum, and her memories of growing up. I could tell that she loved you very much.'

'I loved her too.' Jason's voice held a slight tremble. 'But I couldn't help her.'

'You were always there for her,' said Laura. 'She told me lots of times.' It was a white lie, but it was needed. 'She was obviously a bright girl and was trying to cope on her own. It got too much, even with talking to an independent person.'

'So why didn't you get her any help?'

'My job was to listen. I was there for Ashleigh, someone she could talk to whenever she felt low.'

'But you didn't help her, did you, because she killed herself.'

'I tried to help!' she insisted.

'No.' He shook his head. 'You took my child away from me. She was my life, my hope, my future. That's why I took your daughter, so that you could feel the same pain as me. After losing Vanessa—'

There was a thud outside. It sounded like a car door. Jason dragged her to the window and peered around the side of the curtain. There were no police cars in sight and her heart sank. But just before he dropped the curtain, she spotted a black and white chequered roof. It looked like Eden's Mini.

Jason pushed Laura onto the settee and pulled the duct tape out from under the cushion. 'Put out your hands,' he told her, holding the knife out towards her.

She held them out and he wrapped the tape around twice, pulling sharply to rip the end with his teeth. He glared at her before moving away. 'Now sit there and don't move. You and I are going to talk. And you are going to listen to what I have to say.'

# SEVENTY-THREE

'Was Vanessa the name of Ashleigh's mum?' Laura asked as the room fell silent.

Jason nodded curtly. 'She died of cancer. That was when everything started to fall apart. I couldn't cope with Ashleigh. I was working full-time – what did I know about raising a child, a girl? But we got by – we survived. Until she started to starve herself. It was a while before I read up on anorexia and tried to get her some help. Vanessa would have known what to do – but me? I was clueless.'

'Ashleigh said you were very supportive.' Laura realised a few more white lies wouldn't go amiss.

'I tried to make her eat, but she wouldn't. She said it was the only way she had control of anything. I would make her all her favourite meals, but she would either play with the food, making it look as if she had eaten something when I hadn't seen anything go past her lips, or she would eat it all and then I'd have to try and keep her out of the bathroom.

'I loved Ashleigh very much. She was so beautiful but that – that FUCKING disease made her look like a junkie.' He pointed at his face. 'Her eyes were all black, her hair all lank and dirty. Her skin was too, and her clothes stank. I couldn't allow her out of the house as she was in such a mess. I'd try to stay awake all night to stop her from bringing her food up again. I even tried locking her in her room after a meal, but it seemed too cruel. She wouldn't go to the doctors either. She became very devious.

'Her teeth began to suffer as the weight dropped off her. And then social services got involved because some bitch of a teacher said I was neglecting her! She said that Ashleigh always looked malnourished and dirty. And she'd stopped going to school. I never knew about that until I realised how poorly she was and tried to get help.'

Laura stayed still while he became more volatile. As he paced the room, she kept her eyes on Jess. She looked so scared, so vulnerable. What the hell was she supposed to say to him?

'You shouldn't blame yourself,' she said.

'She wasn't washing.' Jason ignored her. 'That's why she looked dirty. She wasn't eating, that's why she was thin and always looked tired. She would bruise easily – but that was nothing to do with me.

'In the end, I lost my job because I was always off with her, trying to make sure she looked after herself. I couldn't leave her alone for too long. I didn't want to either. I was the only family she had. But it affected my work because of my bad timekeeping. And then social services were going to hold a case conference, and we both knew that they would take her into care. I couldn't cope with her deteriorating alongside me. I couldn't understand that it was her way of coping after losing her mum. My way was hitting the bottle. Her way was surviving a whole day on an apple and a cracker. A game of wills.' His laugh was cruel. 'She won every time. She got it down to a tee. I gave in every time I saw a bottle. I was useless. I was weak. She was brave.' He glared at Laura. 'But you. You could have helped her. Why didn't you?'

Laura raised her eyes to his. What did he mean by that?

'I checked Ashleigh's phone records. She called the helpline at least twice a week. Always at the same times. So I guessed she was talking to the same person, made a connection there.

'When she died, her phone was missing and I found a new one she must have bought herself. It wasn't a smartphone. It was a really old model. She must have lost hers. I don't know why she couldn't tell me.

'I watched the office for a few weeks and found out she'd been ringing during the times you were on your shift. I suppose if there were lots of people working there then I would have struggled.'

'I – I thought I was helping,' Laura said.

'I thought Ashleigh was doing okay when we moved in here. But she just gave up. And now I know why. She was talking to you, so you must have let her down.'

Jess shook her head vehemently. Jason glanced her way for a moment before continuing.

'Ashleigh killed herself. She took an overdose and I' – his voice broke with emotion – 'I came home to find her dead.' His shoulders dropped. 'I'd let her down. I tried so hard to be a good parent, but I couldn't cope when her mum died. Ashleigh starved herself as a way of control, I guess. Losing her mum was hard – on both of us. Her friends dropped off one by one when they didn't know how to deal with her. One minute she would be fine and the next she would be in fits of tears, and she became so angry.'

'But you ' – Jason pointed at Laura with the knife – 'you should have been there for her. Ashleigh rang that helpline for support because she couldn't get it from me. She should have got it from you!'

Laura had let him talk. He had needed someone to listen to him, put his side of the story forward, and she had provided this. Because she knew Ashleigh so well, he was hoping for answers that she didn't have though. She couldn't tell him what he wanted to hear. He shouldn't be blaming her.

But she did feel like she was liable. She could have done more. She looked up at him and said what he needed to hear.

'I'm truly sorry,' she said.

# SEVENTY-FOUR

As Laura listened to Jason, Eden and Amy crossed Davy Road towards number 269. Eden put a hand on the gate.

'Sarge, you can't go in yet!' Amy whispered loudly, grabbing her arm. 'Sean said to wait for backup.'

Eden raised her eyebrows. 'You really expect me to wait?' She looked up and down the street. 'Uniform will be here soon. But there's no one here yet so I'm going in. But you' – she pointed at her – 'you're staying outside. I'll take a bollocking for disobeying orders, not you.'

'You *really* expect me to wait here?' Amy shook her head. 'If you're going in, I'm coming too, whether you like it or not. Proctor could be doing almost anything to your family inside there.'

Eden paused. 'Stay behind me,' she said eventually, 'and be careful. They'll have my badge if anything goes wrong.'

'We're a team,' Amy responded. 'I'm right behind you.'

'No bloody heroics,' Eden warned.

She opened the gate and strode up the path. The curtains were closed at the downstairs window, allowing them easy access.

The front door was open. Eden pulled out her baton and trod carefully, trying not to make any sudden movements that would alert anyone. Hearing a male voice coming from the living room, she turned back to Amy and pressed a finger to her lips, urging her to stay quiet.

The living room door was partly open too. Eden couldn't assess the situation through what little she could see. She knocked, pushing it open as she did.

'Jason?' she said. 'Jason Proctor?'

He was in front of the fireplace. Eden had expected to see an angry man, a dangerous man, a callous individual who didn't give a shit if he hurt anyone as long as he got his own way. What she saw was someone who was broken, grief-stricken and seeming remorseful. Someone who was volatile but vulnerable. Someone who was out of control and scared.

Someone who had a knife in his hand.

She glanced across the room, appraising both her sister and her niece and assessing any injuries. The situation was hostile yet stable, but Eden knew that could change in an instant. She took a step into the room.

'She turned her against me.' Jason pointed at Laura with the knife, looking at Eden with so much sorrow that in any other circumstance it might have brought a lump to her throat.

'It wasn't like that,' Eden replied, one hand in the air and the baton ready at her side. 'Laura thought she was helping. It's her job to listen to young teenagers, and she does it very well.'

Silence fell on the room. Eden moved a step closer, sensing Amy doing the same behind her. Her eyes locked with Laura's for a moment, hoping to appease her. Keep her calm. Allay her fears.

'Did you find Ashleigh?' She turned back to Jason, taking a step nearer.

He nodded. 'I got home from the pub about eight. Ashleigh was in her room. I could hear music. I knocked on the door, but she didn't answer. That wasn't unusual. If she didn't want to speak to me, she would stay in her room.'

'A typical teenager. Just like my daughter.' Eden tried to build up a rapport. But Jason ignored her. It was as if he didn't know anyone was there.

'I fell asleep. When I went to see how she was, that was when I found her.' His voice cracked with emotion. 'She was face down on the bed, an empty bottle of painkillers and an empty bottle of vodka on the floor. I found a note beside her. It said "*I can't do this any more. I love you, Dad, but I miss Mum so much.*" '

Eden said nothing but thought about that poor child. What must have been going through her mind to be in such turmoil?

'Her phone was by the side of the bed,' Jason continued. 'If I had gone into the room when I got home, she might have. . . she might. . .'

Eden glanced at Laura again, wondering if she would have time to get to the door if she herself tackled him. But he could hurt either of them then. She couldn't chance it, especially with both their hands bound in tape.

'That's when I found her diary,' said Jason. 'I found out that she didn't want to live any more. It said she'd tried to end her life twice already but hadn't taken enough tablets, only enough to make her sick. I found out how her friends had turned against her and how lonely she was. But I also read about her phone being stolen and some bastard who shared photos of her online.'

Eden took a step closer.

He glared at Laura then and the air turned dark. 'Why could she speak to you but not me?'

There were sirens in the distance. Eden hoped he would stay calm as they became louder.

Jason looked towards the window and pulled back the side of the curtain. 'I never meant for this to happen,' he said, his face racked with guilt. 'I just wanted to talk to her, see if I could understand why Ashleigh killed herself.'

'It was the system that let her down,' said Eden. 'There was no one for Ashleigh to turn to when her mum died. That's not your fault. That's not anyone's fault. We all tackle grief differently. And who's to say how a teenager will handle the death of a parent?'

'When my husband died, my girls were eight and eleven,' said Laura. 'It was hard. I know what you were going through.'

'No, you don't.'

'I do! I had to rely on antidepressants and sleeping pills. There were times that I thought I might not ever get through it. If it weren't for my sister, I'm not sure I would have been able to cope. Everyone needs someone to listen to them.'

Eden glanced at Laura. She hadn't known any of this, and she didn't need to hear it right now. But she put her faith in her sister as she continued to talk.

'I was a nervous wreck when he died. I thought I'd never cope on my own. But gradually each day got better. My children got me through it. Just like you,' Laura looked at Jason, 'I put on a brave face for them. Ashleigh seemed very close to her mum, was that true?'

Jason nodded. 'I just couldn't cope. I couldn't help it.'

'Of course you couldn't.'

Eden watched the knife fall to his side. She took another step forward.

He looked at them all in turn. 'What have I done?'

'You were grieving,' Eden said, 'and you had no one to look after you.'

'I was.' He began to weep. 'I wasn't a bad father. I just couldn't be Ashleigh's mum *and* dad. It was too much.'

'You did your best. Ashleigh will know that.'

'Did she speak about me?' he addressed Laura.

'All the time,' she replied. 'She said you were a kind and gentle man.'

Eden wondered if that was the truth or a lie. Either way, Laura was very convincing.

'She said she wished she could talk to you more, but she didn't want to share her grief,' Laura added. 'Not with you, not with me, not with anyone.'

'What have I done?' he repeated, the knife still in his hand. 'I didn't mean to hurt anyone. I just wanted to teach you a lesson. You should have helped her more.'

'I couldn't. We tried – we all tried – but you know Ashleigh. She was strong willed. I was as shocked as you when I learned of her suicide.'

'It was a cry for help!' Jason had spittle at the corners of his mouth. 'She told me she didn't want to die. I told her I would make her better. Can't you see? I lied to my daughter, and now she's dead!'

'Why don't you put down the knife?' said Eden, knowing enough was enough, worried that he would lash out. 'You should think carefully about what you're going to do next. You've taken someone's daughter and held her against her will for nearly two days. I can hear my colleagues arriving outside. If they come in, I won't be able to help you.'

Jason paused for a moment, staring at a photo of his daughter that he had thrown on the settee next to Laura. Then he moved towards Jess with the knife. Eden rushed at him, pushing him into the wall. He pushed her back and she flew into Amy, who was coming up behind her. Before she could do anything else he was in front of Jess.

# SEVENTY-FIVE

'Stop!' As Eden rushed to her feet again, Jason started to slice the knife through the tape wrapped around Jess's feet. He was cutting her loose.

She came round to the side of him, hoping to take the advantage. 'Give the knife to my colleague, Jason,' she said. 'Amy can do that.'

With a shaking hand, Jason gave the knife to Amy. Once he was weapon free, Eden reached for his arms and took out her handcuffs. As she read him his rights, Amy loosened Laura's hands. Once she was cut free, Laura raced to help Jess. Amy went round to the back of the chair and began to cut the tape at Jess's hands as Laura pulled the tape from her daughter's mouth as gently as she could.

'Mum,' said Jess, her voice croaky but breaking with emotion.

'Jess, love.' Laura ran a hand over her face. 'Are you okay?'

Jess nodded. 'I just want to go home.' As her hands came free, she threw her arms around Laura's neck.

'I'm sorry,' said Jason, standing by the side of the chair as Eden caught her breath after she had cuffed him. 'I just feel so. . . so. . .' His shoulders shook as he broke down again and dropped to his knees.

Once her feet and hands were free, Jess tore across the room. Remembering the other knife that Jason had hidden behind the cushion, she reached for it and pulled it out.

'You fucking bastard,' she screamed, running at him with it.

'Jess, no!' Eden tried to take the knife from her, but as it swung back it sliced the top of her hand. She cried out as blood dripped over the carpet.

Weakened by sitting in one place for so long, Jess dropped the knife. Behind her, Amy kicked it out of the way. Eden sighed with relief.

But Jess, adrenaline fuelled, hadn't finished. She drew back her foot and kicked Jason in the stomach. He groaned as she kicked him again. The scream that came from her was animal.

'Jess, stop!' cried Laura.

Eden grabbed for her arms, frightened and horrified in equal measure at her niece's rage. 'It's over.'

Laura reached for Jess and turned her round, held her tightly in her arms. Jess collapsed into them.

Eden stood there for a moment, catching her breath as three uniformed officers rushed into the room. Two of them took Jason into the kitchen.

'It's over,' said Eden, looking at everyone. 'You're safe now, Jess.'

'I just want to get out of here,' she whispered, her teeth chattering, her eyes wide.

'He didn't. . . do anything to you, did he?'

Jess shook her head. 'He only attacked me when I went to escape. So I gave it him back.'

A strangled sob escaped Laura, and she began to shake. Eden rested a hand on her arm. Seeing her daughter laying into another person like that must have been a shock. After Jess had been kept captive by this man for nearly two days, Eden had expected her to be scared, vulnerable, anxious. But instead she'd wanted to give as good as she'd got.

'There's an ambulance outside.' Eden ushered them towards the door. 'We'll get you checked out. That eye and your lips look sore.'

Jess turned to her and flew into her arms. Eden hugged her fiercely. Her family were back as one again. Well, almost. She pushed back the tears she would cry alone that night and smiled at Laura, holding a hand to her cheek.

Laura put a hand over it and smiled too.

When Sean turned up a few minutes later, Eden was sitting on the steps of the ambulance as a paramedic tended to her wound.

'You okay?' he asked.

Eden nodded. 'Yes, sir, thanks.'

'Does the hand need checking out?'

'It's fine. The cut is superficial and a gauze and bandaging will suffice.'

He stared at her. 'I told you to wait.'

'Sorry, sir, but I just couldn't stay outside.' She grinned shyly. 'Did you really think I wouldn't go in?'

'No, but that's not the issue.'

There was a silence between them, but it wasn't awkward. Eden knew he would have done the same as her in the circumstances, but she was prepared to take her bollocking when it came.

Behind her in the ambulance another paramedic was tending to Jess. She seemed okay apart from a few bruises and the delayed reaction when shock set in. She'd been lucky. Lots of kidnap victims never came home.

Sean saw them behind her. 'Go home, get some rest and come back in the morning when you've spent some time with your family.'

'I'm fine, sir.' She smiled gratefully. 'Besides, there's a ton of paperwork to do now. And, if I'm honest, I'd rather keep busy at the moment. How's Proctor doing?'

'He'll live,' he replied. 'And that's the main thing. Did he say why he did it?'

'I guess he needed someone to blame, so he took Jess so that Laura would listen to him. When he was brought out of the house, he said he intended to take his own life tomorrow but that he didn't have the guts to go through with it. It would have been his daughter's sixteenth birthday.'

'That's sad.'

'He might get help now though.'

Amy came walking across to them with two mugs. 'Tea.' She gave one to Eden. 'From Mrs Davies at number 271. Apparently we've made her day by something happening next door. And she gets to be on camera. She's just gone to do her hair!'

Eden rolled her eyes. 'Some things never change.'

# SEVENTY-SIX

Eden parked the car in the drive, switched off the engine and sat in silence. A huge sigh escaped her. It was good to be home. If things had been different she and Casey would have spent a pleasant afternoon at Laura's over a delicious Sunday lunch. But at least Jess was safe now.

The day had gone in a whirl of paperwork and interviewing Jason Proctor. Although she could understand that he was grieving, and emotionally unstable because of it, he had been wrong to do what he did. He would have to suffer the consequences. She hoped tomorrow wouldn't be too painful for him, knowing now that it would have been Ashleigh's sixteenth birthday. He'd been put on suicide watch until he went in front of the judge.

And now she had to prepare herself mentally to go to court in the morning for the start of Deanna Barker's murder trial. There was never a dull day in this job.

She reached over for her bag and winced. Her bandaged hand was sore, but it wouldn't need any more medical attention since the paramedic had seen her. A good dose of painkillers and a couple of whiskey shots tonight would do the trick.

There was something she had to do before she went inside the house. She reached for her phone, located Danny's number and typed out a message.

*Where are you? Are you okay?*

Her finger hovered over the send button. Did she really want to put herself through this again? Every few months she would send the same message. Every few months she would be disappointed that there was no reply. She couldn't understand why she still gave him so much time, so much head and heart space. Two years ago, she had been working on a case involving a local gang who were running a loan shark racket. Two men had been murdered and she'd been tasked with gathering and analysing intelligence from the Financial Unit. She'd thought she'd been safe bringing paperwork home. She'd done it for years. But Danny had taken a look at it, used some of the information and tried to blackmail one of the players. After it all went wrong, he had fled.

He hadn't told her any of that. She'd had to work it out for herself. Yet despite that, she still cared for him, still needed to know if he was safe. She could never trust him again, and there was nothing left between them but the happy memories they had shared. But if she had learned something over the past three days, it was that family was so important.

She pressed send.

She let herself into the house, shrugged off her coat and hung it up. Staring back at her from the hall mirror was a tired but happy face. The day had turned out better than she had dared hope.

She could hear voices in the kitchen, and if she wasn't mistaken an undercurrent of Taylor Swift. It sounded like there was laughter too and light-hearted banter. Eden wondered if Casey had friends round. No doubt every one of them had been on their phones, Snapchatting and sending pictures and texts to keep each other informed of the gossip.

She opened the door to see Casey sitting at the breakfast bar. Behind her the table was set for three people. Joe was wearing an apron and taking a chicken out of the oven.

'I think you should leave it for another half an hour. Mum always likes a crispy skin and—'

'Mum would eat anything right now,' said Eden. 'I'm starving.'

Casey jumped down from her stool and ran into her arms. 'Joe was cooking dinner. I was helping, but he seems to have most of it under control.'

'I can see.' Eden hugged her back.

Joe came over too. He hugged her and then kissed her gently, then a little more. She wrapped her arms around his neck, pulling him close.

'Mum, don't be so embarrassing!' Casey made vomiting actions. 'Get a room, why don't you?'

Eden and Joe smiled at each other and all at once guilt overwhelmed her for sending the message to Danny. Maybe she needed to try harder to make *this* relationship work. She had her demons, and she couldn't move on from them yet, but maybe Joe could be good for her. And it seemed that Casey was trying to get on with him. That could be a one-off, after the shock of what had happened to Jess, but at least she was willing to be in the same room as him without storming out.

Eden pulled out a chair and sat down at the table. Right now, all she wanted was a cup of tea and a chicken dinner with the people that she loved.

# SIX WEEKS LATER

THREE CONVICTED FOR MURDER OF DEANNA BARKER – Ryan Copestake, *Stockleigh News.*

*One teenager was convicted of murder and two more were convicted of manslaughter over the death of Deanna Barker, sixteen, on 14 April 2015. Sentencing Nathan Lucas, eighteen, to eleven years and twin brothers Thomas and Craig Cartwright, also eighteen, to six years each, Judge Kerrigan said that he had never witnessed such a brutal attack on a helpless girl in his time and hoped never to again.*

*Kathryn Trent, also sixteen, was acquitted of both murder and manslaughter charges. The judge said it was a difficult case to prove but with only circumstantial evidence, he had come to the decision that she had been trying to help Deanna and had nothing to do with her death.*

*To continue reading, click here*

It was 8.30 a.m. on the morning after the trial had finished. Eden had called at Laura's house to grab a coffee before starting her shift. The last few weeks had taken their toll on everyone, but it was all over now. They could get on with their lives as before. Okay, not exactly as before, because nothing was ever going to be the same again, but looking forward to a new future. A different way for them all.

'Is it really over, Eden?' Laura asked, as she sat down next to her on the sofa and handed her a mug.

'For us, yes. For some, it will never be over. Today is just the beginning. How's Jess been this week?'

'Better.'

Since the kidnap, Jess had spent more time at home than out with her friends. She'd been clingy at first but had now taken to her room most nights. Cayden was still around, but they didn't seem to be as much of an item as before. Eden reckoned the relationship would run its course now. She hoped it would peter out sooner rather than later. He wasn't the right person for her niece.

'And Jason?' Laura asked.

Jason Proctor had been placed on remand for kidnap and assault.

'He'll get the treatment he needs,' Eden replied.

'In prison?' Laura scoffed. 'How is that in anyone's favour? He was grieving the loss of his wife and daughter. If it were up to me, I would have let him go and got him some help.'

'Are you forgetting what he did to you and Jess?'

'Of course not, but. . .'

'He held your daughter hostage for nearly two days.'

'And that means that I shouldn't have sympathy for him? He was a parent, trying to do the best for his daughter, on his own – just like you and me. We can't always get everything right.' Laura looked away, tears in her eyes. 'And – and. . .'

'What is it?' Eden pressed.

Laura looked ahead for a moment and then back to her sister. 'It was my fault that Ashleigh died.'

'Why, because you couldn't talk her out of taking her own life?' Eden shook her head. 'That's not how it works.'

'You remember the night that Deanna was murdered? My phone went wild with text messages coming in from Jess. I took my eye off the ball. I think Ashleigh might have been reaching out to me, and I should have been listening. But instead, I was wondering if my own daughter was okay.'

'It doesn't mean that you had anything to do with Ashleigh's death.'

'I'd been sending messages to Jess. She was ill, and I was keeping an eye on her. She was upset about something that had happened at school, but she wouldn't tell me what. But then messages kept coming in from my friends, as well as Jess, about Deanna. That could have been the night Ashleigh decided to take her own life.'

'You're being too hard on yourself.' Eden tried to reassure her.

'I'm not. I failed Ashleigh because I wasn't there to listen.'

'You wouldn't have stopped the crisis. Ashleigh was a vulnerable child, and she was hell-bent on destroying herself. Maybe there was no way that talking to her would have got through to her, but you did try. You didn't fail her.'

The room went quiet.

'I've thought about resigning from my job.' Laura spoke quietly.

'But that's ridiculous!'

'I can't have that sort of thing on my conscience. And maybe I should be home more for Jess. I'd have to get something more solid around the daytime. Everyone else I know works nine to five.'

'Except me.' Eden smiled. 'Look, don't do anything rash. You love your job. You've helped a lot of teenagers in crisis – their parents too.' She finished her drink and placed the mug on the coffee table. 'I'm getting far too comfy on this settee. I'll just nip to the loo before I go.'

Hoping to catch Jess before she went, Eden slipped upstairs. The bedroom door was ajar so she knocked to get her attention.

'I just thought I'd see how you were doing.' She went into the room and sat down on the bed.

'I'm okay.' Jess smiled. 'It's great to have Katie back. I can't wait to see her later.'

'There's something I want to say to you first.' She patted the bed. 'Sit down a minute.'

Jess frowned but sat down next to her.

'When we interviewed Jason Proctor, he told us about some photos that had been shared online without Ashleigh's consent,' said Eden. 'Your mum told us a bit more about them, that they were of Ashleigh in her underwear. So I started doing some checking up. It seems when her phone was stolen, the images were shared.'

Jess blushed in an instant.

'We traced the information back to your Facebook account.'

'I'm sorry.' Tears welled in her eyes. 'I was just angry.'

'Well, that explains everything.' Eden shook her head. 'You were just angry.'

'And jealous,' she admitted. 'Cayden was spending a lot of time looking at the photos and showing them around, and I didn't like it.'

'And in that split second, you caused someone a lot of hurt and anger. Ashleigh felt ugly in her underwear so it was a double whammy for her,' Eden explained.

'I didn't mean to do any harm.'

'And attacking Jason Proctor?'

'I was scared. Anyone would have done the same.'

'I'm not so sure.'

'You would. I know you would. Mum says I have your daring streak.'

Eden tried to roll her eyes. Trust Laura to say that. But now was not the time to joke.

'I'm sorry about your hand,' said Jess.

Eden rubbed a finger over the remains of the wound. It had healed nicely and would fade in time.

'I think maybe you need to find some new friends.' Eden reached for Jess's hand. 'I don't think that Cayden is a particularly nice person if he can laugh at someone who clearly had mental health issues. And was it your idea or his to get involved in thieving the phones?'

Jess looked at the carpet for a moment.

'You made a lot of money out of other people's misfortunes. We don't have evidence to charge you, nor any of the others. But it stops right now. Okay?'

Jess nodded. It seemed sullen, but it wasn't. Eden knew it was more of an 'okay, I know I messed up' nod.

'You're young enough to move on and forget this,' she added. 'Just like Katie will be able to put everything behind her eventually. Use this opportunity to knuckle down for the rest of the months you have left at school and do something with yourself. Do you still want to go into interior design?'

Jess nodded. 'I'd like to.'

'So you'll need to go to college first to learn the basics. You want a clean record for anything like that. Let that be your goal.'

Jess gave half a smile. 'You won't tell Mum what I did, will you?'

'No, but I think you ought to.'

'I can't.' She gasped.

Eden raised her eyebrows before standing up. She rejoined Laura in the living room and was saying goodbye when Jess came in.

Laura beckoned her to sit down next to her. She put an arm round her daughter and drew her in close. 'I'm glad everything is resolved.'

'Me too,' Jess replied. 'And I'm so pleased Katie got off.'

'She didn't get off,' said Eden. 'She wasn't involved in Deanna's murder.'

'I know, but—'

'You mustn't forget the innocent people in this,' added Laura. 'Deanna didn't deserve to be killed. You have your whole life ahead of you. Deanna doesn't have that – neither do her family.

So whatever happens from now, remember that. Do your best, and you can't go wrong.'

Jess looked sheepish.

'We all make mistakes,' Eden added. 'It's how we learn from them and move on that makes us who we are.'

'Well, I won't go far wrong with you two as my role models, will I?'

The remark brought tears to Eden's eyes.

Laura hugged Jess, but she pulled away.

'Mum,' she said. 'There's something I have to tell you.'

Eden left them to it. She didn't need to be here to share this. Laura was going to be angry with Jess, but at least she was going to come clean.

Eden had been surprised about the photos – especially when she had found out it had been the reason that Jess and Casey had fallen out. Casey had thought it was wrong and had told Jess. Jess had defended herself and they'd had an argument.

To Eden, from what she had seen of him, Cayden had come across as a bully. She'd known something like this would most probably tear the two teenagers apart in time. And they were only sixteen – they didn't know about real love and heartache. At sixteen, all Eden had been interested in was getting a date and keeping a boyfriend longer than two weeks.

She let herself out and headed off towards the Hopwood Estate. She had an appointment to take a statement from a woman who had been seriously assaulted.

Some things never changed.

# ACKNOWLEDGEMENTS

My books might have my name on the cover but there is an awful lot of teamwork happening in the background to make it happen. Thanks to my super agent Maddy Milburn, and my super editor Keshini Naidoo, two talented women I have the pleasure of working with. Thanks to everyone at Bookouture, Oliver, Kim, Kate, Natalie, Hannah and the rest of the gang.

Thanks to Alison Niebieszczanski, Caroline Mitchell, Angela Marsons, Talli Roland and Cally Taylor for writer chats – a support group second to none. Thanks to all the bloggers and reviewers who give up their time to help me. I can't mention every one by name as there are far too many and I would be afraid to miss one out. But each and every minute you spend reading my books and spreading the word about them means so much more than I can ever put in to words. Thanks also to Helen and Max for their research around Youth Offending Institutions and also to anyone who has helped with police procedural questions.

Thanks also must go to a certain group of cockblankets who make me smile every day, and also give me genuine support amongst the tears of laughter.

Finally, thanks to Chris. Behind every writer is a long suffering partner-in-crime, and he truly is a star. Thanks for being on the journey with me, fella.

# A LETTER FROM MEL

First of all, I want to say a huge thank you for choosing to read *The Girls Next Door*. I have thoroughly enjoyed writing about Eden and her team. I had so much fun creating a Doc Martin wearing, scooter driving Detective Sergeant and I hope you enjoyed spending time with her as much as I did.

If you did enjoy *The Girls Next Door*, I would be forever grateful if you'd write a review. I'd love to hear what you think, and it can also help other readers discover one of my books for the first time. Or maybe you can recommend it to your friends and family…

Many thanks to anyone who has emailed me, messaged me, chatted to me on Facebook or Twitter and told me how much they have enjoyed reading my books. I've been genuinely blown away with all kinds of niceness and support from you all. A writer's job is often a lonely one but I feel I truly have friends everywhere.

You can sign up to receive an email whenever I have a new book out here:

www.bookouture.com/mel-sherratt/

Keep in touch!

Made in the USA
San Bernardino, CA
16 February 2017